SUPPER FOR SIX

Also by Fiona Sherlock

Twelve Motives For Murder

SUPPER
FOR SIX

FIONA SHERLOCK

HODDER

First published in Great Britain in 2023 by Hodder & Stoughton
An Hachette UK company

This paperback edition published in 2023

1

Copyright © Fiona Sherlock 2023

The right of Fiona Sherlock to be identified as the Author
of the Work has been asserted by her in accordance with
the Copyright, Designs and Patents Act 1988.

A CIP catalogue record for this title is available from the British Library

Paperback ISBN 978 1 529 36004 2

Typeset by Hewer Text UK Ltd, Edinburgh
Printed and bound in Great Britain by Clays Ltd, Elcograf S.p.A.

Hodder & Stoughton policy is to use papers that are natural, renewable
and recyclable products and made from wood grown in sustainable
forests. The logging and manufacturing processes are expected to
conform to the environmental regulations of the country of origin.

Hodder & Stoughton Ltd
Carmelite House
50 Victoria Embankment
London EC4Y 0DZ

www.hodder.co.uk

To granny, for sitting me halfway down the stairs.

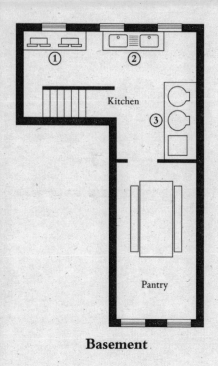

①

②

③

Kitchen

Pantry

Basement

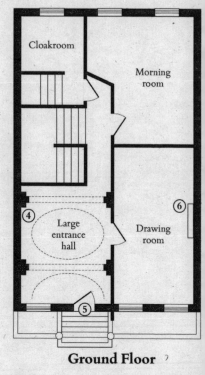

Cloakroom

Morning room

④ Large entrance hall

⑤

⑥ Drawing room

Ground Floor

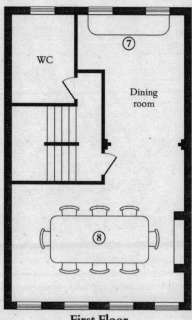

WC

⑦

Dining room

⑧

First Floor

Number
26
Bruton Square

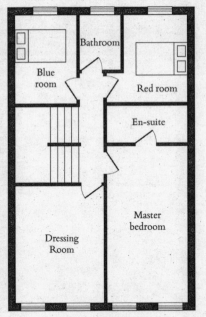

Second floor

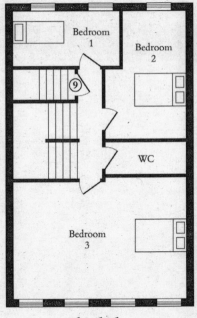

Third Floor

Lorem ipsum

① Tape machine
② Sink
③ Aga
④ Telephone
⑤ Front door
⑥ Portrait of Sybil
⑦ Sideboard
⑧ Dining table
⑨ Landing conceals entrance to attic
⑩ Chest freezer

Attic Floor

CAST

Lady Sybil Anderson	*Hostess*
Earl of Edale, Anthony Anderson	*Husband*
Elizabeth Chalice	*Detective*
Dr Agapanthus Langford	*Neighbour*
Francois Langford	*Lawyer*
Jeremy Crowley	*Musician*
Chrissy Crowley	*Make-up Artist*
Lady Marjorie Anderson	*Anthony's Mother*

Preface

Prefacing her novel, *Gaudy Night*, Dorothy L. Sayers asked readers to overlook that she had amended the movements of the stars, moon, sun and weather to suit her story. She also warned those familiar with the book's setting in Oxford that she had created a college where there was none. Although I can only seek to aspire to the success of Ms Sayers, in the matter of facts and locations I will beg for a similar understanding for *Supper for Six*. Mayfairians may wonder where on earth Bruton Square is. I have summoned from the ethers a small, Victorian square between the north-east corner of Berkeley Square and Grosvenor Street to house the residence of Lord and Lady Anderson. Whilst many of the issues at play in 1977 are based on actual facts, I have manipulated the weather and local events to write this story.

Fiona Sherlock

EPISODE ONE:

An Invitation to Mayfair

BBC NEWSREADER:

Good afternoon, this is the BBC News at 1 p.m. on Friday, 8th April 1977.

The body of Lord Anthony Anderson, the second Earl of Edale, was discovered at his home in Mayfair this morning. The thirty-eight-year-old peer and his wife were hosting a party for friends in the hours before his death.

The only son of the first Earl of Edale, Lord Anderson died without an heir to inherit the title.

London, 1977. A grand house in Mayfair. An aristocrat's dinner party begins with avocado salad but will conclude with two stone-cold dead bodies. It's the seventh of April, and white blossoms gather in the gutter outside 26 Bruton Square, the residence of Lord and Lady Anderson. Lady Anderson is hosting supper for her closest friends, for the first time. No one is expecting any other guests. Before the evening is out, the elaborate plasterwork and Chippendale furniture will be lost to a blaze, and along with it, any forensic evidence. Only the word of her four remaining guests can explain what happened that evening. But can any of them be trusted?

Although overshadowed in popular consciousness by the disappearance of Lord Lucan three years earlier, the events that took place behind the glossy black door of the Mayfair mansion utterly changed the lives of the guests at Lady Sybil Anderson's dinner party.

To lose one Lord Anderson may be regarded as a misfortune. To lose both looks like carelessness. Welcome to Supper for Six. *I'm your host Felix Caerphilly, an investigative journalist. In this era of true crime, podcasters exhume the carcasses of old corpses searching for an inch of gristle to examine for hungry listeners. It's June 2023, and I've been working on the Anderson case for the past forty-five years, since I was a cub reporter for the* British Herald. *My suitcase is full of tapes with the suspects statements – I have been obsessed with unravelling what truly happened to Lord Anthony Anderson who died in 1977. That's where we begin.*

Anthony Anderson was a controversial figure in the late 1970s, reputed as a dilettante playboy. A compulsive gambler, in the months before his death Anderson racked up enormous debts and was at risk of losing his home in London. A connoisseur of fine clothing, in the weeks after his death it was reported that in the first three months of 1977 alone, he had spent over £30,000 on custom-made suits and shoes, which he refused to wear more than once. His father may have been a hard-working businessman born into a lower-middle-class family who ascended to the rank of noble through his contribution to national security, but his son certainly was not.

The inquest into Anderson's death was delayed until 1978 in order not to overshadow the Queen's Silver Jubilee year. By the time the coroner's court heard the details in January of 1978, it was met with little sympathy or interest from the British public, who were then dealing with double-digit inflation and high rates of unemployment. For this case wasn't the first time an aristocratic murder had hit the headlines. Just four years earlier, Lord Lucan had disappeared after his suspected murder of his children's nanny, Sandra Rivett. Lucan was spotted in the glamorous spots he used to frequent years earlier, from Monaco to St Moritz, evading the proper administration of justice. Eventually in 2016, he was declared dead. Even today, the mystery of his disappearance is unsolved. In many ways, Anderson resembled Lucan, with his Mayfair residence and propensity to spend money faster than it came in.

As far as the British public were concerned, Anthony Anderson was another rotten apple undeserving of sympathy from those whose lives were hard enough. For in 1977, Labour's James Callaghan served as Prime Minister and the Yorkshire Ripper claimed his fifth victim, a sixteen-year-old shopgirl. 119 people died when firefighters went on strike that winter. Tensions over Northern Ireland spilled into mainland Britain, with constant bomb threats from the IRA. The Irish aspect to this case is one we will return to. But the most striking thing about how this case was perceived at the time, was the sense that another profligate elite had got his just deserts for life in the fast lane. The true events of that night did not receive the critique or commentary many expected. Even with a case of mistaken identity, the story failed to get traction.

But I was hooked on the tale from the beginning. As an idealistic teenager, I wanted to launch my journalistic career by solving this mystery. Initially an editor at the Herald *gave me a bit of free rein to poke around in the case. I'd nabbed a number of exclusive interviews and gained his confidence. What I hadn't told him was that I had come into a bit of money. I heard that Elizabeth Chalice had a number of tapes from the evening, and I decided to pay for her help.*

FRANCOIS:

There was no doubt Anthony was murdered.

AGAPANTHUS:

The rest of us were excluded from society. It was all anyone could talk about.

There you hear recordings of Francois and Agapanthus Langford, both long-time friends of the younger Anthony Anderson. This high-flying pair, a lawyer and a doctor, have refused to speak since my initial investigation a few months after the crime. Another couple, Chrissy and Jeremy Crowley, were invited to dinner that night, along with private investigator Elizabeth Chalice. Returning to England after three decades in Italy, Elizabeth sought a fresh start. Her funds were exhausted. She reluctantly accepted a thousand pounds to share her recordings with me a few months afterwards. Nowadays, it's essential to be transparent about these arrangements, but there were different standards to tabloid journalism in the 1970s.

So we begin this tale with our lady detective, the owner of the recordings. Born Elizabeth Cowperthwaite in Bolton in 1917, the private investigator hired by Lady Sybil Anderson started life in comfortable but humble beginnings as the daughter of a wool merchant. At the outbreak of the Second World War, she moved to London to train as a nurse at the Chelsea and Westminster Hospital. Chalice quietly supplemented her nurse's salary by conducting investigations for private individuals, mostly members of the aristocracy. Throughout her nursing career, she became noted for her intuition in determining the appropriate course of treatment for a patient, before even the most experienced doctors. Chalice relocated to Milan after the war in an effort to find her husband, who had been missing in action. As a woman living alone, she relied upon her wits to secure investigative work. She gained a reputation as an unabashed hedonist, a chain-smoker who preferred the company of men despite the negative view society held of such independent women in the 1950s.

She became a regular fixture at the copper-and-marble bar of Milan's British Bankers Club. Negroni in one hand, a filterless cigarette in the other, she was the woman that suspicious wives and mistrustful officials would seek out if they had a little matter to be solved. Throughout her thirty-year career, Chalice was the go-to sleuth of the jet set, solving numerous murders, negotiating ransoms, even uncovering financial crimes in the banking industry. She often worked closely with local and international police forces, and was famed for locating a 67-carat ruby that had been stolen from a Russian princess whilst skiing in St Moritz.

As far as an external observer like Elizabeth Chalice could see, the dinner party was the first time the Crowleys and Langfords had met. But it didn't take long for her to see through the class tensions, different accents and the matter of where their clothes were bought.

I've put together the following episodes using a combination of Elizabeth's own covert recordings from the night of the fire, Anthony Anderson's covert recordings of his wife, and interviews she recorded with the other guests, which I've interspersed with my own recordings of my interviews with Elizabeth. For time loosens one's ties to one's own secret.

It was a dreary, wet day in January 1978, almost nine months after the night in question, when I first met Elizabeth in a small function room of the Over-Seas League at the back of the Ritz. (I'd been signed in by my rather officious aunt to a private dining room.) Swatches of silky grey strands mingled with her black curly fringe, from behind a head-scarf and her complexion had the permanent tan of a woman who had spent thirty years under the Italian sun. Her eyes carried a sprightliness of a younger woman, and a question sat permanently on her *raspberry-red lips. She had just returned to England when Lady Sybil Anderson, with whom she had become acquainted ten years earlier in Paris, invited her to supper. But the detective's reputation was not completely unblemished by the time Lady Anderson invited her. Elizabeth sat down in her mackintosh, her fringe frazzled by drizzle. She removed her red headscarf to shake loose a thick head of sleek, dark curls. Her Sphinx-like gaze burned into me; I felt embarrassed at the cheap suit I had worn, concerned my cowlick had not settled into place.*

ELIZABETH:

You're younger than I expected.

FELIX:

I could say the same to you. Have you had lunch? I'm taping us, I gather that's OK?

She nodded and looked to the window where a laundry truck had pulled up at the back of the Ritz, which was located directly in front of the Over-Seas League clubhouse. I'd listened over Elizabeth's tapes of the evening, but needed her to embellish the facts. I was meant to be here to investigate a murder; instead I worried how this woman, the same age as my mother, would view me. Her reluctance to look at me betrayed a disappointment, perhaps a dissatisfaction, that there had been no conviction for the murder of Lord Anthony Anderson.

FELIX:

Why did you bring your tape recorder to dinner that night, Elizabeth?

She placed her handbag, a boxy crocodile-skin number, on the table and searched for a cigarette. The box was almost empty.

ELIZABETH:

Oddio, am I glad that I did! You see, Sybil had mentioned that she had a matter she wanted me to investigate. I had purchased the recorder when I arrived in London – I'd planned to begin work on my memoirs, but the thought of all that typing! I got some peculiar glances when I was recording in Hyde Park, I'll tell you! I decided to record my recollections, and then pass them along to a writer or a publisher to see, well, to see if there was anything there. Enough time had elapsed in my career that I could tackle some of my earlier cases, the Conte case of the missing child, for example. I'd also heard that a Scottish chap was writing about the Caswell-Jones case in Lake Como from 1953. So I'd been walking around for a few days with the recorder and my tapes, ready for any convenient window to make those recordings, but I suppose I wasn't wholly proficient in using the equipment.

She lit the cigarette and flattened her headscarf on the table. I knew this case bothered her deeply, but I sensed she did not want to simply hand over the reins to me. Why would she let a young upstart take the credit for her work on the case?

FELIX:

Why didn't you give the tapes to the police?

ELIZABETH:

Oh, I tried! I made copies for them. In the run-up to the inquest, I bloody spoke to anyone who would listen.

FELIX:

But the inquest concluded that Anthony Anderson died by accident.

ELIZABETH:

The Director of Public Prosecutions was convinced that the evidence was circumstantial. Given Francois's connection to another case that involved a police officer at Belgravia station, I would say that the entire investigation was rushed and then, of course, there was the fire which destroyed much of the house.

We'll look at Francois's involvement in a later episode, but for now, let's have Elizabeth introduce us to the events of that night.

FELIX:

How did you feel when you arrived for the dinner party?

ELIZABETH:

Oh, I didn't want to be there, if I'm honest. I felt jaded. I'd moved back to London as I no longer wanted to work as an investigator. But it's terribly hard to say no to an old friend, so I agreed. First of all, I wasn't expecting anyone else to be there. She asked for my help investigating something, but she didn't say what that was. Sybil answered her own door to me and another guest. There was no housekeeper, no butler. This really struck me right away as being quite unusual for a five-storey mansion in Mayfair. Was she running the place single-handedly? Or did she have staff, but had given them the night off? If so, was there something she was planning that she didn't want them to see? From the very start of the night, this perturbed me. She didn't entertain. In the ten years she lived there, she hadn't hosted one dinner party or afternoon tea. And socialising is the currency of these people . . .

She paused, eyeing me up and rightly concluding that I was not a man of means. I was an outsider. Just like her. I needed her to explain what I could hear on the tapes and to provide the background context. So, I allowed her to lead, like a hunter playing games with its quarry.

ELIZABETH:

Sybil imposed loneliness upon herself.

FELIX:

Tell me what happened when you arrived.

ELIZABETH:

No more questions, for now, Felix. Just let me tell my story.

Using Elizabeth's recordings of that evening, interspersed with her testimony to me, you'll now hear what happened, in Elizabeth's and the guests' own words, as they arrived at Lady Anderson's house that fateful evening.

ELIZABETH:

The strangest thing about that night is that no one was expecting a dinner party, or for there to be other guests. I was invited to help her investigate something but was highly puzzled to see others there. What did she want us all for? The second I arrived on the doorstep, I felt that something wasn't right. It was at that moment that I decided to press record early. Thankfully I'd brought enough tapes with me, knowing how long Sybil can talk for . . . but I thought it worth my while catching everything, in case there was something I needed to know in hindsight. And, I'm very glad I did.

As soon as I arrived, there was Chrissy Crowely, a make-up-artist pal of Sybil's. I met her on the front doorstep. She had the round, pretty face of someone in her thirties, but she was not well. I was a nurse in the war, so I could tell. Her hair was just a tad lighter than the paint on the door. She didn't look like she *belonged* in Bruton Square – wearing a plain black sheath dress, hiding a slight bulge. She was expecting and looked like she was suffering from prolonged morning sickness. At first I thought she must be there by mistake, or an appointment was running late.

And yet, when Sybil brought us upstairs, the towering Dr Agapanthus Langford was there too, drink in hand, looking thoroughly at home. A bobbed and coiffed medic, her lips were tight like the knot of her pussy-bow blouse. Clearly my name was familiar to her and her eyes narrowed. She reminded me of someone, but I just couldn't place it. Her diamond tennis bracelet rattled as she topped up her own wine glass.

AGAPANTHUS:

Oh, I thought it was just us for dinner, Sybil. Who are these ladies?

SYBIL:

This is Chrissy Crowley, a West End make-up artist. Chrissy and I are bosom buddies, she knows where all the bodies are buried!

ELIZABETH:

Chrissy's eyes grew wide at Sybil's introduction, accentuating the feline eyeliner that flicked along up from her lashline. The hostess's remark about knowing where the bodies were buried seemed to have embarrassed her. When I first heard it, I imagined they'd had some wild nights out together, but recalling it is all the more chilling now. Chrissy had gone a little heavy-handed on the blue eyeshadow and bright-red lipstick, but her sallow and broad features were striking enough to be accentuated by the cosmetics. She was a professional after all. But Dr Langford remained staring directly at me, ushering Sybil to mention my name. Again, Sybil spoke in a pointed way that made Chrissy shift in her seat.

SYBIL:

And this is Elizabeth Chalice, a private investigator. I gather she also knows where quite a lot of bodies have been buried, isn't that right?

AGAPANTHUS:

Elizabeth Chalice. Let everyone hold on to their husbands and their purses around her.

ELIZABETH:

Sybil stopped pouring the wine as she watched the doctor in horror. I realised my own jaw was hanging slack at the accusation. It was not the first time I've been accused of stealing someone's husband. You know, I'm rather an old lady now, so it wasn't a recent rendezvous she was referring to. And historically, there were rather a large number of seductions, so I didn't automatically think whose marriage she might have been referring to. Her face did look familiar, but I was surprised at how forthright Agapanthus was. Not even an attempt to apply a veneer of manners. Chrissy seemed nervous to even be in the room, but that remark really shocked her.

SYBIL:

Now, Agapanthus, that's not very nice, is it? It seems your reputation precedes you, Elizabeth.

AGAPANTHUS:

Oh, I suppose I'd better play nicely.

Agapathus laughs sarcastically.

During that first interview, Elizabeth was reluctant to discuss the details of her love affair. It was clear from Agapanthus's scathing remark that she not only knew Elizabeth, but despised her. This was the first of many question marks I held over Elizabeth's account of the evening, but we will come back to that later. I asked her what she thought Agapanthus meant.

ELIZABETH:

I couldn't know what she meant! She brokered a smile, so I decided to let it go. But I was on edge, trying to see how we were connected. You see, a private investigator gathers a lot of enemies along the way. But I have always had a thick skin, and would not let that horrible woman think she had upset me. So anyway, squares of light patterned the white linen tablecloth as the fading daylight bounced off the large, silver disco ball that hung from a hook beside the window. The doorbell rang again. and I noticed the dark circles under Chrissy's eyes. Agapanthus smacked her lips to conceal a slight hiccup. She made no attempt to make Chrissy feel welcome. But I couldn't dwell upon the ladies for too long, as Sybil welcomed a six-foot punk to the table, sporting an eight-inch mohawk, torn T-shirt and studded leather jacket.

JEREMY:

Well, it's not every day you get invited to dinner by the aristocracy. However, I wasn't expecting a crowd.

ELIZABETH:

The moment he clapped eyes on the doctor, his bellicose stance softened in surprise. I saw a flash of recognition in Agapanthus's eyes too. In that instantaneous exchange, they agreed not to know one another, to play the part of strangers. But after three decades as an investigator, that's all it took for me to realise there were multiple currents seated around the large, mahogany dining table in that beautifully appointed first-floor room. Not even the twenty-foot ceiling could dispel the charge that ran between Crowley and the doctor, yet the pretence continued through the evening. Who was this woman?

SYBIL:

Please, don't worry, Jeremy. It's wonderfully good to see you. Now, for introductions. Jeremy, this is Dr Agapanthus Langford.

JEREMY:

I'm Jeremy Crowley. How do?

AGAPANTHUS:

Pleased to meet you.

ELIZABETH:

Jeremy placed a familiar hand on Chrissy's shoulderblade as he took the seat beside her.

JEREMY:

A pleasure. Hi love, I'll sit here—

SYBIL:

Oh, not beside your wife, Jeremy. Gents at either end of the table; you sit up here between Elizabeth and Dr Langford. Jeremy, this is Elizabeth Chalice, an old friend of mine. Elizabeth has recently returned to England from Milan.

ELIZABETH:

Sybil flicked her eyes across the table like a tennis umpire, checking for any further disturbances. But I played the role of pleasant dinner guest. I watched carefully to see if Chrissy detected anything between her husband and the doctor. But the poor woman was staring at her glassware, bamboozled by the variety of receptacles. For the table was exquisitely set with polished silver-ware, fresh roses and pearlescent crockery. I looked again at the doctor, but she would not meet my glance.

JEREMY:

Cheers, Sybil, nice plonk. This bottle's already empty, though.

ELIZABETH:

Good evening, Jeremy. I hope you don't mind me saying but your apparel is quite striking. I'm particularly impressed with the safety pins.

JEREMY:

You don't have punks in Italy? I'm a punk guitarist.

ELIZABETH:

Well, not in my circles.

JEREMY:

And what circles might they be?

FELIX:

How did the others respond to that remark?

ELIZABETH:

Agapanthus sneered at that, rolling her eyes emphatically. So, our connection was linked to Italy, which did not narrow things down greatly. Sybil did not seem to mind his brusqueness. Instead, she padded across the Persian rug, the full skirt of her golden gown swishing as she grabbed a bottle of Kangarouge from the sideboard. A slight tremor in her hand forced her to pick up Jeremy's glass for a refill, leaving a drop or two to land on the pristine white linen tablecloth. Sybil moved around the table as if she were a waitress instead of châtelaine of a grand Mayfair mansion, leaving us to our small talk.

ELIZABETH:

Oh, primarily expats, bankers, but I'm glad to be back in Blighty, even if it is somewhat chilly.

AGAPANTHUS:

Rather balmy tonight, though, isn't it?

SYBIL:

Oh, I am positively frozen this month, Agapanthus. Perhaps that wine is keeping you warm. Jeremy and I go quite far back, you know.

ELIZABETH:

Oh, yes? Were you born in Ireland too, Jeremy?

SYBIL:

No. We went on tour together in the sixties.

CHRISSY:

They didn't just go on tour together. Sybil and the Sandmen were huge! From one seaside resort to the next. They very nearly got a record deal.

ELIZABETH:

Sybil reached Chrissy last, and placed a friendly hand on her shoulder. Both she and Jeremy had patted her down like a puppy. Sybil's armful of gold bangles clinked, almost the same colour as her frock. Her wealth was apparent from the diamond-studded leopard brooch pinned to her breast. Jeremy's unshaven chin hardened at his wife's comment. It seemed that the memory of his brush with success was not a pleasant one. Or was he confused? Had his memories eluded him? For a man not afraid to be outspoken, he seemed almost to be swallowing the comment with a gulp of wine. Sybil laughed nervously and placed a basket of bread rolls in the middle of the table.

SYBIL:

I'll get more—

JEREMY:

Allow me.

ELIZABETH:

You've very good nails for a guitarist, Jeremy.

JEREMY:

Oh, I been doing a lot of drumming lately is all. What's the story, Sybil? I'm bloody starving!

AGAPANTHUS:

Is this everyone for dinner, Sybil? I must say I was very intrigued to get your invitation.

Although all the guests were eager to discover why Sybil had summoned them, that tiny comment from Elizabeth about Jeremy's nails becomes very important later on. You see, Jeremy was a punk guitarist, and the detective expected to see broken nails and hardened fingertips. Instead, his hand was smooth and manicured.

SYBIL:

Yes, apart from Francois this is everyone. I'll explain – all in good time! First, let me tell you about this evening's starter. Bread fresh from the Italian bakery in Harrods, to go along with a prawn cocktail. I have a special ingredient too, it's a thing called an avocado. A large sort of fruit with a stone.

AGAPANTHUS:

Oh yes, the *Galloping Gourmet* had avocado on last week.

CHRISSY:

And *Woman's Way* had a recipe not so long ago.

AGAPANTHUS:

So, we are all familiar with that special ingredient. In fact, it must be rather common.

ELIZABETH:

Why had Sybil refused to tell the story of how their band lost their record deal? Neither Sybil nor Jeremy was interested in sharing the details, but it was not misplaced humility. Sybil's shoulders sloped with the put-down from the two women. She'd put a great deal of effort into the preparations. Agapanthus might be the type to assert her worldliness, but the snipe from Chrissy surprised me. All was not as well between these two friends as Sybil might think.

SYBIL:
Oh, er. Well, I don't usually watch television or read magazines—

ELIZABETH:
It sounds delicious, Sybil.

SYBIL:
Now is there anything Francois won't eat?

AGAPANTHUS:
Oh, my husband has a ferocious appetite. He'll eat whatever one sets in front of him – terribly good grubber.

SYBIL:
I'll just unload the dumb waiter. Back in a second.

AGAPANTHUS:
I'll top up the wine.

ELIZABETH:
Sybil bit on her lip at that point, almost quenching a smile. She opened a hatch beside the fireplace and began to remove the salads, with the avocado slices neatly splayed into a semi-circle.

SYBIL:
(*distantly*) No one go anywhere; it seems I forgot the salad dressing. I'll just run down for it.

ELIZABETH:
Oh, I'll keep an eye on them, don't you worry. I wouldn't want anyone stealing . . . your decor ideas. This disco ball is quite fabulous.

JEREMY:
I hope you wasn't implying anything else, Elizabeth?

ELIZABETH:

Of course, not—

JEREMY:

Because people jump to conclusions about punks, alright.

ELIZABETH:

Just as when she had rushed Chrissy and me up the stairs, Sybil seemed very protective about the rest of the house. She lingered by the door for a moment, as if it pained her to leave us there without her presence. The vein in Jeremy's neck was still throbbing with anger as he tore open his bread roll. I had been joking, not implying that there was any real risk someone would steal anything from the house. But this wasn't a table of aristocrats. Agapanthus rolled her eyes, making a humpfing noise as she swirled the sediment around her wine glass. I nibbled my lip in frustration at not being able to place her face. There were so many tensions prevailing around the dinner table, I could not think straight. The grandfather clock by the fireplace rang out seven o'clock, and Chrissy caught her husband's eye, blinking as she looked intently at him. Were they watching the time carefully? She was hopelessly sawing at a miniature loaf with her butter knife.

JEREMY:

Just tear it with your hands, Chrissy. Don't make a show of us in front of the doctor here. You feeling better?

ELIZABETH:

The comment was abrupt and only served to fluster Chrissy more, who shook her head to respond submissively. He smiled a snakelike grin at the doctor as Chrissy dropped the gnarled loaf and tears plopped down her cheeks.

CHRISSY:

I need the loo.

JEREMY:

Sit down!

CHRISSY:

Leave me alone.

ELIZABETH:

She padded heavily across the rug before her heels clacked angrily on the wooden boards beside the door. Sybil appeared with the jug of dressing in her hand, and raised her hand to block her exit.

SYBIL:

Stop! Where are you going?

ELIZABETH:

The two women thudded into each other, the oil splashing across Chrissy's hair and face. She raised a hand to survey the damage as another wave of tears erupted with a low moan.

SYBIL:

Good God! I didn't see – oh where were you going? Chrissy, are you OK?

CHRISSY:

My hair! I was just going to the loo.

SYBIL:

Here, let's get you cleaned up. I remember you once told me the benefits of an oil-and-vinegar hair mask!

ELIZABETH:

The pair found some friendly ground, but I noticed Agapanthus scowling at me. I refused to be baited. She would spew her spiteful comments eventually, but I was concerned at how the others at the table might take it. Judging from what I could see, no one there particularly warmed to Agapanthus. Especially not me.

CHRISSY:

Just show me to the toilet please. (*quietly over footsteps*) Oooh, tell me how is the new freezer working out?

SYBIL:

Shhh, let's get you to the bathroom.

ELIZABETH:

Her spine curled up at Chrissy's mention of a freezer . . . there's nothing to be ashamed of with buying a perfect state of preservation, if you ask me. She abandoned the jug on the sideboard and reached around her friend, who pushed her sharply away as they walked onto the landing. Jeremy helped himself to another bottle of wine from the sideboard. Agapanthus lifted her empty glass in the air to summon him.

FELIX:

Didn't you suspect something was amiss?

ELIZABETH:

I told you, I felt, no I knew, that things were not right. The lack of staff. Nobody looked happy.

FELIX:

So, why was no one asking Sybil what was going on?

ELIZABETH:

Bloody politeness. I can't stand that stiff upper lip. Everyone did know Sybil, and she was always a shy little thing. I didn't push her because I hadn't wanted her to feel embarrassed. I think we were all very conscious of walking on eggshells with Sybil.

I sipped my wine, nothing like the great slugs that Jeremy and Agapanthus were taking. I thought the Italians drank a lot, but the British could be the worst of them all. There was something about Jeremy's proficiency in table manners – he picked up the correct implement without hesitation – well, it made me wonder if the Cockney accent was a facade. Chrissy, on the other hand, was clearly overwhelmed by the dinner table.

With Sybil and Chrissy gone to the bathroom, there was an air of intimacy about how the doctor and punk seemed in each other's physical presence. She elbowed a teaspoon from her place setting, and without looking at her – in fact, the pair were looking in opposite directions – he caught it. I thought it was time for me to put her under the microscope.

ELIZABETH:

Do you know each other well?

JEREMY:

Nah, never met her before.

AGAPANTHUS:

I'd know this chap if I'd seen him before. Tell me, Elizabeth. I was expecting to be alone with Sybil tonight, she asked for my help with something. I didn't expect a dinner party, did you?

ELIZABETH:

Oh, so now you want to be civil with me? Aren't you scared I will steal your husband once he arrives?

ELIZABETH:

She coughed back her wine, shocked by my frankness. She had to realise I was strong, and wouldn't take flak from her or anyone. In the distance, I could still hear Chrissy crying and Sybil's muffled voice trying to soothe her. It seemed quite dramatic. The doctor smiled warmly, crow's feet the only sign of ageing on her unblemished face, her earlier spitefulness muted. Without realising, I had put a hand to my own neck, feeling the creases that hadn't always been there. Jeremy looked down to the street, from the window at the other end of the room. It was quite a striking image, the spiky hair and general unkemptness of this musician against the elegant and polished panes of glass in the sash window. He lit a cigarette and I considered Agapanthus's question. I lowered my voice so he wouldn't hear.

ELIZABETH:

She's asked for my help too.

AGAPANTHUS:

Hmm. It's rather strange. You know this is the first time she's invited me in?

ELIZABETH:

That caught Jeremy's attention. He strode back over to the sideboard looking for an ashtray.

JEREMY:

Well, what I want to know is where on earth is Anthony?

ELIZABETH:

The door knob squeaked for a moment before Chrissy managed to open it, returning to the room alone, but for the embarrassment betrayed by her flushed cheeks. Sybil had gone to the kitchen at this point. But just like the rest of us, Chrissy's eyes flew up to the ceiling. There were footsteps on the stairs above. Not high-heeled shoes. But the flat thuds of a chap's Oxfords. A fellow who knew his way around this house. Anthony loved his shoes; I remember that much from our brief meeting in Paris. I stood to embrace him as the door opened, but it wasn't him at all. It was a squat, sallow-skinned fop with long brown hair tied into a ponytail that hung limply over the collar of his brown suit, and a minor aristocratic lisp.

AGAPANTHUS:

There you are. Ladies and gentlemen, meet my husband. Francois Langford. How was court?

FRANCOIS:

How'd you do? What's your name?

ELIZABETH:

He couldn't take his eyes off Jeremy and Chrissy. At first I thought it was because Jeremy was quite a sight to behold . . . but there was more to it. If Agapanthus knew Jeremy, wouldn't her husband know the couple too? Why were they pretending to be strangers?

Elizabeth couldn't dwell too long on the potential link between the Langfords and the Crowleys. What happened next was to further disturb Sybil's guests. It was the moment the terror set in.

ELIZABETH:

Then we were all very much taken off guard by a sound I had not heard in two decades. It was the insidious whine of an air-raid siren. My body reacted before my mind caught up, my heart was racing. I could not catch my breath, as the room began to spin. Agapanthus dropped her wine glass. Francois tripped over the rug as he ran to the window, pulling at the catch to stick his head out to the street. As the whine rose and fell, Sybil ran in from the landing. The last thing I saw before I blacked out was our hostess yanking a portable radio from the sideboard. Then the room went dark.

BBC NEWSREADER:

Air-raid sirens are sounding across parts of London this evening to warn people to remain indoors as a precaution, after a chemical fire broke out in Soho. All residents of Westminster, Mayfair and Marylebone should take care to close all windows and doors pending evacuation, if required, by the army. Do not go outside to drive or take the Underground. Experts are not certain just how deadly the chemical smoke is to humans and animals. Both the Metropolitan Police and London Fire Brigade have called in all members of staff, with police officers and fire teams working to restore safety to the streets of London.

ELIZABETH:

When I came round a few moments later, my skin prickling with sweat and nausea, Agapanthus had my head on her lap. I was so disorientated, my first thought was that I had been drugged. I can get paranoid. It's an occupational hazard. I was embarrassed at fainting, but my terror at what I was hearing from the radio

overwhelmed me. The slow drawl of the newsreader took me back
to a time I thought had passed long ago.

AGAPANTHUS:

Here, Elizabeth, have a glass of water.

ELIZABETH:

A chemical . . . fire? How could a chemical fire mean air-raid siren?

ELIZABETH:

Agapanthus sat me upright with a firm hand. Crawling to her knees
with agitation, she was shrieking. In that moment, I realised what she
reminded me of, but the intensity of the noise distracted me.

AGAPANTHUS:

It's nuclear. It's not a chemical fire at all . . . At the hospital, they
have cancelled leave for weeks now. They knew something was
coming . . . dear God. Francois, we must go home now.

FRANCOIS:

My dear wife, you have been drinking too much! If it was nuclear,
they would tell us. We would get the four-minute warning and
chaos on the streets. Now there isn't a peep happening outside. I
have had a long day and am loath to pass up Sybil's hospitality. The
windows are all shut, God knows when we'll eat again if we are
evacuated. So, I say let's tuck in.

JEREMY:

He's talking sense, love. Come on. Be a shame to pass up this grub.

AGAPANTHUS:

We need to build a shelter – an attack must be imminent!

ELIZABETH:

Agapanthus grabbed the straps of her Chanel handbag, pulling
out her house keys. She was ready to go. Sybil stood silently in
front of the door as if to block her exit.

FRANCOIS:

You can leave if you want, but that avocado salad looks simply delicious. At least I think it's avocado, I left my bloody glasses on the Tube and can't see a thing.

AGAPANTHUS:

Oh yes, didn't want to put off any potential lady friends with a pair of specs.

FRANCOIS:

My wife, the comedian, ladies and gentlemen.

ELIZABETH:

Hanging on Francois's every word, Sybil was chewing her lip. Jeremy was standing tall, untroubled by the noise, checking his watch. The doctor glared at her husband, her eyes searching for an ally from the rest of the guests. The siren stopped. Sybil looked overwrought, tears pricking at the corners of her eyes. I could see Agapanthus was being turned off by the show of emotion, but really I'd have to say Sybil looked desperate.

SYBIL:

Do stay, Agapanthus. You simply cannot leave now. You see . . . gosh, I wanted to at least give you a decent meal before asking so much of you all. But it really is an emergency. *Sybil starts sobbing.*

AGAPANTHUS:

Oh, spit it out, Sybil.

SYBIL:

I invited you here to help me find Anthony. I can't even . . . well look. He's missing.

AGAPANTHUS:

This is terribly worrying. But we won't be able to find him if we're dead. So, the radio stays on and if the siren goes again, we are leaving.

ELIZABETH:

Oh, dear. When was the last time you saw him?

ELIZABETH:

Feeling stronger, I took my seat beside Sybil. Despite Jeremy's vocalisations, his hand was shaking as he lifted the fork to his mouth. Chrissy stared at her starter but shoved the avocado around the plate. The absence of sound was chilling, it reminded me of when the raids stopped during the war. You'd emerge from an Underground station into a smoking abyss, streets pockmarked, fires burning. Or nothing. An eerie silence if you hadn't been bombed. But I poured myself another glass of wine and sought to enjoy the meal.

FELIX:

Why did you do that? Didn't you want to stay sober?

ELIZABETH:

Were we all about to suffocate? Where would the army take me? None of the answers to these questions came to me, so I took Francois's cue, and decided to enjoy the setting of Sybil's glorious home, even if the atmostphere was rather . . . emotionally charged. It wasn't long until I was to have another reminder of how short life can be. Sybil was laughing, even though her mascara had begun to run down her cheeks. She was bubbling over with nervous energy . . . and sadness.

SYBIL:

Well, we might not have too much time, so I'd best tell you about the last time I saw Anthony. It was only five days ago. But there is something seriously wrong this time. I can feel it. We'd been at Aintree, you remember, Aggie, Francois? It didn't go well. He lost a lot of money. Which never usually bothers him. But he wouldn't even stay for dinner after the racing! The entire way back, he didn't say a thing to me in the car. He wouldn't even speak to the driver. Insisted we drive the whole way home without stopping. He's usually very pally with everyone, you know. Well, we arrived back here, I went for a bath. I was so exhausted . . . I fell straight into bed. In the morning, he was gone. A few shirts and things were missing from his wardrobe. But no note or anything. From time to time, he would disappear off for a few days, and not tell me where. So, at first, I tried not to worry. But now almost a week has passed—

FRANCOIS:

I hope nothing has happened to my old pal. He could have been in an accident, or anything. Did you tell the police about that scar on his left leg from when he came off his moped on the King's Road—

SYBIL:

Please, Francois! I can't bear to think it's gone that far.

AGAPANTHUS:

Francois, he's your oldest friend, how can you be so blasé?

FRANCOIS:

I'm just a realist, darling. Either he's gone and run away from you, Sybil. Or he's been in an accident. You know him, he'd never carry a licence. Marvellous bread rolls, by the way.

ELIZABETH:

Sybil slammed her glass to the table with a thud. Francois had really upset her. But she'd asked for our help, hadn't she? That was my first indication of that man's emotional comprehension.

SYBIL:

He was always loath to air his dirty laundry in public. I could imagine him hating the idea that I had spoken to strangers about this.

FRANCOIS:

We're hardly strangers, he's been my best friend since boyhood, but why *would* you air his dirty laundry like this?

SYBIL:

Well, you see, each of you has something that I need to help find him.

ELIZABETH:

The overhead lights were bright. Due to the windows being closed and curtains drawn, Sybil had turned them on so we could see each other, but it reminded me of sitting on a stage. Chrissy brought the radio to the table, the upset still visible on her face, although it seemed like she was hiding it from her husband. When she looked in his direction she wore a smile, but the sides of her lips strained, as if she was struggling to keep her emotions under wraps. Francois was as blithe as they come, gobbling down his appetiser like a goose after winter. Epicureanism alone did not explain his calmness; why was he not more perturbed at the order to remain indoors? And at the idea of his friend perhaps being no more?

CHRISSY:

Like Agapanthus said, we can't find anyone if we're all dead. I . . . I don't know how you can all just sit here, there is an emergency! Jeremy, don't you think we should go home?

ELIZABETH:

Now, dear, the instructions are to remain indoors. Smoke from Soho could surround the house in a few minutes, depending on which way the wind blows. You have the radio there, if there are any further developments, you'll be the first to know. Seeing as we're all here, and Anthony is missing, I think we ought to hear Sybil out. When's the last time you saw him, Francois?

FRANCOIS:

Yes, on Saturday as well. But I spoke to him, oh it must have been Tuesday or Wednesday.

SYBIL:

He's called me a few times. I begged him to tell me where he was, but he just said not to worry, that he would be back soon. But here we are almost a week later and no one has seen him anywhere. I've asked you all here specifically to help me find him. Now, I know you were all expecting to meet me individually, but I was worried that you mightn't like the other guests whom I had asked to help me.

ELIZABETH:

She spoke directly to Agapanthus, as if highlighting she was the subject of the remark. But Sybil seemed genuine, and remember, she spent an awful lot of her time alone. I've seen how those who live without much interaction with others cook up ideas about what other people might think that aren't a bit true.

JEREMY:

We ain't the usual crew you'd be expecting to Mayfair alright.

AGAPANTHUS:

Will you bloody sit down, Jeremy! And close those doors.

JEREMY:

(*mocking Agapanthus*) Close those doors. Don't get your knickers in a twist, doc. Close those doors.

FRANCOIS:

Woah there, don't speak to my wife like that.

JEREMY:

Oi, we ain't been properly introduced. Jeremy Crowley. I take it you're this dodo's old man?

FRANCOIS:

Oh, don't be tiresome, save that punk animosity for the street. Sit down.

JEREMY:

Or what, you'll take me outside for a duel?

ELIZABETH:

The way the doctor shouted at Jeremy, the familiarity with which she spoke so contemptuously. In times of stress and ominous terror, people do tend to act strangely. It was only afterwards that I began to ponder that relationship, but at that moment, I just wanted to know if Sybil had a job for me or not. Francois scraped his chair back to square up to the punk, who stood inches taller, but Chrissy seemed to hold a power over them both.

CHRISSY:

Gentlemen, please. You convinced us to sit out the fire here. Don't make me regret it. Sybil, have you even called the police?

SYBIL:

Oh, yes, I have, but they weren't much use. They have his description, but as he's stayed in contact with his employees, well they don't really consider him a missing person. So, I thought you could help, Elizabeth. And really, Francois, why aren't you more worried?

ELIZABETH:

Well, dear, could it be the case that if he's not missing to anyone else, he is just missing to you? But if you don't think that is the case, I will try to help – how did he seem to you, Francois?

FELIX:

How did Sybil react to that?

ELIZABETH:

It felt a bit harsh, on my part. She looked rather hurt. Chrissy seemed concerned about her. But not Francois.

FRANCOIS:

Um, well, I perhaps suspected he wasn't staying here much.

AGAPANTHUS:

Well, I haven't seen him come or go, which is a little unusual. But it's not as if we gawp out of the window at our neighbours.

FRANCOIS:

I certainly don't.

AGAPANTHUS:

What are you insinuating? I'm no curtain-twitcher.

ELIZABETH:

Please, let's just focus on helping Sybil. Go on, you were saying that you hadn't seen him coming or going.

SYBIL:

Yes, yes . . . Stop your bickering. I need *you* to tell me why my husband has disappeared from my life, yet nobody else's.

FRANCOIS:

I, well, I had no idea, Sybil.

JEREMY:

You're this geezer's best mate, and he never told you about the trouble with the missus. I don't buy that for a minute, mate.

FRANCOIS:

Well, Anthony is a private person about that sort of thing. I suppose I felt that something might have been . . . off. But whose marriage is perfect?

JEREMY:

Something is off with my stomach, excuse me, ladies and gent.

CHRISSY:

Dear God, can't you be civilised for one evening?

SYBIL:

Jeremy, you go and do what you need. I need your help, all of you. I need you to help me work out why on earth my husband is avoiding *me*. Why has he vanished from my life, yet nobody else's?

ELIZABETH:

With Sybil's final words ringing out around us, we watched Jeremy leave the room, plodding across the Persian rug in his black boots, mohawk barely missing the doorframe. It was the last time we saw Jeremy Crowley alive. But we weren't to know that then.

I realised that in telling the story, Elizabeth had dropped her guard. She stretched back in her chair, breathing a sigh of relief, and for the first time since she walked into that little room, a smile crossed her face. This was Elizabeth's investigation. I had to let her lead me in the little dance to get the truth out of her. But I could not let myself become too complacent. For all I knew, at that point in my investigation, she was the very culprit of the crime.

Behind the doors of the Anderson residence at 26 Bruton Square, this murder was another stitch in the complicated, knotted tapestry that would become the Anderson family mystery.

For a man died in the house of a missing person. And this was the first time Sybil had ever admitted guests to her house. It is too significant to disregard this as coincidence. Before the evening is out, another diner will meet their death. What made this evening so perilous for those who attended? In the next episode, we shall embark on the deadliest part of this mystery with the first murder of the evening. I'm Felix Caerphilly, and you've been listening to Supper for Six.

EPISODE TWO:

Dining in the Dark

7th April 1977. In a quiet, Victorian square in Mayfair, the night was clear. Behind the inky-black door of number 26 Bruton Square, a five-storey stucco mansion, six diners were met with the terror of hearing an air-raid siren. Private investigator Elizabeth Chalice was one of those guests. Welcome to episode two of Supper for Six. *I'm your host, Felix Caerphilly.*

It wasn't very long until there was another sign that it was not a normal dinner party, as the electricity in 26 Bruton Square was apparently cut off. When did a seasoned sleuth like Elizabeth become suspicious?

ELIZABETH:

Well, blackouts were common. I'd been living abroad so hadn't fully understood that the worst of them had happened about five years earlier and were usually scheduled. It wasn't until later that I began to be suspicious that someone had deliberately caused the blackout.

FELIX:

How did the others react?

ELIZABETH:

It was quite a job to settle everyone down. Dr Langford had wanted to leave; she had some idea that the situation was very dangerous, that it could have even been a nuclear or a terrorist bomb. Chrissy Crowley, the make-up artist and Jeremy's wife, had been very nervous indeed. I had fainted at the sound of the sirens. But somehow, Lady Anderson served up her avocado salad, and we began nibbling away. Then it all happened so quickly, as these things do. Jeremy, who had the get-up of a punk – but of course that was really only a disguise – stood up and announced to us all that he needed the bathroom. About five minutes after he left, when we'd been just making awkward chit chat, the electricity cut off with a buzz. Chrissy was sitting with her head between her knees, taking deep breaths. She seemed very unwell, with a veneer of sweat. No one else seemed to care or notice, not even Dr Langford.

Even with the overhead lights off, enough daylight crept in
around the edges of the curtains so that once my eyes adjusted—

FELIX:

At one point, in your early observations, you thought you saw
the orange glow of a fire on the horizon. What was that?

ELIZABETH:

Yes, it was the fading daylight. You see, I hadn't been used to
these long drawn-out dusks of the north, after living in Italy for so
long. And, I suppose my mind believed that there was a fire, so my
eyes confirmed it.

*In the moments before the first murder, the whereabouts and behaviour
of each of the potential suspects was critical.*

FELIX:

What was everyone doing?

ELIZABETH:

I've mentally reviewed everyone numerous times. To be honest,
my attention was captured by a tiny gesture between Francois and
Chrissy. I don't remember seeing where Sybil and Agapanthus
were until a few minutes later. You see, as Francois stood from his
place, he placed his hand between the shoulder blades of Chrissy
Crowley. They had pretended not to know one another. Just like
their spouses Jeremy and Agapanthus allowed us to think of them
as strangers. I knew that there was an intimacy between Francois
and Chrissy. That was the moment the penny dropped for me that
nothing about this dinner party was as it seemed.

AGAPANTHUS:

Dear God! I can't see a bloody thing.

CHRISSY:

Oh no!

FRANCOIS:

Any more avocado, Sybil?

AGAPANTHUS:

Would you snap out of this, Francois? Don't you see, the electricity has gone off, an attack must be imminent.

CHRISSY:

Well, couldn't the fire affect the electricity supply? You really think it's a nuclear attack?

ELIZABETH:

I doubt it is nuclear. If anything it's probably the IRA . . .

AGAPANTHUS:

Elizabeth, I'm surprised at you. There hasn't been anything since those terrible Birmingham attacks . . . thank God.

FRANCOIS:

It's rather fresh in my mind; you know we were in Scott's the night they shot through the windows. That wasn't even two years ago.

AGAPANTHUS:

And that terrible siege that went on in Balcombe Street . . .

FRANCOIS:

Total beasts. Murderers. Where is that wine from? I forgot my glasses.

ELIZABETH:

They have my sympathies, if you ask me. You can't expect people living under oppression not to break . . . the wine . . . it's erm, Kangarouge, I believe.

SYBIL:

No politics or religion, please! Agapanthus, I understand you're worried, but it's really not helping anyone. Let's hope it's not a nuclear war or the IRA. Please, everyone, stay calm. The wiring was not replaced, this happens more often than you'd think. I'll just go and check the fuse box – no need to panic. I'd better check the main course, it's been in the oven rather a long time. Elizabeth, would you mind lighting these candles? Won't it add to the atmosphere? Francois, would you please call Anthony on whatever number you have? Perhaps this emergency will be enough to encourage him home to safety.

FRANCOIS:

Oh, very well. But my address book is in my briefcase, beside the coat stand. I'll come down with you and use the telephone.

CHRISSY:

I need to use the toilet again.

SYBIL:

Go upstairs to my room, I gather your husband is still in this loo.

So Elizabeth's tape stops after Sybil's mention of Jeremy still being in the loo, meaning that Elizabeth, at this time, had no alibi for the time of Mr Crowley's murder. This detail becomes important later. For now, we will leave my interview with Elizabeth Chalice to hear an eyewitness account of what lay on the upper floor of number 26 Bruton Square. The following is testimony from Dr Agapanthus Langford, then hospital doctor at Chelsea and Westminster Hospital. She recalled finding the body. Dr Langford was at the time married to Francois Langford. They lived six doors down at number 20 Bruton Square, where I interviewed her, in early 1978, a little over a year after the death of Jeremy Crowley. Francois and Anthony had been friends since boyhood. I've included some recordings from Elizabeth, when she joins the scene having fixed her recording device issues by this time ...

AGAPANTHUS:

I warned her not to come into Sybil's dressing room, you know. The wife. Chrissy. I might not have liked her, but I knew she didn't need to see ... well let's just say a dead body is never pretty. Sybil tried to stop her, but she could not. Sybil was bellowing to me to refuse Chrissy entry, but Chrissy just shouted back 'Get your hands off me, Sybil, you bloody idiot. Open that door now. Do you hear me, Jeremy?' I remember it like it was yesterday.

The transience of life is something I've come to be acquainted with, watching patients fade after surgery or die in an ambulance. The sight of a body bag or the chaplain is one I've seen too often to let it cause a stir in my emotions. Resolute, I stood there in service of Chrissy if she needed it. Realisation settled across her face as she sat on the floor, cradling his head, wiping aside his snot and vomit. She looked at him in disbelief.

She simply repeated, over and over again, 'Jeremy? What you doing? Jeremy – answer me.' Then she turned to look at me, and I'll never forget her face – the look of desperation. And she asked, 'What's wrong with him, doctor? Will you help him?'

I'm afraid, all I could say was 'It's too late, I'm afraid. He has no pulse.' I sometimes wonder now if I should have been softer with my words. But I was, and still am, very matter-of-fact about these things. I have to be, in my line of work. She refused to believe me, it seemed, and started miming resuscitation techniques. 'Push his chest or something,' she was saying. 'Don't just stand there! Sybil, will you tell her?' But Sybil simply sided with me, echoing my sentiment, with a softer tone: 'It's too late, Chrissy. He's dead. Come on.' Chrissy's hand was shaking as she raised it to her mouth to swallow the shock of what was in front of her. I knew she wouldn't be a fainter, although the hypothalamus may kick in. Suddenly she started shouting, 'He's not my Jeremy. No this is not him!'

I did my best to calm her down with softer words, acknowledging what a shock it was.

But it is a very normal reaction. Disbelief. In fact, I almost thought Sybil would be the one to keel over, she couldn't look at the chap's body. Her arm was on the crook of Chrissy's back, more to steady herself than to offer comfort. Sybil had a nasty bruise coming up around her ankle, she had twisted it on the stairs, apparently. But she was the least of my worries as I tried to explain the truth to the grieving widow. Although knowing what I do about her now, I needn't have been so careful with Christina Crowley.

She kept beckoning me over, telling me to the bring the candle closer to him just to prove it wasn't him, all the while Sybil was telling her to trust me.

'Somebody ring a bloody ambulance,' Chrissy said, unheeding of Sybil's words. 'He isn't an addict. He didn't do this to himself. He couldn't have. Oh, no, Jeremy, what has happened to you? I don't understand, he hasn't been using any sort of drugs in the past two years.' I responded with soft words again, something like 'Now, I know this is very difficult for you, Chrissy, but let's get you a glass of water, eh? Give you some time—' I was just trying to give her some sympathy, but she responded harshly. 'Shut up, you stupid woman,' she said. 'For all of his failings, Jeremy was a good man. I insist we call the police.'

That wasn't the time for me to correct her. Her husband was a heroin addict, but one that was rather good at concealing it. But there's only so long you can be a messenger boy to the damned without falling victim to the product. Fat blobs of tears were rolling down her cheeks. But I remember seeing something off in her face. As much as she was distressed by this scene, her shoulders weren't hunched over like most grieving relatives. The edges of her mouth betrayed a smile and she rubbed that baby in her belly. She was relieved. Happy even. This was just before the old nurse Elizabeth poked her nose in.

Thankfully for us, Elizabeth had her tape recorder back up and running at this point . . . so once again, we can hear footage from the night in question. Listening back now, I'm struck by Elizabeth's businesslike nature. It is what one would expect from a professional detective, who is no stranger to manipulating those she interviews. I do wonder if she can turn her emotions on and off as quickly as one might think . . .

ELIZABETH:

Everything OK? I heard a cry from downstairs so came up to see what the matter was . . . Oh, no, Jeremy. Have you taken his vitals, Dr Langford?

AGAPANTHUS:

I'm afraid there are no, erm, signs of life.

ELIZABETH:

Who found him?

AGAPANTHUS:

I did – he was already gone. Just. It would have happened within three or four minutes. There was nothing I could do. I came up here to check the windows were all closed.

ELIZABETH:

I didn't see you leave the dining room, why did you creep off so quietly? Agapanthus, I'll need to speak to you alone about this.

ELIZABETH:

I know it sounds strange now, when there was a dead body in the room, but I was in a hyper-alert state . . . And noticed that Sybil's ankle was rather swollen and straining at the straps of her sandals.

ELIZABETH:

What's the matter with your ankle, Sybil?

AGAPANTHUS:

Ankle sprain. Nothing serious but she couldn't bear any weight on it. Anyway, I came to check the windows up here were all closed and this is what I found. Sybil, do sit down or you'll make that sprain worse.

ELIZABETH:

I'm so sorry for your loss, Chrissy. Let me take a closer look. Hmmm. Shall I close his eyes? What a disturbing scene for you all. The tourniquet, was he on medication, Chrissy?

AGAPANTHUS:

There's an empty vial of morphine there.

CHRISSY:

I said he was no addict. He wouldn't have come up here and just injected himself. Why would he?

ELIZABETH:

Well, I do wonder what he was doing up here . . . never mind. Well, there's no need to distress you any further, Dr Langford and I will call the undertaker. I'm sure they'll come as soon as they can. I'm sure the emergency services are delayed by this chemical fire.

CHRISSY:

I said he didn't do this to himself. This isn't my Jeremy. Why aren't you listening to me? He was *murdered*. That's the only explanation.

AGAPANTHUS:

That's when Francois shoved his way through the door like an otter in a dam.

FRANCOIS:

Hello, Sybil, it's no time to show off your jewels, perhaps it's the fire, but it rather smells like the main course is burning— Oh, this is where you all are. Oh, no. Oh, no. The poor fellow. What's happened to him?

SYBIL:

Come on, Francois, leave Chrissy for a moment. They don't need us on top of them. Whenever you're ready, come on down. Let's go.

AGAPANTHUS:

London was burning, the house was plunged into darkness and still my husband was only worried about his bloody gut. I didn't even want to be there, I wanted to get home. If the fire was as big as they said on the radio, the hospital would need all the staff to come in. But I hadn't had a day off in almost a week. I'm ashamed to say that's why I ensconced myself in the scene in Sybil's dressing room. If I was indispensable there, I wouldn't have to go in.

CHRISSY:

Are you listening, Elizabeth? You're an investigator, can't you see that this wasn't an overdose?

ELIZABETH:

Chrissy, I'm so sorry for your loss. You must be in absolute shock. Don't you worry, though, we will make sure this situation is looked into. I think we should call the police.

AGAPANTHUS:

No. No police. It wouldn't look good—

CHRISSY:

You mean to your neighbours? Can't you think of anyone but yourself?

ELIZABETH:

It's important now that we don't move him. There may be finger-prints or other forensic evidence explaining what happened here. Let's leave him for now.

AGAPANTHUS:

Indeed. Why don't we go downstairs and talk about it? I can't see what there is to be done here. Unfortunate though it may be, the man is dead.

CHRISSY:

I just know Jeremy didn't do that to himself. Everything about tonight felt off. And now, I'm a widow! Did you do this to him, Sybil? Did you murder him?

Chrissy starts to sob.

ELIZABETH:

Don't worry, my dear. As we are all stuck inside for the foreseeable, I'll speak to everyone to ascertain what happened. If it is murder, I'll find out who the culprit is. Now, your job is to try and stay calm for your sake. You won't do the baby a bit of good by being so over-wrought. Isn't that right, doctor?

AGAPANTHUS:

Listen to Elizabeth. We will talk about it downstairs over a strong drink.

CHRISSY:

But we are stuck here with a killer! Whoever did this . . . I mean Sybil was the one who organised this dinner party. She had some falling-out with Jeremy years ago – who knows, maybe she's been biding her time all along. She doesn't seem right in the head, if you ask me! And now we're just sitting ducks. What if she's planning to kill all of us?

AGAPANTHUS:

Now, now, you've had rather a big shock. It's natural to feel anxious and confused. You're right, Sybil doesn't seem . . . quite herself. But we shall stay together and try not to worry. I may have only been a child during the war, but I can tell you the greatest enemy one faces is the mind turned on itself. Elizabeth, I'll leave you to see to Chrissy—

ELIZABETH:

No. I need to take some pictures. You have a drink and then we need to speak, doctor?

CHRISSY:

I don't want to leave him alone.

ELIZABETH:

He won't be alone. Now, you're in shock. You need to let this horrific news settle in.

AGAPANTHUS:

Come along, dear.

AGAPANTHUS:

Call the police! Wait in the dining room! Nobody bossed Doctor Agapanthus Langford around like that. I bet Elizabeth thought she was the cleverest of us all – but I came top of my class in Cambridge. I had to, of course, as one of only three women in my college. But now even Mayfair wasn't safe from the infiltration of the lower classes.

Imagine, Francois and I broke bread with an addict. Perhaps I had been wrong about Sybil. She wasn't the right sort of woman to fall in with. And the wailing started again, as I shuffled this new widow down the stairs! Good lord, why must women be so prone to dramatics, even if her husband did die? At that point, I thought there could be a case for sedating Chrissy, or indeed Sybil, if she posed a danger to the rest of us or herself . . . There was a peculiar sense of gloom at number 26 that had been there before the body was found. A smell of mould, despite the recently papered walls.

Faced with disaster, Dr Langford was adamant that the police should not be called. This is one point Elizabeth found suspicious at the time, but it wasn't until the following day that Elizabeth discovered the true relationship that existed between the doctor and Jeremy Crowley. After the doctor left, Elizabeth went to great pains to document the scene, as you're about to hear in the third tape, where Elizabeth whispers into her own microphone after the death of Jeremy Crowley. However, the photos she mentions were lost. In the absence of any official police report, here is a report she recorded on the evening. The most striking difference between the doctor's and Elizabeth's accounts is whether or not the victim was a drug addict. By 1977, work was thin on the ground for Elizabeth. In a last-ditch attempt to save costs, she had just returned to England after almost thirty years on Continental Europe. Elizabeth's capture of the scene is not by any means objective. In fact, it is full of conjecture and her personal musings; at points it seems that she is relishing the opportunity, and shares very frank thoughts about Francois Langford.

ELIZABETH:

(*whispers*) It's just me and the victim now, I've sent the other guests, or should I say *suspects*, downstairs for a snifter of Courvoisier. At least I don't have to worry about them going anywhere. I'll sit down here on the plush velvet stool and document what I can see. Visibility is extremely poor as there is an electrical outage in the area and I'm relying on a single candlestick to illuminate the scene of the murder. This room is better lit than downstairs, benefitting from the yellow glare of the streetlamp outside. I'm in the dressing room of Lady Sybil Anderson, at her home in 26 Bruton Square. It's approximately 8.26 p.m. on Thursday, 7th April 1977. I've taken a few pictures with my flash Kodak, but best make written notes while the details are fresh in my mind.

The victim lies on his back and his pupils are dilated. No pulse or signs of life. Just beyond his left arm sits an empty 20mg vial of morphine. I did not lift the item to inspect it further for risk of rubbing off any fingerprints. Beside the empty vial is a glass hypodermic syringe, measuring just under half a fluid ounce. The metric measurement is on the underside of the barrel, I can't see it. The studded black leather belt of the victim has been fashioned into a tourniquet around his right biceps – but there is no evidence of other marks on his body that would indicate he regularly injected himself. There is no puncture wound on this arm at all. In this light, I cannot say where he was injured.

Some facts do point to signs of a struggle. A small box for earrings has fallen under the seat. In his pocket is a small bottle of saline solution, and a prescription . . . Wait a minute, it's from Dr Agapanthus Langford, for Anthony. For morphine. What's Jeremy doing with this? The dressing-table lamp has been knocked to the floor – but given the relatively small disturbance, our killer either got lucky, or this is not their first time. It's my belief the scene was made to look like an overdose, but that's where our killer slipped up. This is a case of murder. There are clothes scattered over the cream-carpeted floor of this second-floor room, which measures about 12 feet square, in the front of the house facing Bruton Square. I'm not sure if our hostess dressed hastily and left the room like this. A number of Lady Anderson's jewellery boxes are open on the dressing table. She seemed ill at ease all evening, despite her posh frock.

Oddio, I miss my evening Negroni under the shadow of the Duomo, but there is no room for what I want any more. Especially not tonight. A chill gathers around me as the darkness of night settles over this house. There is no respite within these four walls. I will expose the wickedness of our killer. But perhaps I ought not limit my scope to what is in the house, but also what is outside? The fire that rages through the streets, a poisonous smoke that stops us from leaving Sybil's house. A beige car is parked in the empty street. Now that I look through the sash window . . . I notice the darkness of this house is unique to this house. I can see televisions and ceiling lights between the gaps in the curtains across the great mansions of Bruton Square. So, our killer wants to keep us in the dark. I should never have accepted Sybil's invitation.

Oddio, poor Jeremy. As his body lies in front of me, in the candlelight he looks almost childlike. His mother would have watched him sleep as an infant. That reminds me, I must ask Chrissy to provide more details about his family life. Who was he before he became a punk? I'm interrupted by a knock at the door.

FRANCOIS:

Elizabeth? May I interrupt?

ELIZABETH:

I'm recording the scene here, what is it?

FRANCOIS:

Well, it seems that Sybil has locked us all in. Agapanthus was quite keen to go home, but when we tried to leave, well front door, back door, they're all locked. Given what's gone on here, a dead body, the lights out, well it's beginning to look like a Miss Marple novel. Perhaps you could come and talk to Sybil?

ELIZABETH:

She's done what? Have you heard the radio—

FRANCOIS:

No update on that front, the wind is blowing towards the west, thankfully, but one never knows.

ELIZABETH:

Try to keep everything calm, I'll be down in a few moments, I just need to take a few details.

He slithers off into the hallway; there's something I don't like about that fellow, and the way he seems to leer. The appetite his wife described as hearty may not end at his belt. But why would Sybil deliberately lock us in? With all of London ablaze, she has denied her guests the agency of leaving. Perhaps she means to protect us against ourselves? But when considered alongside the question of Anthony's absence, I must interrogate her version of events. There is a killer in the house – one who needs to be apprehended. Until that is done, none of us is safe. It boils down to two questions. Who had the means, the motive, and the opportunity? Was it a chance coalescence of circumstance or a planned kill? As our hostess, Sybil must be considered first.

The woman who never entertains invites a party of acquaintances in. Why has it taken her so long to ask for help if Anthony's been missing for five days? But the real question is, what is it about this particular group of people that she thought could help find him? Although herself living alone, her house and appearance are well maintained. Composed. Even the menu was carefully considered. It is only once the body was discovered that she began to unravel – which in itself is understandable. It's widely accepted, by Francois, those in the Anderson company and Sybil herself – he is accessible by telephone, indeed a Mayfair number. Could it be that he deliberately abandoned her, and that out of desperation and loneliness she locked us all in?

But to scratch beyond that superficial appearance of events, could Anthony be residing within the house? There are four floors, a basement and an attic – and the possibility of a second telephone line. If he is here, the chances are that Sybil would be party to it.

Where else would he source his food? And if that is the case, could this evening's dinner be her attempt to rouse him from his isolation? Or is this a ruse between the two of them to kill Jeremy Crowley? Might she be lying when she claims Anthony is missing? So long have I sifted through the psyches of individuals like Sybil, that I remain cautious about settling upon one argument until everything else has been ruled out.

The second possibility is that Anthony's disappearance is ancillary – just a plot to get Jeremy under her roof. Sybil selected these guests for a particular reason; could it be she selected persons with an underlying history with our victim, intending suspicion be placed at their door, and therefore directing it away from herself? Providing alternative suspects with equal means and opportunity is a method I've seen killers use before.

Someone in this house murdered Jeremy. Now, I have four suspects to interview. Even at this stage, I must keep an open mind. Even his own wife may have wanted him dead.

Despite barely making it out of 26 Bruton Square alive that night, Elizabeth managed to keep these recordings safely in her pocket. Whilst these crucial pieces of evidence survived, her Kodak camera did not. It was not included in the bundle that I purchased from her, and I was only informed of its existence by Francois Langford, several months later. It offers the portrait of a sleuth in love with murder, not necessarily concerned with the truth or protecting the other guests of Lady Sybil Anderson. In the forty-five years that have passed since that night, and those later interviews – I could find no link between the victim and Elizabeth. I do not believe that she was capable of murdering someone to make a job for herself, and have accepted her version of events to be as close to the truth as could be. I have never uncovered evidence that Elizabeth lied, or concealed the truth, apart from when it came to matters of the heart. We will hear about this in time. But what were the other suspects doing whilst Elizabeth was documenting the murder? Join me in the next episode as our focus remains on our mysterious hostess. I'm Felix Caerphilly, and you've been listening to Supper for Six.

EPISODE THREE:

Black Forest Gateau

Chocolate sponge cake, layered with cream, cherry liqueur and grated dark chocolate. Sybil Anderson was about to serve up dessert at her deadly dinner party on 7th April 1977. Candlelight glinted off the edge of the solid-silver cake knife as she sliced the Black Forest Gateau into five. Where she had served six portions of avocado salad, now there were only five gilt-edged plates to fill. But no one had an appetite for food, despite Sybil's insistence. Their main course, a Country Captain chicken dish, had been burned to inedibility. The sixth dinner guest, Jeremy Crowley, was now dead, sprawled across the cream carpet of his hostess's dressing-room floor, a few feet from an empty bottle of morphine. I'm Felix Caerphilly, welcome to the third episode of Supper for Six.

What had happened to Jeremy? Had it been an overdose? Or was he murdered? Several unusual things had already happened that evening to cause Lady Anderson's guests to fear that their hostess was acting irrationally and might even intend them harm. Elizabeth, who was not in the dining room to watch her serve the carefully chosen cake, had her own suspicions about Lady Sybil Anderson. For this episode, let us step away from Jeremy's death to the question of Anthony's disappearance. This mystery entwines both men, and to understand Sybil, we must understand her husband.

How well did anyone really know Sybil? The night of the murder was the first time in a decade that Elizabeth had seen her in person. The Langfords were old friends of her husband's and before Aintree the previous weekend, neither claimed to have seen her for many months. Jeremy had played music with Sybil in the sixties. It was only his wife, make-up artist Chrissy Crowley, who had spent any time with her recently, and even their coffee appointments had dried up months before. The residents of the square considered Sybil a recluse. And now they were locked up together with a dead body upstairs. Private investigator Elizabeth Chalice tried to get help from the authorities, despite an emergency situation which had sent Londoners seeking refuge indoors. In this next tape, recovered from 26 Bruton Square, is Elizabeth's phone call to the police. Firemen found an open-reel recorder in the basement which captured audio from the telephone line, similar to the system used by President Nixon earlier in that decade. Elizabeth's theory was that

*Anthony had tapped the phones to try and find proof that Sybil was
being unfaithful, in order to secure a divorce. The small portion of the
tape was not damaged by the fire had recorded Elizabeth's phonecall to
the police. Notice the tone of the officer taking the call – it's almost
comical and certainly not fitting to the gravity of a woman in danger,
reporting a murder. Despite London's size as a large city, the police and
legal system are too entwined. The officer taking the call was linked
closely with one of the dinner party guests. There's a sense the officer was
toying with Elizabeth, with his comical tone.*

*Elizabeth's conversation was not the only recording of a telephone call
recovered from number 26 Bruton Square. Anthony had been recording
every thing on the phone line to and from the house. However, it is not
known for how long Lord Anderson had been recording his wife's telephone calls, as only that evening's tape was undamaged by the fire. The
Anderson family made their money in automobiles, but Lord Anderson
had begun to import audio equipment from Japan. Sybil, forbidden to
perform in public by her husband, had taken to recording herself singing.*

POLICE OFFICER:

Good evening, Belgravia Police Station. What is the nature of your
call?

ELIZABETH:

I'm calling to report a murder.

POLICE OFFICER:

OK, I'll just take your details, madam. But first can I confirm that
you aren't in danger?

ELIZABETH:

Well, I'm stuck in a house with the killer. She's locked us in.
Number 26 Bruton Square.

POLICE OFFICER:

Not a chance we'll get to you anytime soon, can you make your
way to safety somewhere inside the house? Failing that, you could
lock her in a room? Why don't you tell me what happened?

ELIZABETH:

There were six of us. The other three are with her now so I could put the call through. My name is Elizabeth Chalice, private investigator. Five of us were invited to dinner this evening at 26 Bruton Square. One of the party went missing in the house, just as the electricity went off, about quarter past eight – that's just an estimate. A short while later, he was found dead in one of the upstairs rooms. It looked to me like he was injected with morphine.

POLICE OFFICER:

Very Agatha Christie. Let me guess, did it happen with a candlestick in the drawing room?

ELIZABETH:

This is no laughing matter, officer. A man just lost his life. We are stuck here with his killer and no way out.

POLICE OFFICER:

If you're safe for a few minutes, I'll take some details and try and get someone over urgent. What was the victim's name?

ELIZABETH:

Jeremy Crowley, aged approximately forty-one, I'd say.

POLICE OFFICER:

And the names of the other people present?

ELIZABETH:

The victim's wife Chrissy Crowley, the hostess Lady Sybil Anderson, and her neighbours Agapanthus and Francois Langford.

POLICE OFFICER:

Lady Sybil Anderson? There's been a murder in Lord Anderson's house – the Earl of Edale? Fact of it being the abode of a gentleman should appeal to Scotland Yard. Right ho, repeat the names again.

ELIZABETH:

Agapanthus and Francois Langford.

POLICE OFFICER:

All right, Langford, is it? He a lawyer?

ELIZABETH:

Er, yes, I believe so, why?

POLICE OFFICER:

No reason. On a scale of one to ten, ten being in abject fear of your life, and one being not concerned for your safety whatsoever, how concerned are you for your safety?

ELIZABETH:

I've never been asked to rate . . . I mean, I am certain the killer is here with us, and I hope we can keep our guard up, but we really do need a team down from Scotland Yard as soon as possible.

POLICE OFFICER:

So, let's say, you're at about a four.

ELIZABETH:

More like an eight. There are four other people here, I can't keep tabs on them all.

POLICE OFFICER:

You're a private investigator, you say? I ain't never heard your name around here before. You must have some street smarts? Tie her up, lock the door and sit tight.

ELIZABETH:

You wouldn't have . . . I live in Italy, usually.

POLICE OFFICER:

OK. Well, if I was you . . . what was your name again?

ELIZABETH:

Elizabeth Chalice.

POLICE OFFICER:

If I was you, Liz, I would take my chances staying indoors with your Mayfair dinner party lot. I'm getting in awful, awful reports of dead birds falling out of their nests and all sorts with this gas in the air. Do what you can to preserve the scene, take statements and we will have someone with you as soon as we can.

ELIZABETH:

OK. Can I ask if there is a senior officer to whom I can relay this information?

POLICE OFFICER:

Ma'am, you happen to be speaking to a detective sergeant here. I'm only on the phones because I did my knee in and can't barely walk and everyone else is out on jobs. I will be in touch with Scotland Yard now about this. In the meantime, do what you can to keep things secure where you are.

ELIZABETH:

How long do you think you'll be?

POLICE OFFICER:

It's impossible to say. Ring me back if there's any more dead bodies.

ELIZABETH:

Oh, officer, before I let you go, I'd like to report a missing person. Well, he's already been reported but please, if you have officers on patrol, Lord Anderson has disappeared from the house. There's a chance he may not be in his full capacities.

POLICE OFFICER:

You've got your hand's full there, love. When was he last seen?

ELIZABETH:

Well, he hasn't been seen for approximately five days.

POLICE OFFICER:
Why hasn't he been reported missing before now?

ELIZABETH:
Well, his wife did report him, but he is still using the telephone.

POLICE OFFICER:
He ain't missing then. Listen, love, if he's run off, tonight is not the time to try and find him. All regular patrols are suspended on account of the fire, I told you we was understaffed. But I've made a note of it here. Anything comes of it, we know where to find you. Now, love, I hear my kettle singing, best go. Cheerio.

FELIX:
What did you think of how the police handled the investigation?

ELIZABETH:
I'm glad the tape of my call with the officer was recovered – as you would have heard, the bobby didn't take us seriously at all. He took the whole thing as if it were some sort of joke. Now, I rang them as soon as I'd recorded the murder scene. I suppose they must have a lot of innocuous calls in Belgravia. Paranoid millionaires, but still – this was murder! I decided not to let the others know about the delay. I decided to let on they would arrive any minute to keep the others calm and so Sybil would feel the pressure. She'd already shut off the lights, and locked us in. Was the house booby-trapped? She'd been in such a bloody rush to get us upstairs when we arrived.

At the same time as Elizabeth was calling the police, Francois Langford was amongst the party who remained in the dining room, maintaining the dinner party's facade. Later we will see how Francois' case was also connected to this police officer, further explaining his strange reaction to Elizabeth. When the lawyer finally agreed to let me interview him the early 1978, I was keen to learn more about what happened in the brief moments before the lights went out. Next you'll hear recordings of my interview with Francois, followed by some more of Elizabeth's invaluable recordings of the night in question . . .

FRANCOIS:

When I arrived, I was immediately concerned about the other guests at the dinner party. It was not like her to entertain, so I had been wary from the moment I walked in. But I was quite taken off guard to see Christina. She caught my eye like a doe in the headlights. Don't say a word, she seemed to say, breaking the glance before anyone else could notice. I knew she was an old friend of Sybil's. But us all guests at the same dinner party, here in Mayfair? In Bruton Square? I wasn't ever good at pulling off deceit. The best thing was to get through the meal and leave as soon as possible, before Agapanthus suspected a thing.

FELIX:

You had been having an affair with the victim's wife, Christina Crowley?

FRANCOIS:

Well, she'll be my wife soon. We're engaged to be married. But our affair began a few months before the dinner party. She'd er, fallen pregnant and by April, she was about five months gone. I'm ashamed to say when she first told me I panicked and ended things. But as she was tidying the plates away after the avocado, just before the lights went off, I saw the curve of her belly. It was real. This child of hers. Growing inside her.

FELIX:

Why did you think Sybil invited her? What was her motivation in hosting the dinner party?

FRANCOIS:

Anthony had been planning a ivorce. I thought she must have found out about it, and engineered this evening to strengthen her own position. Was she going to blackmail me? I was still in regular phone contact with Anthony; he'd said she was clueless about his impending plan to end their marriage. Lord Anderson, millionaire, entrepreneur, my best friend. I suppose if I were his wife, I'd be expecting a big pay-out. But Anthony didn't intend to give her one. Now we know what happened, I think there's a strong chance Sybil was the murderer. That she planned the entire event for Anthony to be murdered. She was awfully tied to that house, you see. It was Sybil's refuge. She would have killed to keep number 26 Bruton Square.

Anthony was keen to keep his assets away from Sybil, but in my experience, all hell breaks loose when the other party finds out. He had only recently updated his will – which provided well for Sybil – so I wondered what had changed his mind to go for all-out divorce? It was also a professional opportunity for me. For years I'd been slaving away in general practice, not picking up much more than a few wills. It had started to look like that would change. He put me in touch with a senior barrister for a murder case – I'd always wanted to try criminal law. Anthony always looked out for me.

I remember when I arrived, I was late. Sybil was in high spirits at the door, but upstairs the mood was tense. And moments after I came in, that blasted air-raid siren rang out, sending the women berserk.

Let's cut to Elizabeth's tapes again. Listen carefully, for Francois Langford contradicts the accounts of the others. Now we rejoin the group at the dining-room table where Sybil is serving dessert to hear a different part of the tape. Elizabeth has just returned from telephoning the police. It begins as a strangely polite conversation, considering both a killer and a dead body are in the house.

SYBIL:

Thank you all for coming here this evening. Before I explain myself, I'd like to raise a toast. To getting answers.

ELIZABETH:

To, uhm, getting answers.

AGAPANTHUS:

To getting answers . . .

FRANCOIS:

I felt like I was toasting my own doom. I was working on the murder trial and expected to be in court first thing. Between Christina and Sybil, well, I'm ashamed to say I just wanted to leave the mad women together and get a good night's sleep. I became conscious of how nervous I must have looked. The trouble with having a thick head of hair is how flattened it gets when the sweating starts.

FRANCOIS:

Is it a big secret you want to share . . . or . . .

AGAPANTHUS:

Francois, can you please make some attempt to control your verbal incontinence?

SYBIL:

Now, now, Agapanthus. Your husband is right. I really had better tell you what I wanted to ask for your help with.

FRANCOIS:

Sybil was fiddling with her rings, spinning that enormous engagement ring around and around. I thought there was something about Elizabeth Chalice I couldn't trust. That she'd be capable of illicit activity. Or accidental manslaughter. She had eyes that were too ready to look away. It was as if she wished for some great drama to happen, but was prepared to avert her gaze if it did. She had a peculiar habit of not looking where you'd imagine one would look. She was distracted by something over my shoulder. I wondered where Mr Chalice was. And then it dawned on me. She'd had a bloody affair with Agapanthus's sister's husband, twenty years ago. They'd been in trouble for years, but Elizabeth had brought Sally a lot more trouble. Anyway, that's a story for another day. Sybil spewed up the whole story about Anthony.

SYBIL:

Very well. It's just rather, erm, personal. It's rather difficult.
Embarrassing. I've known you all for a few years now. Jeremy and I
go back quite a bit farther. Francois, you're Anthony's oldest friend.
Elizabeth, we haven't seen each other much over the years.
Agapanthus, despite living so closely we are still getting to know
each other. Chrissy, although we go for our coffees, you know I've
always held something back. My attempt at a stiff upper lip, I
suppose. You see, since I met Anthony, I feel that I've been
conducting this grand performance. Acting at being Lady
Anderson. I've been so busy playing this part that I've sort of
forgotten about Sybil Ní Chríodáin. In striving to be an aristocrat,
I've been avoiding my own entrance into the world. Anthony has
never felt anything other than belonging.

FRANCOIS:

This was clearly another one of Sybil's attention-seeking bits.
Well, I just drank my Kangarouge, and tried not to let my feathers
get ruffled. The others, of course, were champing at the bit to hear
Sybil's tale. I've gone over that evening in my mind many times
since. Because Jeremy was acting strangely. I know trouble when I
see it. His fist was clenched like he was about to thump someone. I
reckoned that he'd clocked up a few public order offences, petty
larceny, offences against the person.

SYBIL:

In fact, he's the only member of the Anderson family confident in
who he is. Remember, his parents weren't born aristocrats either.
Anthony was their entrance into high society through his school
friends. A strategic union with an old family and he would have
secured the dynasty. Well, instead, he chose me. You can imagine
how disappointed they were. I often wonder if that disappointment
at Anthony's choosing me killed them. Because without something
to strive for, they had nothing to live for. Well, Anthony had wanted
to understand the world his parents came from. We said it was love,

of course, at the time. It was the sixties! But I think we are all old enough to know that love is just the excuse we use for the actions we take to fix ourselves. Anthony needed to play the guide with me, just as he had done for his parents. Sybil Pritchard was young enough that he could mould her into his idea of a wife, whilst always sitting in the driving seat. He knew then as now of his charisma, his ability to charm anyone—

FRANCOIS:

A lock of dark hair fell across Christina's face as she sat back to watch Sybil. Mother Nature had planted some extra pregnancy weight about her face; thankfully that's all gone now. But she was still quite beautiful. Those dark eyes, with hair as rich as a cup of Nescafé. She almost looked like a waitress in her straight black frock, quite the contrast to Sybil's yellow dress, as if they were the personification of day and night. Obviously, her attempt to look slim. But all eyes were on Sybil as she told us about Anthony's disappearance. I knew she was lying, but couldn't be sure until later.

SYBIL:

Anthony married Sybil Ní Chríodáin. Little mousey Sybil from Ballyglass. My dad was a builder, my mum is a secretary at the local school. I wasn't a polo-playing, privately educated daughter of society. That's for sure. When we married, I was very conscious of meeting his expectations but also of retaining myself. My own essence. Yes, I could stop singing and wear different clothes, but that little flicker of myself, well, it would still burn. Over these past ten years, sometimes it's been hard to keep it alive. I miss the stage. I *wish* I could perform. Though I suppose I am in a way. I am playing the part of Anthony's wife. So, the last time I saw him was five days ago. We'd been at Aintree, you remember, Aggie, Francois? It didn't go well. He lost a lot of money. Which never usually bothers him. But the entire way back, he wouldn't say a thing to me in the car. He wouldn't even speak to the driver. He's usually very pally with everyone, you know. Well, we arrived back here, I went for a bath. I was so *exhausted* from the day . . . I fell straight into bed. In the morning, he was gone. A few shirts and things were missing from his wardrobe. But no note or anything. From time to time, he would disappear off for a few days, and not tell me where. So, at first, I tried not to worry. But then on Monday, I got a telephone call. From someone at the company. A fellow came for all of the papers in his desk.

FRANCOIS:

This was after the sirens went off, before the lights went out.

ELIZABETH:

Do you think you could get a message to Anthony, Francois?

FRANCOIS:

I will try . . .

SYBIL:

He probably wishes I'm dead, so that he can move back here and forget the whole sorry affair.

FRANCOIS:

Now, now, Sybil. It oughtn't to come to all that . . . drama. All roads will lead home for him eventually, you'll just have to be patient. Ultimately, he'll respect a cool head from you more than some half-cocked plan to force him home.

FELIX:

How did the others react?

FRANCOIS:

Jeremy started to swing back on his chair, sniggering with his lip curled down. Everyone at the table was looking at him. I'm not one to start a row but I was raised better than to allow such poor table manners. So, I called him up on it. Agapanthus was drunk, I could tell by the flush across her neck. And when she's like that, there's no way I can rein her in.

FRANCOIS:

Did I say something funny, Jeremy?

JEREMY:

Nah, mate. I'm just taking you all in. This little dinner party of yours, Sybil, it ain't panning out like I thought. I reckoned it would be white linen tablecloths and fresh flowers – no one wanting to speak their minds, stiff upper lips sort of thing. But instead, you're all giving it the bleedin' heart.

AGAPANTHUS:

If you don't like it, no one is stopping you from leaving. I like the casual atmosphere you've created, Sybil. If we could all just enjoy our food without, well the bad smell that's lingering, I can literally smell the stale perspiration from you—

FRANCOIS:

Now, Agapanthus, I don't think we ought to descend to personal insults.

JEREMY:

You going to let her say that to me, Sybil?

SYBIL:

Jeremy, will you shut up! This is a serious matter. Francois, aren't you worried that your best friend is missing?

FRANCOIS:

Well, yes. I suppose I am. If what you're saying is true, then really no one has seen him for a few days. That's no big deal – and I spoke to him the day before yesterday and he sounded rather chipper on the telephone.

JEREMY:

If this is what he has to listen to I don't blame the bloke.

SYBIL:

I didn't realise you were so easily offended. Look, I'm sorry that you're not getting the aristocratic dinner experience, but I've done my best. My husband is missing. I need your help. If you can just cool your heads 'til we figure it out.

AGAPANTHUS:

How do you expect this criminal – punk, whatever – to be of assistance is beyond me.

FRANCOIS:

All eyes fell on my lady wife. She'd even surprised herself by saying more than she meant to. I watched her spin the base of her glass in circles, crinkling the white linen tablecloth. It was then I realised that my wife knew Jeremy. I'd been so concerned when I saw Chrissy there . . . I hadn't noticed. Agapanthus's shoulders slouched back and her pout softened. She was backtracking.

AGAPANTHUS:

Well, musicians are often arrested, that sort of thing. Apologies, I shouldn't have said anything. Too much wine.

JEREMY:

Sure, that's what you meant.

ELIZABETH:

Look, I know that we have found ourselves in a strange situation, there are tensions running high. But you have all been invited here by Sybil to track down Anthony. Can we just agree to put whatever disagreements you may have on ice, whilst we get to the bottom of it? We are all adults here. So, let's act like it. Sybil, you said that you've devised a list of places he could have gone. I'll make a few telephone calls. Francois, perhaps you could have a think about where he might be? I know it's only been five days, but hasn't the thought crossed your mind?

FRANCOIS:

He's a multi-millionaire, Elizabeth – he's probably renting somewhere we would never suspect.

SYBIL:

Show me that telephone book, Francois. That's a Mayfair number. But his number is local to here. He really can't be far away. You know he can be very volatile. He is liable to lash out. And then they'll take him straight into custody, or worse, to the loony bin. My mother . . . that's where she ended up and it killed her. Those doctors and nurses, no offence, Elizabeth, as I know you were a nurse.

ELIZABETH:

I nursed in Chelsea and Westminster throughout the Second World War—

SYBIL:

Yes I do know, Elizabeth. But as I was saying, about my mother. At that time, all they wanted was for her to die. It was barbaric how people were treated in there. Francois, I want you on hand in case he does get violent and attacks someone.

AGAPANTHUS:

He would be as much use as a chocolate teapot.

FELIX:

What was Christina doing?

FRANCOIS:

By this stage, Christina had started to look a bit peaky. She was sweating under the dark dress. Having her husband and lover in the same room was difficult for her. There was so much tension around that dining table. Things were on a knife edge. Agapanthus made her way to the sideboard and poured herself a brandy. Even that didn't stop her from chewing down those manicured nails of hers. Sybil was perched on the very edge of the fine fainting couch showing Elizabeth the phone book. Her yellow dress stuck to her back. Rings of sweat showed the dress was clinging to her underarms.

FRANCOIS:

Shut up, woman, will you? Anthony? Violent? Apart from one or two small run-ins after a lot of alcohol, I've never seen that side of him. I really do think you're making an awful big fuss out of nothing.

SYBIL:

Well, that's why I chose you all to come here. Please help me find him. I hoped you'd understand how this is a private, family affair. I'm trusting you with the information about Anthony, because he would not be happy to have that in the public domain.

AGAPANTHUS:

We will find him. Don't you worry about that.

FRANCOIS:

My wife was making such a great effort with Sybil in a bid to distract from her earlier exchange with Jeremy. I may have enjoyed an affair or two over the years. I know it was unfair of me to judge her . . . and well, perhaps I could have let it go. But his apparent murder shortly after kept the revelation in my mind. Maybe I wasn't a barrister, but I knew my wife and how to push her.

FRANCOIS:

She's only saying that to shut you up.

JEREMY:

Why would I help you? I have enough to be doing looking for work with a baby on the way.

SYBIL:

Yes, I know, Jeremy. But despite this act you—

JEREMY:

It ain't no act!

SYBIL:

I know how intelligent you are. Please. Just give me a few hours of your time. I'll compensate you for it. Aggie, you know everything that happens on Bruton Square . . . you're well connected in society. And then there's your work at the hospital. If he had turned up . . . I thought maybe you might have heard something from the Residents' Association . . . perhaps there's been talk about him?

AGAPANTHUS:

No, nothing like that. If he came into the hospital, I would have known about it.

FRANCOIS:

From my seat on the edge of the table, I could see right out into Bruton Square. There wasn't a single person out there on the street. You could be forgiven for thinking it was the dead of winter, with smoke hanging in the air like the blue fog of a December night.

The large glass chandelier inside the hall door of number 26 hung in darkness when Francois made his way downstairs. Finding Anthony's office number in his address book, he dialled his titled friend from the rotary telephone in the hall. He knew exactly where his friend was. Or did he?

FRANCOIS:

I thought I heard his voice saying his usual 'Hullo?', and I immediately said 'Tony – Frankie here, I really think you ought—' But the electricity went off within seconds, cutting us off. In the dark, I tried to call back, using the light from the street to read the numbers. The next call just rang out. I wondered why he would just hang up on me? I wondered, was there another woman? But Anthony wasn't too bothered about members of the fairer sex. The *real* reason I was calling was because I knew he loathed the news and radio. Even with the air-raid siren, I was worried that he hadn't heard the indoor warning. Knowing Anthony, he would have had all the windows open wherever he was holed up, inhaling the noxious miasmas everyone else was avoiding, I thought. Constitution of an ox, that man had. I could picture him in a satin robe listening to old Beatles records, sipping on an Irish coffee. Bachelorhood suited Anthony.

Francois's primary assertion was that Sybil killed Anthony to keep their Mayfair townhouse. We'll learn about Sybil's fate later in the story, but now it's worth noting that after Anthony's death, the house reverted to the ownership of Anthony's mother, the original Lady Marjorie Anderson.

So who exactly were the Andersons? As my investigation into the Anderson Affair grew legs, I began to realise that the foundations for the events that took place on 7th April were dug a decade earlier. I met Francois six times in the spring of 1978. The man relished the opportunity to talk. Where Elizabeth Chalice had been initially reluctant to talk to me, Francois was very keen. In fact, he sought me out, numerous times. But he was a narcissistic interviewee, and I was forced to record dozens of hours of tapes. Eventually, I managed to convince him to reveal more information about number 26 Bruton Square. And he made a shocking admission that directly related to the death of Jeremy Crowley. Is what you are about to hear a coincidence? Sybil was concerned about her husband's disappearance, but wasn't there anyone else who loved Lord Anderson, the Earl of Edale?

The following interview was recorded in January 1978, in Lamb Chambers.

FRANCOIS:

That house was no stranger to unseemly death. I wouldn't even say that Sybil knew the truth about what happened to Anthony's father and his second wife, Idabel. The papers reported an unfortunate car accident. They reported that, because Anthony's godfather was the editor of the *Daily Chronicle*, and that's what he instructed his minions to report.

FELIX:

What really happened to Anthony's father and his second wife, Idabel?

FRANCOIS:

The truth is, they died in this house. Anthony senior was a self-made man; he was used to taking risks . . . But not those sorts of risks. He divorced Anthony's mother and remarried. A glittering socialite. Not much older than myself and Anthony. She was young, but of good stock. She relished the opportunity to introduce her husband to the heights of society. Wealthy Americans were her favourite pals. She'd been pally with the youngest Getty son. In fact, she was rather ashamed of their townhouse. Measly by the standards of those she socialised with. When her delinquently wealthy pals were using drugs to escape the ennui of extreme wealth, it was less a case of keeping up with the Joneses, more like keeping up with the jags. Injecting the stuff, you know.

Anthony's stepmother managed to maintain a relatively decent facade, although she could not hide the gauntness the constant late nights gave her. Whatever her mistake, Anthony senior had not been into drugs. I mean the man died in robust full health. He'd managed to close a huge government deal just days before his death. These ministry officials wouldn't overlook drug use if it had been apparent in the chap. Anthony senior returned to drawn curtains and unemptied ashtrays; things had overtaken his young wife.

FELIX:

Was Anthony junior involved in their death?

FRANCOIS:

Oh no, Anthony found them, amidst the entropy that had beset number 26. He had been convinced that his father had acquiesced to the encouragement of his druggie wife, perhaps he'd wanted to celebrate the deal. Took a little taster of his wife's delectation. And not being used to it, he overdosed? Anthony didn't think that was likely. But what was the alternative?

FELIX:

Why did Anthony hide the details of their deaths?

FRANCOIS:

Anthony was no fool, even at that age. Despite what he found that day. He acted quickly to take over his father's business. That he could ensure something like that was kept out of the papers, himself only twenty-six, just goes to show the acumen the fellow has. When he met Sybil, that was his main motivation in having her retire from the stage. In case she got wrapped up in the showbiz drug use that was already starting to bother him about Idabel.

FELIX:

What did you do when you found out about the cover-up?

FRANCOIS:

He kept the entire situation to himself for days before he told me what had happened. I was finishing my legal training. He nabbed me out of the office for a pint – marching me into the Seven Stars. Anthony didn't ordinarily drink beer. He looked dog rough. It was one of the hottest days of the year, where the pavement stays red hot until closing time, creating this electric energy of office workers capitalising on the fine weather. Indeed, many people had started drinking with their lunch. He was manic, I had never seen him like that.

He drank his pint in large gulps, telling me how he'd found them. Sought his kingmakers – contacted his father's best friend in the Home Office. The chap in the *Daily Chronicle*. Arranged an undertaker. Had the bodies removed. The place cleaned. He'd done it all on his own . . . but had to tell someone. I mean, I had qualms about knowing. But I hadn't fully qualified as a solicitor and knew the fellow as a child. So, I listened. At first, I thought he was jacked up on something . . . until we teased out the various details. I knew then, he was telling the truth. He himself had always lived cleanly . . . and after that, his health became an important focus.

Sybil would speak about unusual things she'd seen in the house.

Pots being moved around, paintings crashing to the floor, exactly what you'd expect from the ghost of Anthony senior. Maybe that's why he didn't like staying here. In fact, that was the longest time I'd spent in those four walls since I visited the nursery as a child. Anthony never wanted any visitors. He left the place damn near abandoned for years, until eventually he moved Sybil in. When Agapanthus told me that she'd discovered Anthony's young bride poking around in the square gardens, I was sure she'd got it wrong. But there you have it.

FELIX:

So how was this linked to the night of the murder?

FRANCOIS:

Well, that night it all came back to me. As soon as the electricity went off, I felt around for some matches. I found them beside old Anthony's Waterford Crystal ashtray, on the lacquered side table beside his regal chair. That's where he would hold court. I can just remember him there, reading the paper and dictating messages to his secretaries. He used to work 'til midnight, every single evening. Regal with a shock of thick dark hair, a substantial moustache. He'd have factory workers bring samples over all the time.

One day, oh, we were about ten, Anthony came in to ask if he might go out to Hyde Park. I daren't enter his demesne, but I remember there were four car doors leaning up against the wall-paper rail. Same duck-egg blue. That decor was all Anthony's mother, Marjorie, of course. Rather sounded like margarine – that's what Anthony senior called her before the divorce. She wasn't terribly glamorous. But then his second wife was far too concerned with fluttering her socialite wings to bother about pelmets and Chippendales. Anthony never spoke of his mother after his parents divorced.

But here's where Francois's testimony just doesn't add up. He says Anthony never spoke of his mother after the divorce, but that's plainly untrue. Marjorie is an unseen presence at the dinner party that night.

Although she was not present on the evening, ordinarily she was employed as Sybil's housekeeper. Not for the money, it seems, as she would have been well provided for in the divorce from Anthony's father. But for the access to Anthony and to help Sybil. Why would Francois lie about a fact he knew to be plainly untrue?

FRANCOIS:

Tea is man's greatest asset for mental acuity. Doesn't cause the servant to defect, as you say. That's why I brewed a pot. Elizabeth was downstairs in the drawing room interviewing Agapanthus. Chrissy was unwell in the morning room. Everyone was feeling terribly . . . on edge. There was a sense of dread in the air. But there was no sign of Sybil, so, what was a fellow to do for a cuppa? If I'd realised that was bloody Anthony lying up there instead of Jeremy, well I wouldn't have done it. But I bloody didn't know. But let me tell you – what I'm about to reveal will shed light on the sort of woman Sybil was, not that I'm an angel.

FELIX:

Was this after the lights came back on?

FRANCOIS:

Yes.

FELIX:

But before you started playing cards?

FRANCOIS:

Yes. Tell me, you seem to know exactly what happened already. Have you fallen under the charms of Ms Chalice? No need to answer, for I already know the answer is yes. Elizabeth was interviewing my ex-wife, Agapanthus. Throughout our marriage she did have a tendency to be . . . violent. She is a hot-tempered person, so I was expecting Elizabeth to really rile her up. So, there I was downstairs boiling the kettle – why Sybil hadn't a cook to help, I do not know – reviewing the evidence I still needed to prepare for court the next day, although by this time, with the fire, I was starting to think it would be held over anyway. I tried to call my counsel, but the line was engaged. Seeking an update from the sky itself, I returned to the kitchen and peeked through the window. The moon had come out from behind the night sky clouds. There was no smoke that I could see. But then Sybil appeared. Teeth bared like an animal in search of its prey. I have to say, I don't scare easily but I was genuinely terrified. It was quite disgusting, mascara running down her face, a distinct scent of body odour as she crept soundlessly into the room.

At this point, Francois scrunches his nose as if in disgust at the very memory. But I can tell he's enjoying putting on a show for me, as though his own performance can convince me of the truth.

FELIX:

And what did she say when she came into the room and saw you?

FRANCOIS:

Oh, she looked quite intrigued, and asked why on earth I was poking about in her pantry. 'Are you feeling ok?' she said in a very strange, inquisitive manner. 'I'd like to talk to you.' She pushed her greasy hair off her forehead and smoothed her dress nervously as if she was about to begin a performance. She was acting like she was in control, but it was clear to me she was not. So, I thought I'd play her at her own game.

FELIX:

What do you mean by that?

FRANCOIS:

I simply said, 'Did you kill Jeremy? Is that why you removed the fuse for the lights?' I confronted her with the facts. Told her that I'd seen her hovering at the top step of the basement before the lights went out, giving her time to go down to the fuse box. Then she accused me and Chrissy of working as a team, quite ridiculously. But then her body softened.

FELIX:

What happened next?

FRANCOIS:

A thin little smile emerged as she swept the mascara aside, laughing at something only she was amused by. She stepped closer to me . . . I had a feeling what would happen next. At my age, you develop a sense for these things. And despite the bloody mad circumstances of that night. The tension, the fear, well, I suddenly found the situation incredibly . . . arousing. At that point, I almost wished she was the killer . . . to add to the depravity. Gah – the bloody tape. I hope you'll be judicious in which details you share in your article, Caerphilly. I have a son to think about now. Right, where was I? Sybil was standing only an inch from my face.

The words dropped slowly from her lips. 'I've been waiting for a moment alone with you.' I tried to push her away, tell her it wasn't time for that. But then she hit a nerve. Spoke about how I'd always been overlooked, first by Anthony and then Agapanthus. She knew Anthony was planning to divorce her, and asked me to represent her instead. She leered at me. Grinning at me like a churchgoer to a vicar. I realised she'd changed her clothes. The black dress she'd put on lent her an air of a Victorian mourner. That entire evening was a performance by someone starved of attention. With her fingers clasped, she arched her eyebrows in expectation of my affirmation. I didn't quite notice the teacup had started to overflow. She made me scald myself, the madwoman. Threatened to tell Agapanthus that I'd slept with her and I had been having an affair with Chrissy. My wife . . . she wasn't stupid, she knew there had been . . . indiscretions. But I did not want the whole business strewn out in front of Elizabeth Chalice.

FELIX:

Were you attracted to Ms Chalice, Francois?

FRANCOIS:

Well . . . I mean. I had quite enough on my plate. But it was
highly wrong of her to record us like that. I pointed out the illegal-
ity in the course of the inquest and investigation . . .

FELIX:

I was surprised you didn't want justice for a murder victim?

*Francois grabbed his briefcase and stood from his chair, signalling that
he would end our interview, so I decided to change my questioning tactic
and take him back to the conversation with Sybil in the kitchen.*

FELIX:

You were saying, Sybil asked you to represent her in the divorce.

FRANCOIS:

Yes, she was going on about how wealthy but illiquid Anthony
was, and how I'd get my money far more quickly as her lawyer. But
Anthony was my best friend, it was never going to happen. I'd had
enough of her and tried to leave the kitchen . . . But, well dammit,
she had me all worked up. There was a thin bead of sweat slipping
down her collar bone along the curve of her bosom. I wanted to
taste it . . .

FELIX:

So, you kissed her?

FRANCOIS:

Only for the briefest of moments; I came to my senses then.
Told her Anthony wasn't planning a divorce. She tried to ask me if
I knew Jeremy before, but the real stranger there was Elizabeth. I
asked her how long she'd known her. I reminded her that Chrissy
was her friend.

We were interrupted by a series of shuffles and a loud thud from
upstairs. Agapanthus could always take care of herself, but given
the events of the evening, it would have been negligent not to
check. Sybil snaked up the stairs hissing after me. I knocked on the

door but Agapanthus burst through, her lips drawn together in a
pout as she stood with one hand on her hip, the strings of her
blouse undone. There were even some cobwebs in her hair. Wild
eyes. What did I do to be locked up here with two deranged
women? She eyed Sybil closely. Perhaps I had given some sort of
clue . . . but somehow, she detected that there had been a moment
between myself and our hostess. As we stood in the doorway,
Elizabeth lurked behind my wife, silently observing, her tape
recorder in hand to document every bloody second of things.

*From Francois's interview we return to Elizabeth's recording from the
dining room. Despite Francois mentioning loud banging, we return to a
civilised scene.*

SYBIL:

Would you like some tea, Agapanthus?

AGAPANTHUS:

No, something stronger is needed tonight. Of course, I've known
all about you, Francois. You've treated me like a fool for years now.
Anthony is planning to divorce you, Sybil. I found the papers in
Francois's briefcase. Along with something else. A copy of a trust
Francois established for a client. A wealthy one. And you'll never
guess who the benefactor is. One Jeremy Crowley. Is that tape
recorder on, Elizabeth?

FRANCOIS:

She nodded, summoning us back into the room with an open
arm. Of the three women, Elizabeth had retained her sense of
decorum. True blitz spirit is a rare thing to see these days but she
possessed it in buckets.

SYBIL:

Please, can't we sit down and I'll get you all a drink – what
happened in here?

FRANCOIS:

Then we noticed the broken glass all over the floor, the blood on Agapanthus's trousers. The slur in her speech.

AGAPANTHUS:

Your little detective knows how to get a body worked up, isn't that right, Elizabeth? Here, let me clean it up.

SYBIL:

Please, can we all just calm down and let Elizabeth do her job. I'll take care of the glass. Here – the seats at the other end of the table are clear.

AGAPANTHUS:

Fine. The will was never actioned. Elizabeth already knows this. No such thing as a private call in this house, Sybil. With all the hand-sets you've lying around the place. Well, you know, dear husband, I rather want to stay and find out who our killer is. No one will catch me out with a syringe. Oh, just let them try.

SYBIL:

Well, I'm glad you want to stay. I never meant to lock you all in here with me. But you know, the gas. I don't want my best friends in the world to be burned up, now do I? Look, I must admit I do have access to some source of information . . . quite unsure if Elizabeth will go for it. I know we are all not quite ourselves. Here's a drink for you all.

FRANCOIS:

Not poisoned, is it? No crushed glass or anything?

SYBIL:

Only a good dash of Tia Maria. I'm glad we can laugh about this.

AGAPANTHUS:

Oh, I'm not laughing. I'm not laughing at all. But whatever your plan is tonight, Sybil, you're not going to scare me. And you, Francois? Make a copy of those divorce papers for us, won't you?

FRANCOIS:

Well. Um. Yes. I gather that would be the correct—

AGAPANTHUS:

That is, unless you're going to try and break my neck first.

FRANCOIS:

Dear God! Those two meowing cats. I loathe the drama that accompanies women. This unpicking of a beautiful moment with reality. Agapanthus's frankness took the fun out of it. Now, to go back to your question about Elizabeth. For a woman of her age, I don't know if I'd ever quite seen someone come alive like that. She was a minx of the highest order. God knows what I would have admitted to. And there, Mr Caerphilly, we must leave our interview. I hope I've given you something to spice up your investigation. I'm due back in court now. But everyone loves a lothario, no?

I'd barely taken a bite of my Battenburg when he jumped up and started loading up his briefcase.

FELIX:

But when did you realise that the body in Sybil's dressing room was not Jeremy Crowley?

FRANCOIS:

I told you I'd never met the fellow before that night. Now, I really cannot be late for Judge Winters. He does not like the silk I'm working for and can't afford to risk riling him up.

Francois ushered me down the stairs. I've held a few things back from Francois's interview in the interest of allowing you to experience the evening as the guests did. But I do owe you an explanation. As we make our way through this story, we will pay close attention to each of the other diners that night. Could Francois be trusted? The loquacious lawyer spoke frankly to me about his extra-marital affairs, and revealed his best friend's secrets without hesitation. At the time, I thought him a cad with few morals and little consideration for the women or the children he left behind . . . This made me wonder if his forthcomingness was an attempt to bombard me with information that would conceal his true secrets, including the high-profile murder case he was working on that linked him to the detective sergeant Elizabeth Chalice reported the murder to. Because the policeman recognised Francois's name, and did not report the murder to Scotland Yard. In fact, he did not take notes, and later denied receiving the call. Francois's account of that night took on greater importance when it transpired that Elizabeth Chalice had lied to everyone about her connection to the murder victim all along.

We will explore the dirty secrets of Lady Anderson's guests, including a potential collusion with the IRA. But what happened immediately after Jeremy's body was found? We will return to the scene of the crime in the next episode of Supper for Six, *I hope you've worked up an appetite.*

EPISODE FOUR:

The Hostess with the Mostess

Locked into a Mayfair mansion with a dead body and a murderer, the guests of Lady Sybil Anderson were served more than they expected at the aristocrat's dinner party in April of 1977. As Londoners were instructed to remain indoors due to a fire in Soho, only investigator Elizabeth Chalice knew that the police were too busy to interrogate the suspects and protect the lives of her fellow diners. But who was guilty and who was innocent? I'm Felix Caerphilly and welcome to episode four of the Supper for Six *podcast. Let's return to an earlier part of the evening, where we may have missed some critical clues.*

Lady Anderson had announced her husband had been missing for five days, and that she needed help to find him. As the body of Jeremy Crowley lay cooling in Sybil's second-floor dressing room, detective Elizabeth Chalice managed to take control of events by interviewing each suspect individually. They readily agreed to a private conversation with the sleuth, for behind this veneer, each diner held their secrets closely amidst an intricate web of extra-marital affairs, family secrets and business deals gone badly. In this episode, we discover exactly how Lady Anderson engineered the Mayfair dinner party, from an interview Elizabeth Chalice recorded that night. But how much of it is true? I'll warn you that she makes a number of false claims.

FELIX:

Did Sybil know you were recording her?

ELIZABETH:

No, she wouldn't have spoken so freely.

FELIX:

How did she seem?

ELIZABETH:

She began the interview very composed on the surface. Considering she was essentially a recluse, and it was her first time entertaining, I found that very peculiar. But I could see that it was an act and she was as anxious as me, as she tore a line of flesh from her cuticle with her teeth, wincing as she produced a droplet of blood. I left everyone else in the dining room and interviewed Sybil in the drawing room.

FELIX:
This was downstairs on the ground floor?

ELIZABETH:
Yes. Sybil had vehemently objected so it was quite the job to convince her to open up that room, but eventually she conceded and I interviewed Sybil in the drawing room where the coals were starting to glow in the grate. I'd set a fire to cast some more light as Her Ladyship sat across the large Chesterfield armchair from me. Shadow covered the walls and ceilings of the grand room, and I realised there were no family photographs. As with the dining room, this chamber was lacking in personality, as if it was a house hired for a photographer's shoot.

I had to dab the palms of my hand to hold the pen, I remember that. You see she had masterminded the entire evening, and not only my own life was at risk, but that of the Langfords and Chrissy downstairs. I had to speed through things as quickly as possible to get the five of us back together. I paid close attention to her countenance – committing a murder takes a terrific toll on the body of a killer, most people can't sustain a calm exterior.

FELIX:
How did she seem?

ELIZABETH:
Tears rolled down Sybil's cheeks. The translucent pearls washed away the darker Pan Stik to reveal her pallor underneath. I handed her a tissue. I wanted to finish the interview to check on the others. But this was an important detail in the story.

ELIZABETH:
Now, Sybil, I need to establish some facts this evening. But first, you said that Jeremy is not what he seemed. Can you tell me about that?

SYBIL:

Well, I'm sure Jeremy made a strong impression on you this evening, the mohawk, the accent. Well, it's a bit of an act, really. A show that he's been living for years now, but an untrue life, all the same. You see, Jeremy Crowley was the adopted child of Florence and George Crowley of Castlebar.

ELIZABETH:

I thought he lived in Forest Hill?

SYBIL:

I'm getting there. Jeremy's father was a wealthy farmer and landowner. In fact, he grew up in the countryside of Somerset. He attended a private school. His father was even Master of the local Hunt at one point. But then his parents divorced, his mother moved to London, and he came with her, rejecting everything his father had stood for. I believe George did make attempts to have a relationship with his son, but Jeremy was too angry at what his father had done to his mother – he refused. He did not take an allowance. Eventually George stopped paying. Chrissy doesn't even know what George could have done to Florence to make him act that way – maybe he was just really angry. However, there are several financial instruments in place due to the position of his birth. Trusts, benefits-in-kind, and a life insurance policy. That should make things easier for Chrissy.

ELIZABETH:

Did she know about the estate?

SYBIL:

Oh, yes, she mentioned it all the time. How his death would solve all her problems.

ELIZABETH:

Do you really think Jeremy was murdered? It's far more likely the poor chap died by his own hand, albeit accidentally. What I'm saying is that I have an open mind. It's worth investigating.

SYBIL:

You seem certain that is the case.

ELIZABETH:

I know better than to be certain of anything. So, are you suggesting Chrissy murdered him to get her hands on the money?

SYBIL:

She's a wily woman, Elizabeth. I wouldn't put it past her. Raised in the gutter, she was. Her family had *nothing*. She lived with an aunt who's dead now. Despite that, she's made a name for herself as a make-up artist in the West End. But why she would want to do it in my house is rather annoying. That reminds me. Is ten pounds enough of a down payment for you to start your work?

ELIZABETH:

You mean to pay me for my investigation of Jeremy's death?

SYBIL:

And then for finding my husband. I need more information on Anthony, I feel that he's growing more and more distant from me . . .

ELIZABETH:

I couldn't accept a fee for this business with Jeremy. But ten pounds will cover the investigation of your husband. I can't promise we will find him – that's the thing, there are no guarantees. But I will try my hardest. But it's vital we discuss Jeremy first. Do you mind if I smoke?

SYBIL:

Please, actually, oh no—

ELIZABETH:

Would you like one?

SYBIL:

Oh, go on.

Sound of lighter clicking twice.

SYBIL:

(*inhaling*) Are you sure I can't pay you for tonight . . . I wouldn't want you to be out of pocket?

ELIZABETH:

A woman has her principles, my dear. Tell me, you first met Jeremy in the sixties; what were those circumstances? Neither of you wanted to tell it.

SYBIL:

We met at the local speech and drama group in Forest Hill. I moved to London when I was seventeen and stayed with my aunt for a while. I made sandwiches in the mornings, and looked for singing gigs in the afternoons. Everyone else in that group must have been at least forty. I wondered why he even went, but he was a classically trained musician, so saw the benefits in being a classic- ally trained dramatist. He played the piano, the bass guitar, the regular guitar, even the violin. I have never met such a talented musician. He was synaesthetic you know, when he heard music, he could actually see the colours. It's no surprise he got into art.

ELIZABETH:

So, you struck up a relationship?

SYBIL:

Oh, no, he wasn't my type at all. He carried a bit of extra weight back then but he offered to accompany me at gigs. It became an awful lot easier to get gigs with a guitarist – and then we found two other chaps he'd gone to grammar school with to play the drums and the bass. We had a band.

ELIZABETH:

Jeremy was living with his mother, at that time?

SYBIL:

Jeremy didn't like to talk about it. But I saw Florence a few times, dressed very smartly – pristine white collars and the like. There was an Irish link, that he had been adopted from there, but he never wanted to get into it. It was clear that they had money – it didn't make sense that they were living in this little two-bedroomed house. One day I was behind her in the bank. It was a quiet day in the middle of summer. I'd gone in to take out my cash for the week. She was up with the teller – it seemed that she was trying to cash a cheque but they wouldn't do it for her. She even used the phone in the bank. She was livid, hissing in anger although she was trying to be quiet. I do remember she said 'you're never going to see your son again, after this'. I never mentioned it to Jeremy – it was none of my business. If that had been my mum in the bank, I wouldn't have wanted people gossiping, you know.

ELIZABETH:

When did your own mother die, Sybil?

SYBIL:

Shortly after Anthony and I were married. I was so caught up in being Lady Anderson, I rarely got to see my parents. (They're both dead now.) I'd still not produced an heir, despite our best efforts, and I couldn't bear to leave Anthony's side. And I was embarrassed to let Anthony see the house, with no hot water tap – the knitted toilet-roll holder with my Barbie doll stuck in it. Everything about those trips, from the tinned fruit to my mother's Pan Stik, reminded me that I was not aristocracy. I'd leave and go to some Viennese waltz in the Ritz and feel like a fraud. But I stopped the visits – and my mum, her nerves got worse and worse, so bad that my dad had to have her sectioned. That place they sent her; well, it was the end of her. I should have tried harder. (*starts to cry*) Oh, I'm sorry, Elizabeth.

ELIZABETH:

It's OK to cry, Sybil, you have had a traumatic evening. We'll get back to Jeremy in a moment, but this may help me to find Anthony. Why was your mother sectioned?

SYBIL:

She almost burned the house down. Setting a fire in the living room.

ELIZABETH:

Perhaps the chimney hadn't been swept?

SYBIL:

Not in the fireplace. She lit it right in the middle of the room. Thought she was camping.

ELIZABETH:

Oh, my dear. I see. I see. What an impossible situation for your father.

SYBIL:

I've been terrified of fire ever since. Luckily when Anthony's parents renovated this house they installed rope ladders on the upper floors and lots of new alarms. But my mum never came home after that. I tried to help, you know, like I moved her to the best hospital in Bristol. More like a hotel it was. Friends of Anthony's all sent their parents there. I visited every weekend, but then we went to Paris. He had been patient enough, but we were newlyweds. When it was clear my mum wasn't coming out, he wanted my company. Said I ought to behave like a wife if I wanted a husband. His horse was running in the Prix de Diane in Chantilly.

ELIZABETH:

So, this was the year after we met in Paris?

SYBIL:

The following year, yes. When we were in France, Mum managed to get away from the nurses. Down to the beach. Oh, Elizabeth, it was all my fault, for letting her stay there.

ELIZABETH:

Dear, your mother was mentally unwell. No one could have saved her. I'm terribly sorry you lived through that. Here is a tissue. I know it's just rotten waiting around like this. Just let's go back to Jeremy for a moment, Sybil, is that all right? Why did you fall out of touch?

SYBIL:

After the band broke up, I didn't see Jeremy for years. By then, I'd struck up a friendship with Chrissy backstage. I couldn't perform, but I still enjoyed being at the heart of the action. Then when she introduced me to her husband, well, I didn't recognise him. He'd lost all the weight and taken on this Cockney accent. I don't think he really told her about his family until after they were married. It must have been last year, at one of our little tea meetings that she asked me about it. That's when she told me about the life insurance and er, his inheritance.

ELIZABETH:

Are his parents still alive?

SYBIL:

His mother died a while back. Not long before my own mum passed away. If you ask me, she wasn't able to scrimp and live like that. I think the father is still alive, although I don't know if Jeremy ever made contact with him.

ELIZABETH:

Tell me, why did the band break up?

SYBIL:

Well, we were just going to artistically different places, you know? We had a good run of shows and performances. We were up in Scarborough one summer. Sell-out shows. The hotel was very happy with us. It seemed things were going to, I suppose, take off for us . . .

ELIZABETH:

So, what happened?

SYBIL:

It's a long story, but something changed by the time we got back to London. Jeremy didn't want to play the same music, he wanted to experiment, and so did I . . . but all the interest seemed to be in the ballroom band that we were. Funny, that I ended up as an aristocrat, and Jeremy a punk.

ELIZABETH:

What changed, do you think?

SYBIL:

Oh, Elizabeth, this is ancient history, can't you leave it be? If you must know, I never went to the meeting with the record label. I was the face of the band, you see. That's what they wanted.

ELIZABETH:

Why didn't you go?

SYBIL:

I'd just met Anthony. Just that week. I'd been sitting in the Bar Italia, trying to work on some new material. But it was just not coming. He was chain-smoking cigarettes at the next table and leafing through paperwork. Just as they were going to boot me out for spending too long there, he sat beside me and started to chat. We stayed for lunch, and then walked around Mayfair. In fact, we passed this house. He didn't say anything about it being his house. But he took out a key and unlocked the garden; we sat in there for the afternoon. The housekeeper must have seen him, and brought out a picnic. The next day he invited me to the races. So, I never went to the meeting. He was a Lord, Elizabeth. Courting me. And a damned handsome one. So, I blew off the meeting and the label never offered a deal. Jeremy's never forgiven me.

ELIZABETH:

How was it when he married Chrissy, and you met again after all those years?

SYBIL:

He didn't approve of our friendship. It was a link to the past, to the identity that he didn't wish to perform any more. He had transmuted into this bolshy Eastender, who knows the price of everything and value of nothing. Oh, he was polite enough to me, but it soon became clear that Chrissy and I would be friends, without the husbands.

ELIZABETH:

What did Anthony think of him?

SYBIL:

Anthony would love to be seen out and about with a punk. There was a resemblance between them too. Both men relished being the star of his own show. Anthony has such wonderful confidence. He's never doubted himself, my husband, and he just doesn't care what anyone thinks. Now that I think of it, I'm not sure they've actually ever met. No. They've never met.

ELIZABETH:

When's the last time you saw Anthony?

SYBIL:

I suppose just before I had my bath. He'd been in foul humour since we left Liverpool. So, I'd just taken myself off. I was sitting on the edge of the bath when he burst open the door looking for his gold tie pin. I told him I hadn't seen it and then he grabbed me by the shoulders. Through gritted teeth he shook me, I had never felt strength like that before. I thought . . .

ELIZABETH:

What did you think, Sybil?

SYBIL:

Well, it was as if he meant to drown me. I felt myself slip against the roll of the bath; my nightdress was slippy. But then the doorbell rang. He loosened his grip on me. That was the last time I saw him. When I got out of the bath, I was so exhausted, I climbed into bed still in my towel. When he wasn't there the next morning, I was relieved. It's as if I'd assumed a large debt when he made me a lady. Anthony has been the dominant force in all his relationships. Even his parents worshipped the ground he walked on. I wasn't prepared to live like that. Yes, I've made concessions . . . but there comes a point where you simply have to call time on something.

ELIZABETH:

What sort of concessions?

SYBIL:

Anthony didn't want me to perform any more. (*mimicking Anthony's voice*) 'I'd love to scratch out those vocal cords and take away your suffering', he would say. It was . . . strange.

ELIZABETH:

Why are you so set on finding him if he doesn't want to be found?

SYBIL:

Anthony would never divorce me. There's no possible way he could afford to. He has very little actual cash. It's all tied up in the company and in property. But he often said he didn't want the family line to die with him. Can you imagine?

ELIZABETH:

Do you think it's possible to rekindle things? Even if he did return?

SYBIL:

Of course, I do. I don't want to spend the next fifty years on my own, and affairs aren't really my thing . . .

Sound of a thud in the background.

FELIX:

What was that?

ELIZABETH:

There was a sort of shuffle from behind the door, as if someone had been listening. No one was in the hall when I looked to see. In fact, the house was so quiet I could hear the distant wail of sirens. I couldn't help but peek out of the fanlight of the door, where I saw the orange glare of the fire on the horizon. London was burning, the police weren't coming, and all this time the lives of four innocent people, including myself, were at stake. I had to remove the kid gloves from my interview with Sybil.

SYBIL:

No one there?

ELIZABETH:

Nope. Let me get to the point here, Sybil. Did Anthony have a mistress?

SYBIL:

Ha. I'm sorry, I don't mean to laugh. It's just . . . well. If I don't laugh, I would just simply cry. I don't know. Perhaps. He may like charming the ladies . . . but I don't think he would take it any further. I mean he's no Francois. I even saw him giving you the eye tonight! He's rather shameless. Bruton Square's worse kept secret! Francois picks up any floozy he comes across. They say he's fathered three children, and doesn't give a penny to any of the mothers. Anthony told me all about it. In a way, the fact that Francois was so profligate an adulterer in front of my husband, it put Anthony off. And his own father was like that too. Ran off and left Anthony's mother for a younger, more glamorous model. But maybe I'm the fool for believing that would stop him.

ELIZABETH:

The hall lights suddenly burn bright as we squint our eyes, unaccustomed to the illumination. Sybil jumps up and turns off all but one. There's no sign of a limp as she returns to her seat. Aha, she doesn't even realise her mistake. How could she walk on such a badly sprained ankle without flinching? Morphine is how. And I thought I'd spotted a medicine cabinet in the first-floor bathroom. But I didn't want to let her know I'd made that connection, so I asked her about turning off the electricity.

ELIZABETH:

How did you do that, Sybil?

SYBIL:

I don't know what—

ELIZABETH:

You turned those lights off, all part of your scheme here—

SYBIL:

Do watch how you speak to your employer, Elizabeth. There's a bloody great fire, this house is badly wired—

ELIZABETH:

You've asked me to investigate and I have my principles. A faux electricity outage is the sort of thing that looks suspicious in light of the dead body upstairs. It would have given you plenty of time to make it up to murder Jeremy, wouldn't it? She went to a white marble and copper drinks trolley in the corner of the drawing room and poured us a glass of wine each.

Sybil starts laughing sarcastically.

SYBIL:

Ah. You do have principles after all. Tell me, if you really think I killed him, wouldn't I have a plan to finish the rest of you off too? A poisoned wine glass, perhaps? Tell you what, if you're so bloody suspicious of me, I'll let you choose which glass is mine.

FELIX:

Things took a turn for the worse at this point?

ELIZABETH:

She was standing over me then, looming with a crooked grin. Strands of her blonde hair clung to her forehead. As she took a sip from both glasses, she grotesquely licked the rim of each so that I could see the purple vein under her tongue. With the overhead light behind her, I struggled to maintain eye contact and stood back from her, the chair clanking aside in my hurry. Sybil was more dangerous than I previously suspected, and I had to take back control of the room.

ELIZABETH:

I don't want a drink. Please, sit down. I didn't mean to offend you.

ELIZABETH:

Her eyes fell to the dark corner of the room as she avoided my gaze. There was nothing there, she was just searching the murkiest corners of her own mind for what she would say next. Her frame relaxed and she laughed nervously as she sat down again, smoothing a wrinkle in the rug with her thick platform sandal. Not the footwear of someone with a sprain.

SYBIL:

I'm tired of being misunderstood, Elizabeth. Taken for a fool, a bizzaro. I really ought to serve the digestif now, my guests are waiting.

ELIZABETH:

I know what it feels like to be an outsider too, let me tell you. Let us finish this interview. Now, to tonight. So, Agapanthus found Jeremy? What was she doing up there? Did she scream? Tell me what happened.

SYBIL:

I had come upstairs to find Jeremy first. He was gone to the loo for quite a while . . . I didn't want him to . . . hurt himself in the dark.

ELIZABETH:

But you couldn't find him in the loo.

SYBIL:

Not here on the first floor, no. Which I thought was . . . strange. You know, that he would go upstairs, up to the bedrooms.

ELIZABETH:

Was Jeremy here before?

SYBIL:

No one has been here before. Well, apart from Francois when they were pals as boys. But all the houses on the square are the same. And I suppose Jeremy is a housepainter too, isn't he? So he would be familiar with different layouts. That's why I think it's so strange he snuck up to the bedroom. It's almost as if he was looking for something,

ELIZABETH:

Or someone. I just think it's a coincidence that you both went upstairs – perhaps it was to have a little chat about something? Because, say for argument's sake you were having an affair with Jeremy, that would be the way to do it. That he'd disappear upstairs and you'd come looking for him . . .

SYBIL:

Don't be ridiculous—

ELIZABETH:

Love can prevail in the sparsest of landscapes. You said yourself Anthony wanted a child but you weren't able to have one. Perhaps you're trying to make that happen before it's too late.

SYBIL:

Have you got another cigarette, Elizabeth? I haven't smoked in years but—

ELIZABETH:

I felt around for my lighter, but she pulled one from her pocket. That surprised me as there were matches for the candles and the fire scattered around the drawing-room table. That detail stood out for me, given how the night would end. As I lit myself a cigarette, she reached for one too and lit it. But she let the ash fall on the rug she had so carefully smoothed out moments ago. Rational thought had begun to evade her as I passed the lead-crystal ashtray. I had to calm her down.

ELIZABETH:

Careful there. Put the ash in here.

SYBIL:

Yes, I do want a child. And my time is running out. It is hard to fill one's days alone, with Anthony off at work or travelling about.

ELIZABETH:

How do you spend your days, Sybil?

SYBIL:

Oh, I read, a lot of Agatha Christie, of course. All the detectives – Sherlock Holmes, Harriet Vane, Peter Wimsey. I've read them all but still can't ever guess the killer. I take care of the garden, maybe do some cooking. That's why I don't really have any help come in. I wasn't raised with money – I can't help feeling completely useless when someone else is mopping or dusting and I'm there staring at my navel. Marjorie comes, a few times a week. That's more to give her some money than anything else. I have started writing, lately. Automatic writing. I sort of get myself into a trance, and then let myself be used as a vessel. W.B. Yeats used to do it. The message just comes and I have no recollection of ever writing it.

ELIZABETH:

Do you stay at home all day, every day?

SYBIL:

Oh no, I'm not a total recluse. I sometimes go for tea with Chrissy. Take a walk in Hyde Park – the gardeners there really are very creative, you know; the placing of orange and purple blooms together is quite striking. Or I go for a drink in the Ritz. But I am happier here, within these four walls. You know, despite the horrific outcome for Jeremy, I have realised quite how much I enjoyed having you all here. I must do it more often.

ELIZABETH:

Sybil was lost in the circus of her thoughts and day dreams as she let the ash build up on her cigarette. The intensity of her expression relaxed and I realised that she was simply happiest when lost in her own world. Could such a lonely woman really be responsible for orchestrating an elaborate plan? I goaded her.

ELIZABETH:

Well, why did you remove the fuse?

SYBIL:

Say whoever killed Jeremy did remove the fuse; it's a lot of faffing around. They would have had to get from the basement to my dressing room, that's three flights of stairs, in a matter of seconds, then kill him. Really, Elizabeth, I thought a private investigator would have thought through the timeline a bit more. Isn't it more likely to be an unfortunate coincidence of an old fuse?

ELIZABETH:

Let's leave the matter for a minute. The lights went off at about quarter past eight. You took a candelabra upstairs. What happened then?

SYBIL:

I was just coming out of this room when I heard Agapanthus on the landing. I was distracted and misplaced my step, landing myself with this terrible sprain.

ELIZABETH:

It didn't hurt to walk on it just now and you're wearing platform sandals, Sybil. It can't be that bad.

SYBIL:

Er, no. I took a painkiller. *Il faut souffrir pour être belle*, as the French would say. But before the morphine kicked in, I started to think that something really was wrong. I actually thought that I'd left a window open up there, and smoke from this chemical fire had got in and, you know, knocked her out. So, I was shouting her name . . . I heard a moan, I suppose that's when she found him. Agapanthus was in a state of terror – her mouth was hanging open. She was staring into space – she was thoroughly disturbed. And she's a medical woman, she has seen a lot. So, I knew it would be bad.

ELIZABETH:

How did you get up there? If your foot was sprained?

SYBIL:

Agapanthus helped me.

ELIZABETH:

That must have taken a while. After just finding a body? I'm wondering why she wouldn't come to tell us first? I'm just getting the timeline straight here.

SYBIL:

If someone died in your bloody house, I'm sure you'd want to take a look.

ELIZABETH:

How did Jeremy seem?

SYBIL:

At first I actually thought he was just joking!

ELIZABETH:

At one point Chrissy said it wasn't him.

SYBIL:

I mean she was clearly raving with shock and horror. But he really just looked like he was asleep with his eyes closed. His face was contorted, some foam around the mouth – it was horrific, really. To see my old friend in such a state. But then I noticed the tourniquet.

ELIZABETH:

Which arm was it on?

SYBIL:

Oh, it was on the side closest to the window. His right arm.

ELIZABETH:

And where was the syringe? The other paraphernalia?

SYBIL:

Erm, my first thoughts were about Chrissy and how devastated she would be. I think the syringe was on the carpet beside him. I know it's odd but I did think about the carpet.

ELIZABETH:

People can think about strange things at a time like that. What else did you notice? Anything out of place?

SYBIL:

I suppose there was his cigarette tin on the ground. My lamp was on the floor, smashed. Some of the jewellery boxes had been opened.

ELIZABETH:

I found a pair of your earrings in his pocket. Here.

SYBIL:

Hmm, yes. I did notice they had gone. They'd come in a big orange box, which I kept at the back of the bottom drawer of my dressing table. Well hidden. The box had been taken out, opened, and the earrings were gone. But with the commotion . . . I hadn't wanted to upset Chrissy any more. Poor dear.

ELIZABETH:

I thought the carpet was very thick? Surely the lamp would be unlikely to break, or as you say smash, after falling off . . . where did you say it was?

SYBIL:

On my dressing table. Yes, I suppose it would need to have hit something rather hard. Although with enough force, it would have broken on the carpet. Hmmm.

ELIZABETH:

So, Agapanthus helped you up the stairs whilst holding a lit candle? That must have taken a while.

SYBIL:

No, she put down the candelabra, and then I walked on my ankle. Probably why it's so sore now. Adrenaline took over, I suppose. I just had to get up there.

ELIZABETH:

Hmm yes. A moment ago, you stood up on the badly sprained ankle. Tell me, why would you take morphine for a sprained ankle, Sybil? Are you an addict yourself? Perhaps that's why you invited Jeremy here.

SYBIL:

Don't be so *dramatic*, Elizabeth, I'm just terrible with pain, you know. Agapanthus gave me it. I just wanted to be in my right mind. You know I haven't even served the cheese fondue yet?

ELIZABETH:

It will keep.

SYBIL:

No, it won't. It will go all cold. I've gone to a lot of trouble with this evening's party, you know.

ELIZABETH:

Why do you keep morphine, syringes and such a well-stocked medical cupboard in the house?

SYBIL:

Oh, you noticed that in the bathroom, did you? Oh, that's not me. It's Anthony. He always kept a stash in case of emergencies. He never trusted doctors. Refused to be examined or have any check-ups. His mother was a hypochondriac and he endured all sorts of investigations as a child. No, he always said if something were to go wrong he would never set foot in a hospital.

ELIZABETH:

How was his health the last time you saw him?

SYBIL:

He was perfectly well! As far as I could tell.

ELIZABETH:

Do you think perhaps he could be unwell? And that if he is nervous about medics, he could have found somewhere to stay when being treated?

SYBIL:

I mean, I hadn't considered that. But yes, it would make sense. He would be worried that I'd insist he see a doctor. You know, he saw you in Milan last year.

ELIZABETH:

Anthony did?

SYBIL:

He had to collect some papers from the British consul. They were having a lunch for the local expat community:
Thomas Caswell-Jones, James and Marnie Beresford, as well as a lot of the Americans who have bought these palaces on Lake Como.

ELIZABETH:

The name Caswell-Jones sent a shiver through me. Twice in one night I'd been reminded of an investigation I'd been called to by a family friend. First, Agapanthus cast a slur on me in front of everyone, for the entanglement I'd once had with her sister's husband. Sally had been one of my prime suspects. Then the name Thomas Caswell-Jones. Despite twenty years and thousands of miles, I could not escape that Christmas in Como. With all my resolve, I clasped my hands under my sweaty knees and allowed Sybil to keep talking. I felt the heat of embarrassment rise through me as I foresaw the tale she was about to tell me.

ELIZABETH:

Oh, yes. I don't recall that.

SYBIL:

He was at a loose end, so he went along. The impression you have always given to me is that you're deeply connected with the Polizie, the lawyers and wealthy Italians and English over there.

ELIZABETH:

That is the truth.

SYBIL:

Well, first of all, he spotted you at the entrance to the function room. Some issue with the ticket. Anthony reckoned that you thought someone had already purchased a ticket for you. That you were going to collect it. It was reserved, but unpaid for. Anthony saw you hang back until an old woman – a grand old dame in need of company – came along, and you convinced her to buy the ticket for you.

ELIZABETH:

What about it? Signora Elena invited me there. I don't know what you're getting at.

ELIZABETH:

She was looking for a rise from me. Sybil. Dredging up some event from last year to paint me as some impecunious parasite. Implying my situation is precarious. Highlighting the inequality between us – her the titled lady, and me, the broke and desperate employee.

SYBIL:

Let me finish. His name wasn't on the table plan as he'd only decided to go at the last minute. Anthony got the sense you were on the lookout for a sponsor, so did his best to keep out of your sight. My darling husband said you worked the crowd. Begging cigarettes and offering your services.

ELIZABETH:

Why are you saying this with such vitriol? In this job, I must keep in touch with people. Haven't I always been a good friend to you?

SYBIL:

But you ended up two tables away. Beside the old behemoth. Anthony concluded that not only were you hard up, but desperate. Not the best situation for a woman approaching sixty. That's why I was truly thrilled that you'd returned to England just in time for my supper for six.

ELIZABETH:

Your husband clearly views life through a negative lens. I shouldn't tolerate these accusations. Here. Take your money back. Anthony is dead bloody right to have left you, now I can see why!

At this moment, the pair are interrupted by Agapanthus Langford, which is where we will pick up in the next episode. But for now, let's take a look at what transpired between our detective and the hostess. How much of Sybil's story do you believe? Elizabeth's prevailing impression of Sybil is as a lonely recluse, who spends her days without keeping company. Nonetheless, Sybil orchestrated an elaborate meal, and essentially a stage production for her dinner party. Her mother suffered from poor mental health; could Sybil have inherited the same proclivity?

Something about Sybil's tale of how she knew Jeremy jarred with me. It sounded so perfect, so polished. As if she had been practising it. Not a moment of hesitation. She speaks of her difficulties in her marriage to Anthony, although ultimately wants to find him and even have his child! Did you notice she did not make an outright denial of turning off the electricity? That she herself alluded to the presence of the drugs cabinet? In some ways, Elizabeth's interview with Sybil raises more questions than it answers. Listeners, we haven't quite finished with our hostess. Join me in the next episode where the truth finally comes to the fore.

Our lady hostess, Sybil Anderson. Was she merely an over-excited actress treading the boards, or could she have orchestrated the terror that her guests felt that night? I'm Felix Caerphilly, and you've been listening to Supper for Six.

EPISODE FIVE:

Cocktails and Wine

Welcome to Supper for Six, *this is episode five, and I'm your host Felix Caerphilly. We're about to return to Elizabeth Chalice's recordings of the night of 7th April 1977 and that fateful dinner party. In the last episode, we heard the beginning of Elizabeth's interview with Lady Anderson. We will pick up from that point, when the tense exchange was broken by a knock on the door of the first-floor dining room, now illuminated as the electricity had been restored. Francois and Agapanthus Langford had been waiting in the dining room when five-month-pregnant Chrissy Crowley began to feel unwell. You'll notice tempers are badly frayed, as the tension gets to the guests, who are trapped inside with a killer. Apparently the authorities have instructed Londoners to remain indoors to avoid ingesting an airborne toxin that has been released from a factory in Soho. The body of Jeremy Crowley lies in the hostess's dressing room. It's this moment where the tape begins. Agapanthus Langford, a hospital doctor, opens the drawing room door where Elizabeth and Sybil are unhappy to be interrupted.*

ELIZABETH:
What is it, Dr Langford? I'm in the middle of interview—

SYBIL:
We have already finished, please ignore Ms Chalice.

AGAPANTHUS:
Chrissy here needs to lie down now. Her husband has just died in the most tragic—

CHRISSY:
(*weakly*) He was murdered, I told—

AGAPANTHUS:
Don't think of that now, consider your unborn child! Sybil, will you please unlock the front door so I can take her to my house?

SYBIL:
(*manically*) Impossible. Listen to the radio, I have it here.

BBC NEWSREADER:

. . . reporting from Chelsea and Westminster Hospital where dozens of people are being treated for severe burns to their eyes, lungs and skin as they did not listen to the authority's order to remain indoors. Seventy-four-year-old Timothy set out for his son's house two streets away, wearing a gas mask from the Second World War, not realising the device was compromised. Doctors have sedated him—

CHRISSY:

(with no energy) Please turn that off.

ELIZABETH:

What is it, are you feeling light headed?

SYBIL:

Chrissy! Oh no.

AGAPANTHUS:

Grab her, quickly.

ELIZABETH:

Chrissy? Quick! Catch her, Dr Langford. She's about to faint.

AGAPATHUS:

You're OK. Slowly, Elizabeth, lower her to the ground. That's it. Deep breaths, good girl.

CHRISSY:

Look at the wall – I can't believe what I'm seeing. I didn't notice it earlier.

AGAPANTHUS:

Head between your knees. Deep breaths now, Chrissy. I don't like the décor myself. Marjorie always went too far with the Rococo gold.

ELIZABETH:

Sssh, do be quiet, Dr Langford.

AGAPANTHUS:

Don't bother her, you silly nurse, let her regain her senses. She'll tell us in her own time. Get her a glass of water. Doctor knows best. Sybil, kneel down here and fan her a bit of air.

ELIZABETH:

Here you go, sip on this, Chrissy. You've had a bit of a turn, that's all. It's been a long evening. That's it, drink it down.

SYBIL:

She's opening her eyes. Hi Chrissy, it's your old pal Sybil.

CHRISSY:

(*crying*) Sybil. Yes. Oh no, Jeremy.

ELIZABETH:

Shhh, take it easy, you're looking a lot better now

CHRISSY:

(*crying*) He's dead isn't—

Silence

ELIZABETH:

What is it, Chrissy, what have you seen?

AGAPANTHUS:

She's staring at that terrible bloody painting. It would make anyone nauseous. No, my girl, let's get you up—

CHRISSY:

It's one of his. Jeremy painted that. The vision in this eye hasn't been very good. I can't see very well from this side. Oh, I think I'm going to be sick—

ELIZABETH:

We'd better take her to lie down.

AGAPANTHUS:

Come, help me take her upstairs. I'll examine her. Sybil, get me a fizzy drink.

CHRISSY:

No! You're a two-faced bitch, Sybil. How many painters are there in London? How many artists would be glad of the business? Or maybe it's even worse – he's been painting women on stage for years, right from the very start. They sold well – he told me they were commissions from famous singers. But I never paid attention to the faces. All along, they must have been Sybil.

SYBIL:

Oh, don't be so dramatic. It's not as if I took the chap to bed. I promise. You are my dearest friend in the world, Chrissy. I would never hurt you. Come along. We'll let you take a rest.

CHRISSY:

You killed him, didn't you?

SYBIL:

Of course not. It was her. Agapanthus. Jeremy painted her house. They must have had some sort of entanglement. Who else would know how to do the injection like that?

AGAPANTHUS:

No, I certainly did not. I'm neither an adulteress nor a murderer. Why would I murder a stranger? How would I?

ELIZABETH:

I agree with the doctor, Chrissy must rest. And I need to interview Dr Langford as soon as Chrissy is settled.

There's about ten minutes of dead air after they leave the room. When I listened to that exchange on that chilly, January night in 1978, I did not yet realise the significance of what Chrissy had seen. Not even the steaming bowl of Smash *could warm me up after spending hours listening to the tapes, and I climbed into bed dejected and miserable. There have been many times over the past forty-five years I've conducted this investigation that I've felt helpless or hopeless, but that night I knew I'd never be able to stop chewing over what I'd heard on the tapes.*

Why was Chrissy so upset that her husband had painted her friend? Could I see myself in Chrissy's shoes? Had she been suspicious that they were having an affair? But just before I was about to fall asleep, I heard a hammering at my front door.

It was Elizabeth Chalice – with a suitcase in her hand. Her headscarf was freshly ironed, her mackintosh dry and her hair styled in a tight French roll. She looked decades younger than the woman I'd interviewed earlier that same day in January of 1978. She sat on the edge of the patched orange sofa of my mouldy basement bedsit as I started the tape recorder. I was exhausted but keen to hear what she had to say as we returned to the night of the party.

ELIZABETH:

Agapanthus refilled our glasses from the decanter on the drinks trolley in the corner of the drawing room, casting a judgemental eye on my worn notebook, my outfit – everything about me felt shabby in comparison to her. She'd reminded me of my place when Chrissy fainted, all that doctor-knows-best business. Her gaze was one of superiority. She drank from her glass – by this stage she must have drunk two bottles of wine but didn't even seem tipsy. Behind the steely exterior I could see her vulnerability. The woman had been rejected by her husband. Was competing against her male hospital colleagues in a race she could not win. All this whilst reaffirming her position at the very top of society. Her clothes were beautifully tailored – the bouclé jacket was a perfect square across her shoulders. Money was not an issue for her, unlike the worn-out suit her husband wore. The gulf between the two of them was not unique to a marriage as well established as theirs was. I asked myself, could she take a gamble by committing murder? There are some inconsistencies as to where she was when the lights went out. I recall all the suspects were together in the dining room, but could I have missed something in the dark?

ELIZABETH:

Let's get straight to it. Why did you leave the dining room in such a hurry when the lights went out?

AGAPANTHUS:

Are you forgetting about the bloody air-raid siren that was roaring? The gas attacks?

ELIZABETH:

They are saying it's just a chemical fire. Didn't you want to take Chrissy to your house a few minutes ago? How is she, by the way?

AGAPANTHUS:

Francois told me that Sybil has locked us in. We'll have to get the key off her. God knows what else she has in store for us this evening. Chrissy has gestational diabetes. She must have already been diagnosed with this if she has her own insulin. There are signs of a vitreous haemorrhage, which explains the blurred vision. She's sleeping upstairs.

ELIZABETH:

On her own?

AGAPANTHUS:

Oh, you aren't still convinced that addict was murdered, are you? It was obviously an overdose, Elizabeth.

ELIZABETH:

So why did you wait until the lights went out to leave?

AGAPANTHUS:

Well, it was a distraction, wasn't it? I wanted to go home without my husband or anyone else bothering me. When the rest of you were faffing around, I ran downstairs to leave.

ELIZABETH:

In the dark?

AGAPANTHUS:

It wasn't pitch black; the sun had barely set! Anyway, I realised the door was locked, and I started to feel around for a key. By that stage, Francois had followed me downstairs and was searching the telephone table for the key. He told me to check Sybil's dressing room, so up I went. Even though she said she was going up to check. But that's when I found him. Jeremy was in there, rifling around in her jewellery box. He seemed like a man on a mission.

ELIZABETH:

Was he angry when he saw you?

AGAPANTHUS:

He didn't see me. My lighter ran out of fuel, so I started to look around for a light. I found a candlestick in Sybil's bedroom, and when I came back, well he was dead.

ELIZABETH:

How could he have had enough time to shoot up, inject and die in the time it took you to get a candlestick?

AGAPANTHUS:

Delayed reaction. If he injected himself first then—

ELIZABETH:

Then he would be out of it, not packing up a loot bag like a cartoon criminal.

AGAPANTHUS:

If he had a tolerance for opioids, he would not have been greatly impaired. Here's what I think happened: he slinks off upstairs, having found some of the bathroom stash. He shoots up cautiously, he's a man with a child on the way and doesn't want to die. He nabs a few thousand pounds of Sybil's jewels – the Andersons were always extravagant with diamonds as new money often is – but gets greedy, goes for another hit. Everything is already there so he does it quickly. That's what pushes him into overdose, when I find him a few minutes later.

ELIZABETH:

When did Sybil appear?

AGAPANTHUS:

Oh, I don't know if I recall. I mean she just seemed to appear there.

ELIZABETH:

She says you carried her upstairs because of the sprained ankle.

AGAPANTHUS:

Well, she's lying! Why on earth would I carry someone with a sprain up to see a dead body?

ELIZABETH:

How did you know he was dead?

AGAPANTHUS:

I, um, I had gone up there, found him, *then* Sybil came into the room, and saw him on the floor – immediately pointing out the belt he'd used as a tourniquet and came to the same conclusion as I did. It was an accidental death. The fellow overdosed. And we are all pussy-footing and pretending it's a murder, not an overdose, to spare this woman's feelings. But I could tell from the minute I saw him with his spiky hair. I knew that he was a wrong-un. That's what he'd been rushing to the bathroom for. To get his fix. To think that I dined beside someone . . . someone who would do that to themselves.

ELIZABETH:

But how were you certain he was dead, that he wasn't just unconscious?

AGAPANTHUS:

I'm not a bloody idiot, Ms Chalice. I checked his pulse, it was non-existent.

ELIZABETH:

Yes, but sometimes with opiates, the pulse may be very faint, but they're not quite dead.

AGAPANTHUS:

His eyes were wide open! I've seen a dead man's stare plenty over the years.

ELIZABETH:

Was it then that you gave her the morphine?

AGAPANTHUS:

Morphine? To Sybil?

ELIZABETH:

She said you did.

AGAPANTHUS:

Certainly not. Where would I have found any? Oh. I see what she's doing. She's trying to incriminate me. Well, I don't travel with syringes, ordinarily. My doctor's bag is at home.

ELIZABETH:

How did you give the insulin to Chrissy?

AGAPANTHUS:

She had her own kit!

ELIZABETH:

Why was she so unwell if she was being treated for the diabetes?

AGAPANTHUS:

The dosage wasn't right. She didn't like the injections. That's not really the point though, is it?

ELIZABETH:

Did you notice anything unusual when Sybil saw Jeremy's body for the first time?

AGAPANTHUS:

I'd never been in that room nor met that chap before, and I barely know Sybil. So, how could I possibly say what's usual and what's not? And the circumstances were not exactly usual either. The only thing I can think of is Sybil reached out to his hands, she sort of twiddled his fingers. She rubbed his hand across her palm, then stood back and exhaled.

ELIZABETH:

Yes, Sybil is acting rather strangely tonight. On another matter, did you know the first Lord Anderson well?

AGAPANTHUS:

Anthony's father? No. Francois and I lived in Ireland when we were first married. We visited Bruton Square occasionally, but by that stage Anthony senior had moved out. I saw the wife, Idabel, once. She had a huge canvas, gosh it must have been ten feet, strapped to the roof of her little Anderson Ant car. An artist! She couldn't have been much older than Anthony and Francois. That his father was dating someone the same age as him really galled Anthony, I gathered. I didn't have much to do with her, myself. Her chestnut hair was cropped tight, she had huge sunglasses and seemed to sort of toddle into the car. It looked as if the breeze might knock her over. Then two weeks later, they were dead.

ELIZABETH:

You must have been intrigued by the invitation to come here this evening?

AGAPANTHUS:

Well, yes. I understand that Tony wants to divorce Sybil. Well, if the papers Francois has in his satchel are anything to go by.

ELIZABETH:

How long have you been selling prescriptions to Jeremy?

AGAPANTHUS:

How— you can't possibly. That's outrageous. I never met the man before tonight.

ELIZABETH:

Untrue, Doctor. I've spent decades playing close attention to the people who I am with. Your dislike of each other was obvious the moment he came into the room.

AGAPANTHUS:

I'll have Francois sue you for slander—

ELIZABETH:

There's no one else here. Unlike you calling me a husband-stealer earlier.

AGAPANTHUS:

Well, it's the truth, isn't it? I was wondering when you were going to bring that up.

ELIZABETH:

He was selling your prescriptions to the highest bidder, wasn't he? A crime that would have you struck off as a doctor, maybe even facing criminal charges. But the money from the prescriptions wasn't enough any more, and he'd been blackmailing you, I gather? Let me guess . . . Neither of you wanted to acknowledge this little arrangement in front of your spouses – so when you had a quiet moment in the dark, you snuck into that room and injected him with a dose big enough to kill him.

AGAPANTHUS:

How dare you, Elizabeth! Why would I sell prescriptions in the first place?

ELIZABETH:

Your clothes are this season's Chanel, whilst your husband's attire is in tatters.

AGAPANTHUS:

I'm a doctor; I come from money, finances are not an issue, nor is my husband's wardrobe motivation enough to kill a man.

ELIZABETH:

You're not from money. Your sister, Sally, was a self-made woman. Your father was a brickie! Your entire event is a facade.

AGAPANTHUS:

Really, Elizabeth, I feel terribly sorry for you. I see what you're doing here, trying to go along with this idea there was a murder so you can make a job for yourself. I'm sure you must have been a good nurse, once upon a time, but whyever you took it upon yourself to start investigating crimes is beyond me. Now I have a pregnant woman in need of care, why don't you go and try to calm down Sybil? She's obviously unused to hosting events and is greatly stressed. In fact, a tranquilliser may well be the best option—

ELIZABETH:

Let me stop you there, Doctor. Tell me, is this your prescription pad?

ELIZABETH:

Her eyes narrowed as she sat forward to look at the square prescription pad with her name printed at the top that I had put before her. She rolled her eyes in exasperation but shrugged it off, squeaking backwards into her chair. Her silk top clung to her chest, wide rings of sweat visible amidst the geometric pattern. She may have been trying to act coolly, but her body was betraying her. The decanter was empty – a fact which would have made her uncomfortable.

AGAPANTHUS:

Why, that's not even my handwriting. He must have taken the pad from my handbag, a common pickpocket wouldn't have any trouble—

ELIZABETH:

But Jeremy wasn't a common pickpocket, was he? He wasn't a punk, or an Eastender, or any of the things he pretended to be.

AGAPANTHUS:

I told you; I never met the chap before tonight.

ELIZABETH:

Stop lying, Dr Langford! Look, I don't need to tell anyone about this prescription business, or even your humble beginnings, if you'll just be forthcoming with me.

ELIZABETH:

She suddenly rushed to the window and when I realised she was trying to open it, I flew over to stop her, pushing hard against her bony fingers. I didn't see the glass in her hand, but it smashed right there in her palm.

AGAPANTHUS:

You shouldn't have done that, Elizabeth.

ELIZABETH:

Why on earth were you going to open the window?

AGAPANTHUS:

There isn't anything dangerous about that night air. Good lord, the idea of this noxious miasma is as foolish as Hippocrates' humours. Do you really believe everything you hear on the bloody radio?

ELIZABETH:

Earlier you thought we might have been under a nuclear attack, now you just want to swing open the windows?

AGAPANTHUS:

If it was a nuclear attack, we would be all finished anyway. If that were the case, the best option for all of us would be to go the same way as Jeremy.

ELIZABETH:

Your hands, let me look at them. I didn't mean to push you so hard.

ELIZABETH:

She nonchalantly wiped the blood from her hands on a tissue. Her bothersome little husband burst through the door, before I could confront her with more evidence that she was in fact very well acquainted with Jeremy's father. Oh, Felix, I think your phone is ringing.

FELIX:

You see, Elizabeth, I do have friends. I'll just be a moment. Perhaps I will go to the disco after all.

In this next excerpt, I'm going to share a little bit more about what it felt like to be in the room with Elizabeth, as a seventeen-year-old-boy. I picked up the telephone, trying to ignore the fact that Elizabeth was examining the dust on my mantelpiece. She had many secrets of her own, sewn through the Anderson case like gold thread. Perhaps if I could tug one loose, her entire tapestry would unravel. It was my editor, Roger Stapleton, calling from a bar in his throaty warble. 'Listen to me, boy, have you never heard the phrase "don't shit on your own doorstep"?' he said, interrupting to order two bottles of Krug from whatever watering hole he'd rung me from.

He then said, 'I've had two reports of you conducting yourself in a manner that doesn't befit a member of my staff. The manager of the Over-Seas League complained that you wouldn't leave when asked and started to pester one of their elderly members.'

At one point I held the phone receiver away from my ear whilst he continued his rant, but he suspected as much, and started to call 'Are you there, boy?' I had underestimated what a powerful man he was, as the editor-in-chief of the largest daily newspaper in Britain. I would live to regret making an enemy of him for the rest of my professional career, and it's ultimately the reason I could not tell this story properly until now. But I was a child, I found the whole thing hilarious as he went on. 'You were pestering the staff in the Ritz. Bringing the name of the paper down twice in one day! You know there are times to ruffle feathers and times to toe the bloody line! Seeing as you obviously need more journalistic training, I want you to stop this nonsense about Lord Anderson. The blighter is dead, nothing you do is going to bring him back. You need to be taught a bit of respect, boy. You're back to tea duties from tomorrow!'

I couldn't hide my dejection from Elizabeth as I took my seat in front of the recorder again. This was the man who paid my pittance of a wage. What had I been thinking trying to take down the establishment as a teenager? Having paid my entire savings to Elizabeth for her tapes, I couldn't afford to fall out with my boss.

ELIZABETH:

Don't worry, Felix. The first bollocking you get is always a shock, but it makes you better able to cope with the next one.

FELIX:

I erm. Yes. Where were we—

ELIZABETH:

I have to go now, catching the Caledonian sleeper to Edinburgh.

FELIX:

But we haven't finished—

ELIZABETH:

I'll be back in a few days, but given the call you have just received, perhaps you need to pause the investigation for a while. You have all of my tapes. I'll take your telephone number, and I can fill in the blanks when I'm away.

FELIX:

No, Elizabeth. No more prevarications. We had an agreement, I paid you one thousand pounds – my entire savings – for those tapes and for you to tell me exactly what happened that night. I don't care if Roger Stapleton has me making tea, someone else will take this story.

ELIZABETH:

My train leaves in thirty minutes; if I don't leave now, I'll never get a cab—

She yanked together her things and belted up her coat as she went for the front door. I didn't mean to scare her or anything, but I stood in her way.

FELIX:

You're not going anywhere until you tell me—

ELIZABETH:

Get out of my—

FELIX:

Goddamn it, Elizabeth. When did you realise that the body in Sybil's dressing room was Anthony?

She stood still for a moment, and quietly checked her small gold wristwatch. Her eyes narrowed as she exhaled deeply, the resistance giving way as she stood looking out of the bay window into the dark night. It had begun to rain, which echoed the gloomy atmostphere of my flat.

ELIZABETH:

That thousand pounds does not mean that you own me, Felix. If you ever act like this again, I will go to every other newspaper and pip your story to the post. Do you hear that? Your youth does not excuse you from common decency.

She stepped closer to me, so close I could smell her lilac perfume and the powder that set her Pan Stik. It reminded me of being a little boy, watching my auntie getting ready on a Saturday night. The rain was pelting down by then; I remember thinking it was so loud the tape might pick it up.

ELIZABETH:

All right, I will miss my train and stay and tell you the rest of what happened that evening, but then we are finished. Do you understand? You'll have the tapes, my interviews, but I will not speak to you again. Are you sure that's a gamble you're willing to take?

She reapplied her Yardley red lipstick as I stood there, speechless. Whether it was teenage impatience or my desire to put this case into the public eye, I nodded to accept her bargain. That's where we leave this episode of Supper for Six. *Do come back now, won't you? We really haven't got to the after-dinner games yet.*

EPISODE SIX:

A Surprise Guest

SYBIL:

(*singing the air of* 'Carrickfergus') I wish I was in Carrickfergus /
only for nights in Ballygrand / I would swim over the deepest
ocean/ only for nights in Ballygrand. / But the sea is wide, and I
cannot swim over. /And neither have I the wings to fly.

*Lady Sybil Anderson was a talented singer, forbidden from performing
by her husband. The clip you've just heard was recovered from a tape
that Lord Anderson had been using to covertly record his wife, which we
will hear more of in a later episode. For Sybil, like many of her guests,
had close ties with Ireland. Could the motivation to murder Lord
Anthony Anderson have been political?*

*Whilst the English middle classes were hosting aspirational soirees,
like the one in Mike Leigh's play* Abigail's Party, *which opened less
than a fortnight after Sybil's dinner party, 1977 was a tumultuous
period for the United Kingdom. The death of Anthony Anderson came at
a time of heightened anti-establishment sentiment, as voiced by bands
like the Sex Pistols, whose ' God Save the Queen' record reached number
two in the charts that May. Jeremy Crowley was both a punk guitarist
and an Irishman. The Irish question is one motive that I considered,
given the backgrounds of the suspects.*

*Fiachra O'Donaill, cultural historian and podcaster, discusses the
broader implications:*

FIACHRA:

At this time, many Britons considered Irish people as terrorists.
Even a work colleague or a neighbour with an accent could be
thought of as a suspect or potentially a member of the IRA. Their
individuality was discounted with the derogatory terms 'Paddy' or
'Mick'. In 1971, it's estimated that there were 700,000 London
Irish. They comprised the Mailboat Generation of Irish men and
women who streamed into the capital after the war, and a second
wave of immigrants in the late sixties. The Irish population continued to grow into the late 1970s and 1980s, with men moving into
construction and engineering.

Agapanthus Langford and her sister, Sally Lansdowne de Groot, née McNicholas, whom detective Elizabeth Chalice met years earlier in Lake Como, were the daughters of Patrick McNicholas, a wealthy Irish builder following in the tradition of Sir Robert McAlpine and John Laing. Jeremy Crowley was born in Ireland, relocating to London with his mother when her marriage to George Crowley broke down, where he worked as a painter with Irish contractors.

FIACHRA:

You see, the upper echelons of British society were closely entwined with Ireland too. Prime Minister James Callaghan continued to spend his summers in the West Cork village of Glandore despite death threats. And Lord Mountbatten refused a security detail when he visited Classiebawn Castle in the years before he was murdered by the Provisional IRA in August 1979. There was almost a sense that they were above the petty squabbling on the streets of Belfast. Britain's colonial legacy in Ireland was evident with the Anglo-Irish aristocracy – the landed gentry, titled aristocrats and owners of large estates. They were in no-man's-land, for although born in Ireland, they were educated privately, often in Britain, and spoke with English accents, so their local communities considered them British. They held close ties to London, often possessing London townhouses.

In the 1970s, having an Irish connection would certainly work against a suspect in a murder case, with several high-profile miscarriages of justice following poor policing of those suspected of terrorism. In the next part of my interview with Fiachra, he argues that broader Irish cultural expressions, particularly of music, remain muted by her former coloniser. The following statements may be triggering to those who experienced IRA violence, but as this podcast is being recorded in 2023, I think it's important to consider this conversation. Listeners, be aware, O'Donaill's views are very pro-Irish.

FIACHRA:

Last year, when the Irish women's soccer team qualified for
their first World Cup, a video capturing them singing 'Ooh, ah, up
the RA' from the Wolfe Tones song 'Celtic Symphony' drew international attention – the *Sky News* presenter who interviewed the
team captain in the days after the controversy went as far as to
suggest the team 'needs educating' – demonstrates the gulf in
contemporary discussions on the Anglo-Irish relationship. The
truth is that the Irish people and culture suffered tremendously at
the hands of British rule. Well into the nineteenth and early twenti-
eth century, smallholders were evicted by absentee landlords,
spoken Irish was forbidden and Catholics were discriminated
against. Innocent men, women and children were tortured, raped
and murdered. Inequity between Protestants and Catholics in the
North remained well into the 1960s. There's no doubt that the
cowardly actions of the IRA in bombing and murdering innocent
civilians is and always will be categorically wrong. I want to empha-
sise that, for any listeners who may have lost a loved one at the
hands of the IRA. But there is a far longer legacy of inter-genera-
tional trauma that Britain inflicted on the Irish people.

*But some sympathisers believed the actions of the IRA were just.
Agapanthus Langford, née Agatha O'Callaghan and Lady Sybil
Anderson, née Sibéal Ní Chríodáin, would have been ideal intelligence
targets. Listening to Sybil's rendition of 'Carrickfergus', I was prompted
to explore the political leanings of all of those present at supper that
night. The Official Secrets Act prevents me from identifying the following
individual, whom we will call Mr X, who worked as part of a counter-
intelligence unit between 1974 and 1982. I will now read a statement he
provided me with.*

As early as 1974, we had received intelligence that senior leaders of
the Provisional IRA had identified a number of well-regarded
Anglo-Irish aristocrats as targets to recruit to the organisation. In
particular, those who may have previously voiced Republican

sentiment. Our understanding was, they wanted agents who had the very best connections in British society. There were two objectives to this strategy. Firstly, they wanted the ears of those who moved in the elite circles as government cabinet ministers to gain advance information about defence manoeuvres. Secondly, the Provisional IRA was looking for high-profile locations and targets to bomb. The murder of Mountbatten in August 1979 was one of a number of planned assassinations, but it was years in the works.

Sybil and Anthony Anderson had come to our notice, as Sybil had grown up in a very rural part of County Mayo with strong Republican ties. But we were looking more closely at those from Ulster, instead of the Republic of Ireland. Sybil seemed proud of her Irish heritage; she wore a diamond Claddagh ring and was known to enjoy traditional music, but it very quickly became apparent that Lady Anderson rarely left her house and had an extremely limited social network. When Anthony Anderson was murdered in 1977, our attention was drawn to one of the other guests, Agapanthus Langford, née Agatha O'Callaghan.

So how does this relate to the guests at the dinner party? To see the threads knit together, we return to Elizabeth's tapes of the night of the murder.

FELIX:

What struck you as odd about the other diners?

ELIZABETH:

A few things about Jeremy had bothered me all night. If he was a Cockney, a punk, why did he take such care at the dinner table? His manners were so polished. Chrissy claiming it wasn't her husband. Then there was the matter of the dinner party itself. A last-minute event hosted by a recluse. But I still couldn't put it all together.

FELIX:

What struck you as odd about the house?

ELIZABETH:

Sybil had taken down all the photographs of Anthony from the dining room and hallway. But she forgot the wedding picture on her nightstand, and a photo album from their trip to Italy. You see, it had been ten years since I had seen Anthony. Sybil wanted me to help find her husband, but he was there under my nose all night. I hadn't noticed because . . . well, I hadn't expected to notice.

FELIX:

Where did you go after that?

ELIZABETH:

I left her bedroom, and looked on the landing carpet for any clues or evidence I might have missed when the lights were off. Between the carpet and the skirting board I found a tiny faux-turquoise cabochon stone half the size of my fingernail. It was a piece of a cheap earring or bracelet, so I thought it was probably Chrissy's. Beside it, a gold tie pin. Nothing else was out of place, so I pushed the door of the dressing room open. The brass handle was bright and gleaming.

FELIX:

Did Sybil really clean the five floors of that Mayfair mansion or was Marjorie handy with her tin of Brasso?

ELIZABETH:

This was before I realised that Marjorie was Anthony's own mother. Sybil had spoken of her as if she was nothing more than a housekeeper. How would she feel when she found out her only son had been murdered? So, I knelt beside the body and rubbed off the eyeliner with a dampened hankie. There were Anthony's soft hand-some blue eyes. Through the tears in his T-shirt, I could see the skin around his nipple piercing was red and inflamed, with a tiny crusting of blood. It was fresh. That explained the saline solution I'd found earlier. He had it pierced to complete his disguise as Jeremy. His scalp was red, from where he had bleached the hair to dye it green. I tugged the very end of the construction, and six inches of green hair came loose in my hand. He had glued the extra hair to his own to make the mohawk the same size as Jeremy's.

FELIX:

What else was not right about the body?

ELIZABETH:

I pulled up his right trouser leg, and the gnarled flesh confirmed that it was not Jeremy Crowley. It was Anthony. Realising this mistaken identity, I checked for a pulse again for some strange reason. Of course there was none. Whilst she was learning how to control it with insulin, Chrissy's diabetes could have left her feeling unwell, with the disturbance to her vision as she had told us and distraction, is it really possible Anthony could have fooled her for a few days? Perhaps if he didn't come too close and kept a wide berth he could convince her.

Agapanthus had been drinking heavily all night, so she must have presumed she was checking Jeremy's pulse, not Anthony's. I later came to realise that Agapanthus was not as drunk as she seemed, so in my mind I moved on to consider Francois. But what about Anthony's wife and oldest friend? How could Sybil and Francois not have realised that this was not Jeremy? I could not be sure, at this point. But Francois did not come into the dressing room when the body was discovered. He had peered in from the landing. The lawyer had forgotten his glasses, his vanity more important to the chap than clear vision, and they had only spent a few moments at the dinner table before the electricity went out. I didn't think he would have reminded us about Anthony's scar if he had been in on the scheme. But was Francois just *acting* the idiot?

FELIX:

What did you suspect about the victim's wife?

ELIZABETH:

Sybil invited me and the others to dinner under the pretence of finding Anthony. The fact that she had never entertained in the house before and had removed the photos downstairs, pointed to her being in on the scheme with her husband. In her interview, she told me about Jeremy's potential life insurance policy and their falling out over a record deal. It was all misdirection.

Sybil was a starlet in the shadows. And that dinner party was all one final show. Even the electricity outage when the rest of the square was illuminated. Who else could be responsible for setting this stage apart from Sybil? Did Anthony remove the fuse as part of their plan? But what was their motivation? Had she been expecting Anthony to be pronounced dead? She seemed calm initially, but shortly after became unhinged. If she had wanted to murder her husband, why would Anthony have pretended to be Jeremy?

FELIX:

What had happened a week earlier for Anthony to impersonate Jeremy? And had the killer meant to murder him, or did they think they were killing Jeremy?

ELIZABETH:

These were the very questions that ran through my mind as I sat for a minute with Anthony, now that I saw who he really was. I did not know the answers. If Anthony Anderson was there in Sybil's dressing room, where was the real Jeremy? I realised that I possessed an advantage. The true killer, or killers, did not suspect that I knew the victim's real identity. I quickly stood up, deciding not to call the police again until I could make sense of my discovery.

FELIX:

Where did you go next?

ELIZABETH:

I crept back down the stairs. Halfway down, I thought I heard a woman screaming outside in the street. From the landing window, I looked out and saw it was just a pair of drunk men. In the yellow glow of the street light, I saw they were dressed head to toe in red and blue sequins. The fellow on the outside went over on his ankle in his platforms. As his friend leaned over to help him, he stood on the wide bell bottom and the fabric tore up to his bottom. I knocked on the window to warn them to get indoors, but they had fallen over in an inebriated tangle of arms and legs laughing and could not hear me. I'd been watching them for at least a minute, and there was no sign of any dramatic chemical burn. Across the square, a woman wheeled a pram carefully down the steps of a house. Why would she take a baby for a walk if there was a chemical leak? There was no smoke either, and the fiery glow on the horizon was gone. With the fire over, the police and undertaker could remove the body.

In the dining room, I found all four of my suspects playing bridge at a card table that had been placed at the opposite end of the room, beside the window that overlooked the garden. Disco music was playing on the record player. If a stranger had walked in at that moment, they wouldn't have suspected a thing was wrong. I was still trying to understand why Anthony could have impersonated Jeremy. Who had the chance to kill Anthony? I needed the apparent calmness of the moment to process my thoughts.

Here we return to Elizabeth's recording from the tape deck hidden in her handbag.

SYBIL:

Francois, play a dummy hand, please.

FELIX:

What did you notice about the others?

ELIZABETH:

I sat down between Chrissy and Agapanthus and I saw the tension that existed between Sybil's guests. In front of me, Francois shuffled the deck. He threw two cards in the direction of his wife who snarled a sarcastic thank you. As he lifted his arm, I noticed a drop of blood inside the cuff of the jacket. Was this from injuring himself or could he have been the killer? The embers of the fire were smouldering and the room had grown cold. Francois had put his suit jacket back on.

Arms crossed on her lap, Agapanthus ignored the cards. Her eyes searched the sideboard for a bottle with another drop of wine in it. All signs of the earlier indulgence had disappeared. There was no cheese, no wine. No sign of fondue. Even the candlesticks had burned down to stubs, although they weren't responsible for our light as the electricity was back. Sybil snatched up her cards, frantically laughing as she snuck a look at her bounty.

And then there was Chrissy, the only one sipping a glass of water. Her face was bloated, her left eye swollen. A silk salmon-pink throw had been wrapped around her shoulders. Then the thought struck, could they all be in on the events of that evening? Was it me that they were trying to trick?

ELIZABETH:

Feeling better, Chrissy?

AGAPANTHUS:

I gave her a shot of insulin. I told you. We'll have to make sure you're properly looked after for the rest of your pregnancy, won't we? At least one of your bastards would be safe and healthy.

ELIZABETH:

Agapanthus's remark split open the heavy tension in the room. Francois loosened his ponytail and his brown hair sprawled across his shoulders. Chrissy's mouth gaped open as Francois slapped the doctor across the face. The loud clap sent his wife's earring flying across the table into Chrissy's water glass. It was a long, turquoise chandelier earring. Agapanthus cradled her cheek as the moment snapped Sybil from her reverie.

AGAPANTHUS:

I suppose I deserved that.

ELIZABETH:

There's no call for hitting a woman, Francois. It's quite out of order. It's 1977—

FRANCOIS:

She had that one coming.

ELIZABETH:

He massaged the sting from his own hand as he paced behind the card table. He looked between his lover and his wife, annoyed at both and feeling sorry for himself. A thick vein popped across his forehead. His rage grew. Gone was the smarmy womaniser. The anger bubbled up like the foam from his spittle as he stalked down the length of the room, screaming at his wife.

FRANCOIS:

Who would want to be married to a cold, dead fish like you, eh? What a shame it's not you lying upstairs instead of bloody Jeremy Crowley. I'm leaving now. I've had enough of this pathetic party, Sybil.

AGAPANTHUS:

See, Chrissy, the sort of man who you've lain with? I very much hope the child takes after your own side. I'd rather be a single mother than tied to him.

ELIZABETH:

Sybil placed her left hand on Chrissy's shoulder. She dabbed the edge of her sleeve under Chrissy's eyes to stem the silent tears. I heard the sound of the news and ran to the radio, almost tripping over the rug which had twisted and bubbled. Why had those men been in the street, dressed for a party?

BBC NEWSREADER:

Good evening and welcome to the nine o'clock news. Dozens of fire engines are fighting a blaze in Soho that has claimed the lives of more Londoners than any other event since the Blitz. Sarah Hardwicke reports from Chelsea and Westminster Hospital where dozens of people are being treated for severe burns to their eyes, lungs and skin as they did not listen to the authorities' order to remain indoors. Seventy-four-year-old Timothy—

SYBIL:

Turn off the radio, Elizabeth! We can't listen to it any more—

ELIZABETH:

Sybil pushed the dial to silence the radio. She took the bloody thing, opened the dining-room door and threw it down the stairs, where it clattered on the cold, marble steps.

Back in 1978, my interview with Elizabeth was interrupted by a call from my editor, pulling me from her account of Sybil's dinner table to my mouldy flat as Elizabeth glared impatiently at me.

EPISODE SEVEN:

After-Dinner Games

Realising how she had been duped in the earlier part of the evening,
Chalice resolved to uncover the interwoven dynamics between the two
couples. How could a wife not recognise her own husband? Who was
lying, Chrissy or Sybil? Such queries tugged at Chalice, but more press-
ing was the desire to remain alive. For in their midst was a killer.

The Crowleys and the Langfords were secretly linked in two ways.
Francois Langford and Chrissy Crowley had been involved in an affair
since meeting in a café several months earlier, which had resulted in the
child she was carrying. Chrissy was not the only married woman at the
table he'd manage to bed, for Sybil counted as the most recent notch on
his extra-marital bedframe.

But Agapanthus Langford was hiding a secret from her husband too.
Although Chalice did not know the full details at this point in the even-
ing, she knew enough. Agapanthus had recognised the man who would
become that first murder victim, but did she recognise Anthony Anderson
or believe the disguise and see Jeremy Crowley? Elizabeth had found her
prescription pad, and believed the pair were involved in an illegal
prescription scheme. That both links existed coincidentally was not
acceptable for Chalice.

Three months later, Elizabeth reappeared at my door at dawn one day
in April of 1978. Chain-smoking as we moved through the investigation,
by teatime she was wearing away my carpet as she paced up and down
in front of my fireplace, two electrical bars glowing orange. Dark circles
hung under her eyes, and her hair was scraped severely back off her face
so the line of white were striped like a badger. She gave no explanation
of how she had spent the past three months, and in her absence my work
on the case had slowed. She wanted to talk about Francois Langford.

ELIZABETH:

The lawyer. He was now the only male left at Sybil's little dinner
party. He was a man who sought to assert himself on the others,
but was forced to run along behind. Always on Anthony's coat-tails.
Then behind his wife as she clambered the medical ladder. His
need to dominate was met by the frustration at his lack of agency.

A deadly combination. Such repression can build in pressure until it finds an escape in the most unusual of circumstances.

Was it possible Francois did not recognise a man he knew? One he had lived six doors down from since childhood? Yes, he had arrived without his glasses. But we know each other by more than sight alone. There's the pitch of voice, even when under a put-on accent. Our mannerisms. The way we occupy space. Could someone so led by their physical nature as Francois really be blind to these cues?

Could he really have believed it was Jeremy? And if that was the case, was he really the sort of man to kill his lover's husband? He had the means and opportunity to commit the crime just like the others, but what was his motivation?

FELIX:

Sybil suggested some entertainment that was not just a regular hand of cards, didn't she? How did everyone feel at that point? Francois had slapped his wife, Sybil had thrown the radio down the stairs. Things had really deteriorated and felt violent?

ELIZABETH:

It was terrifying. It felt like anything could have happen. But we couldn't leave! Everybody sat and seethed. Sybil was setting up an Ouija board on the dining table when I pulled Francois aside for the interview in the downstairs drawing room. Sybil hadn't wanted us to split up – but if I didn't interview Francois then I didn't know that it would happen at all. I had to put my gut instinct to work, you see, so that I could keep the rest of them safe. I had my own daughter to think about, I didn't want her to be left without a mother even if she was safe in university in Scotland. Francois brought me a cup of coffee. Black. It was instant, but we were in England so I expected nothing less. I considered that interview as a dance. I would let him think that he was in charge, whilst I led him directly to the spot where I wanted him to be.

This intimate conversation between Elizabeth and the lawyer was covertly recorded by our detective – notice the obvious chemistry between the pair. Elizabeth was not maintaining the distance required of a detective, a tendency Francois references by mentioning a dalliance Elizabeth had conducted in 1953 with Agapanthus's brother-in-law, Ludlow Lansdowne De Groot, then also a murder suspect.

FRANCOIS:

Sybil turned off the electricity. Doesn't that worry you?

ELIZABETH:

Yes of course, that makes sense. The rest of the square was not dark for as long as this house. How did you realise?

FRANCOIS:

It was me who replaced the fuse in the basement. Our fuse box is in the same place.

ELIZABETH:

How do you know Sybil did that?

FRANCOIS:

To help set the scene for this bloody disaster of an evening. This is just typical of her.

ELIZABETH:

He looked at me with a smug smile, clasping his hands as he sat back, splaying his legs apart to take up as much space as possible. The banker's lamp backlit him so I could not see his expressions so well. He flattened his ponytail over the back of the Chesterfield armchair. He pointed his tongue and licked his lips emphatically. He was speaking quietly and softly, with his head bowed. I would have to work hard to get what I wanted.

FRANCOIS:

This whole evening has been quite ridiculous. If Anthony were here, Sybil wouldn't be acting like this. It's all part of her plan to get him to give her some attention, no doubt!

ELIZABETH:

She's rather childlike, isn't she? What do you know about Sybil?

FRANCOIS:

That yarn she spun about her family, that sounds about right, from what Anthony's told me over the years. I'm not surprised at all that she's strung us along this evening, first the story about Anthony. I didn't expect we would encounter a body, though.

ELIZABETH:

The marriage is not a happy one? Tell me about the last time you saw Anthony.

FRANCOIS:

It's natural enough when people have been married for years that they become less enamoured with one another. Anthony has grown tired of her tricks . . . her desire to be in control, to run the show. They had an awful fight at Aintree. He threw a bottle of whiskey at her head . . . He'd backed a few horses heavily, and of course they didn't come in. He should have known better than to rely on tips for the National. I'd tried to stop him. So had Sybil. But we were wasting our time.

ELIZABETH:

He was a big gambler?

ELIZABETH:

His head was tilted to the right and he was running his index finger around the rim of his coffee cup. He set it down and patted his tie, as if looking for something. Loosening the knot, he opened the top button of his shirt revealing a thick curl of chest hair.

FRANCOIS:

Ah, that's better. Oh, Anthony was as bad as Claudius. Worse, probably. Once upon a time he'd had a bit of a knack. But there was no evidence of that recently. He'd been playing games that a gentleman had no business in . . . But you know, I'd better not say

too much more. We all have secrets, don't we, Elizabeth? I say,
Ludlow did well to nab you.

ELIZABETH:

The grin returned as he reminded me about a married man I
had foolishly been involved with two decades earlier. Anyway, there
Francois sat, spouting venom with the loquaciousness of someone
who'd never been stung.

FRANCOIS:

I was glad of your affair, too. Took Sally down a peg or two. Women
have no place in business, if you ask me, or a bloody hospital.

ELIZABETH:

Do you resent your wife's career? Do you think women should be
subordinate? Is that why you hit your wife in front of us all?

ELIZABETH:

He rolled his eyes as his jaw hardened. The sign of a man deliberately muting his reaction. The stiffening of his body and reluctance to look me in the eye told me of the contempt with which he
viewed women.

FRANCOIS:

I don't see what that has to do with anything.

ELIZABETH:

Well, you are both suspects in a murder investigation, let's not
forget that. Someone took a man's life here tonight. Marriage is
such a big part of life; it surely does speak to the killer's mindset.
You see, I understand that you're a serial adulterer.

FRANCOIS:

I wasn't bloody married to the chap, was I? Never met him before!
Infidelity is hardly a new invention and if having a fling made you a
killer, half of the men in London would be in line for the Old
Bailey.

ELIZABETH:

You're the one who made that link, not I. I would say you have a pretty strong motive to want the fellow dead, what with his wife carrying your child.

FRANCOIS:

She's a pretty girl, so I gave her a little pat in the dark. How could you infer anything from that? Honestly this interview has descended into farce!

ELIZABETH:

A man's life has been taken, Francois. It's no minor thing. You are a lawyer; you know they haven't hanged anyone in over a decade, but what is the sentence for murder?

FRANCOIS:

Life. Maybe fifteen, twenty. But the Director of Public Prosecutions would never take the case. Where's the evidence? A junkie overdosed at a posh dinner party. End of story.

ELIZABETH:

So, you don't think there's a killer in the house with us?

FRANCOIS:

Well. No. No, I don't. This whole thing has been blown out of proportion, in the typical histrionic style of Sybil.

ELIZABETH:

You've said that quite a few times, Francois. Now. Do you practise much criminal law?

FRANCOIS:

No. Mostly conveyancing and probate, although my clients have got themselves into a few scrapes with the police, from time to time.

ELIZABETH:

You've never worked on a murder trial?

FRANCOIS:

Not since I qualified, no.

ELIZABETH:

And what will happen to the estate of Mr Crowley? How soon
could his wife access the funds?

FRANCOIS:

Well, I'm sure a chap like that has died intestate. And I doubt he
has a penny to his name . . .

ELIZABETH:

   He rolled his eyes and exhaled in disgust as his bottom lip fell.
Despite myself, I was forced to admit I did find the fellow terribly
attractive. There was an animalis magnetism. He was a man of the
shadows, just like Anthony. The golden light of the lamp highlighted the strength of his jaw and gave definition to his features.
In my youth, he may have been able to sway me. I might have
been old, but I wasn't dead. It was that stupid thought that
spurred me to move as quickly as I could. Upstairs the three
women were waiting, and I was not certain that the killer wasn't
one of them.

ELIZABETH:

Say he does. Humour me.

FRANCOIS:

Well, once the death is announced, if he has left a will, his solicitor
will inform the executors, and the will is read. The executors may
allocate funds to the wife, if she urgently requires them.

ELIZABETH:

And if he dies without a will, how long will it take for the wife to
gain access to his accounts?

FRANCOIS:

You mean his bloody post office account? His possessions,
anything in their joint names will pass immediately to his wife. In

time, so will any funds or assets, but it wouldn't be immediate. It could take months, years even.

ELIZABETH:

What if Jeremy was born into a wealthy family? Say someone had taken out a life insurance policy. How would that change things?

ELIZABETH:

His easy manner shifted at that remark. He sniffed and cleared his throat, looking for a way to buy himself a moment to think. I had been correct in suspecting Francois could have been involved in the murder, given his relationship with the victim's wife.

FRANCOIS:

This life insurance policy. It would be unusual, although not unheard of, for a parent to take a policy out on his son. It's usually the person who pays the premium who is the benefactor. You'd have to see the documents to know who would receive any pay-out and under what conditions. Even then it would take months if not years before the insurance company completed its investigations. They are always looking for ways around pay-outs. If the individual was a known drug user, then I would imagine it would render any policy null and void. I am absolutely certain that there's no criminal misdoing here. Otherwise, I would have insisted on calling the police immediately. And really, Ms Chalice, what is taking them so long?

ELIZABETH:

They will be here as soon as they can. But if Jeremy does have some inheritance, some assets in his name which he may not know about . . . They would be paid directly to his spouse?

FRANCOIS:

Yes, she would be entitled to the majority, along with any children of the deceased.

ELIZABETH:

His response seemed accurate. Perhaps he wasn't involved after all. Why would he speak so freely?

ELIZABETH:

These probate matters, as you say, can take months if not years. By the end of August, Jeremy's son or daughter will have been born.

FRANCOIS:

The same applies. You can't get blood from a stone. Chrissy told me that they live in a squat. She's the breadwinner.

ELIZABETH:

So, she asked you about this?

FRANCOIS:

No.

ELIZABETH:

You see, I can tell you're not very financially comfortable yourself.

FRANCOIS:

Is my Mayfair mansion not sufficient?

ELIZABETH:

Your suit is shabby. Those shoes are worn. You and Agapanthus both work . . . So if you knew there was a large pile of cash on the way. Along with a baby—

FRANCOIS:

Legally speaking he's really considered Jeremy's child.

ELIZABETH:

But your own flesh and blood! A new life, a new wife – plenty of money. It's quite a compelling proposition for a chap like you, Francois. And Chrissy wouldn't give you half the gip you take from Agapanthus.

FRANCOIS:

Oh, I don't know about that. But what is the point of this line of questioning! Why don't you take a closer look at our hostess? Anthony always said she has mental disturbances. I'm no psychiatrist, but her actions this evening are those of a woman who is clearly unhinged, such as with the bloody Ouija board.

ELIZABETH:

His hands were gripped together. His frame was tense as he fought to retain a collected exterior. Push him too far, and he would not cooperate with my questioning. For a moment, I realised the danger I could possibly have been in. If Francois had been the murderer, whether the intended victim was Anthony or Jeremy, he had managed to overpower him long enough to inject the morphine. I unclasped my handbag, pretending to look for my diary, but reassuring myself with the cold blade that I'd kept to hand. Just in case. He watched me very carefully, so I took out the small navy book and pretended to open that day's page.

ELIZABETH:

Let's leave Sybil for the moment. Can you tell me where you were every night for the last week?

FRANCOIS:

I've been working like a dog on this bloody case. Timothy Hall QC is a hard taskmaster. I wouldn't want to get into the witness box in front of him, he's like a dog with a bone.

ELIZABETH:

What is the case that you're working on?

FRANCOIS:

Oh, don't be dull, Elizabeth. You're repeating yourself now. It's of no consequence here.

ELIZABETH:

Indulge me.

FRANCOIS:

Oh, fine. Seeing as you've badgered me into it. It's a murder trial.
My client is innocent, of course.

ELIZABETH:

I thought you don't do much criminal work?

FRANCOIS:

Hardly any. I'm really only there to advise on the probate aspect to
the case. Another solicitor is running the main defence with the
barrister.

ELIZABETH:

Who is the victim?

FRANCOIS:

A fellow – he's accused of murdering his sister-in-law. Some
blighter broke into the house and bludgeoned her to death with a
brick. My client was in the unfortunate position of arriving home
and going straight to his own shed. Only place the fellow could get
a bit of peace and quiet, by all accounts. He hadn't seen a thing; the
killer had come in through the front of the house. He found her
though . . . was covered in her blood. He only came across her
when he heard the baby crying and went to check what was wrong.
The police put two and two together and came up with eleven. All
this talk of the Yorkshire Ripper and the Lucan fiasco, there's no
such thing as innocent until proven guilty if you're an ordinary
chap these days.

ELIZABETH:

Was she the benefactor of a large inheritance? What probate are
you advising on?

FRANCOIS:

You can't expect me to break the confidentiality of my client. You
don't have any right to quiz me on that. Well-bred people aren't the
only people who write wills you know. Even the common man will

try to look after his children. I'm not going to say any more on the matter, this is the private business of an innocent person.

ELIZABETH:

OK. So, who killed her then?

FRANCOIS:

She'd been having a fling with a friend of the family. Lover's tiff went wrong. But he is a police officer. A detective sergeant, so of reasonable rank. His partner provided an alibi for the man. Hence my client is in the frame.

ELIZABETH:

Is that why you've been so conflicted about calling the police here tonight?

FRANCOIS:

Look, Elizabeth. I know you have to justify this investigation and prove that you're earning whatever Sybil is paying you for this evening, but you don't really believe anyone murdered Jeremy tonight, do you? I mean the man was a drug addict like Anthony's stepmother, Idabel. Heroin, opium, morphine, they are all pretty much the same, aren't they? So, he comes across a bounteously full cabinet of morphine. Well, even if he had been clean, the very sight of the thing might have been enough to give him a craving. I know his type, as I'm sure you do. This wasn't a murder. This was an accident.

ELIZABETH:

I'm not sure I agree, Francois. You've lied to me, in the middle of a murder investigation! You have to admit that it is suspicious. You told me you'd never met the chap before.

FRANCOIS:

There's no bloody crime here, Elizabeth. I didn't lie.

ELIZABETH:

Well, you failed to correct your wife.

FRANCOIS:

That's not the same thing as lying.

ELIZABETH:

Oh, it's an error of omission. But that's not the only way you know our victim, is it? Tell me, how long have you owned the house in Mayo?

FRANCOIS:

How did you know . . . ?

ELIZABETH:

I remember when I first met Anthony and Sybil, he told me that his friend had married a builder's daughter from Ireland, a very wealthy one, who had returned to his home county to purchase a large estate near Castlebar. That particular fact came back to me earlier this evening, when I was thinking about just how much Anthony reminded me of Lord Lucan . . . you see that family were also of Anglo-Irish lineage, and also held a baronetcy there.

FRANCOIS:

Well, I don't own it. It's Aggie's family home. The Lucans were long gone out of Gorteendrunagh by the time Patrick O'Callaghan went home to buy his lodge . . . I really don't see the connection.

ELIZABETH:

O'Callaghan. Yes that was the name Anthony mentioned. I have a very good memory for names. It wasn't the first time I'd heard that name. As you alluded to earlier, I did have an entanglement with the sister of Agapanthus, Sally. She'd taken her husband's name, Lansdowne de Groot, when I knew her. And I realised that this O'Callaghan fellow must have been Sally's father. It's incredible, no matter where you go in the world, there always exist these tiny threads and connections that tie us all together. Anyway, that evening in Paris ten years ago, he said the fellow was having a terrible time trying to ingratiate himself with the local gentry. That leads me onto my next point. Do you hunt, Francois?

FRANCOIS:

No. It's a grim business, if you ask me. I'm a city boy, anyway. I
don't share the bloodlust of my wife.

ELIZABETH:

But that's how you know Jeremy's father, isn't it? He's too old to
actually go out hunting, but you both go along for the port and
fruitcake. If Sybil grew up there, spent summers there, she would
have known the Crowley family for many years, isn't that true? In
fact, she probably grew up with Jeremy. Before his mother took him
to London.

FRANCOIS:

Look, maybe she did know Jeremy, but what good is it going to do
dragging my name into this? Don't you realise that a legal career
– that life can be impecunious if you're not born into a legal family?
I've had to work hard to keep my practice going, you know. No
well-known uncles to send business my way. I can't believe you're
homing in on me like this – but it won't do a single bit of good to
ruin my reputation by embroiling me in the death of an addict.

ELIZABETH:

Nice deflection back to yourself. Tell me, Francois, have you ever
been approached by a member of the IRA during your time in
Ireland?

FRANCOIS:

Absolutely not, they are bloody murderers.

ELIZABETH:

And your wife, could she have been swayed to provide them with
intelligence of the movements of the aristocrats? There are plenty
of influential Anglo-Irish families with summer houses and castles
in the north-west . . . Her father was not born into money. Her
ancestors would likely have suffered at the hands of these landlord
families.

FRANCOIS:

Agapanthus is far too concerned about herself to put effort into any ideology.

ELIZABETH:

You've embroiled yourself, Francois. In many ways. Tell me, did you *seek out* Jeremy's wife?

FRANCOIS:

What on earth do you mean—

ELIZABETH:

Oh, for God's sake, do not try and give me the slip-around. Can I make another guess? That you were responsible for setting up all those trusts and wills for Jeremy for his father? I can just imagine it now. You both meet at the local hunt ball. You've already admitted that work is hard to come by, so you work the room. Look for any old codger there with broken veins who might be involved in some sort of strife with his children. Old Crowley sidles up to you. Asks if you ever come across his errant son in London. You lend a sympathetic ear. Maybe you tell him how he's fallen in with a bad crowd. Tell him that even if he won't talk to his father, his father can still ensure he's taken care of. Poor fellow feels sorry for you, wants to give you the business. So, let you draw up all the papers. Then you even offer to get his son up to Mayo, offer a chance to reconcile with the fellow. You had Agapanthus arrange it, didn't you? She offered him the decorating work, and told his dear old dad when he would be at your house. But the plan didn't work, did it? As soon as Jeremy saw the Mayo address he knew what was being planned.

FELIX:

How did you realise the connection?

ELIZABETH:

Here. I found it in Sybil's and popped it into my bag.

She handed me a yellowed page from the Connaught Telegraph from January 1977, three months before the murder. Amongst the spotty black and white pictures, she pointed to one. A photograph of an older rotund gentleman in a solid-coloured waistcoat I took to be red, and the Langfords. The caption read 'George Crowley MH, pictured with Agapanthus and Francois Langford at the North Mayo Harriers Ball last weekend'.

FRANCOIS:

It was her fault. My bloody wife . . .

ELIZABETH:

But you had put that trust in place. Drawn up the insurance policy. You knew Jeremy would be more valuable to his wife dead. And if that was the case, you could replace him. She'd have a respectable husband – a house in Mayfair—

FRANCOIS:

Hold on a minute, I didn't plan to *kill* Jeremy. You obviously have quite the brilliant mind, my dear. Brilliant. But to think that I masterminded something so intricate is frankly incredible.

ELIZABETH:

Let me finish. But the fly in the ointment was, after the meeting with Jeremy didn't happen, his father never signed the papers. There is no inheritance, nor trust for Chrissy's baby.

ELIZABETH:

A man as infantile as Francois could not hide his true concern that what I was saying might be true. Gone was the tense writhing of his hands, replaced by a limpness, a vulnerability that came with the realisation his plan would fail.

FRANCOIS:

How could you possibly know that?

ELIZABETH:

It's my suspicion.

FRANCOIS:

That old bastard.

ELIZABETH:

It seems it was too complicated for you to mastermind, after all.
Poor Chrissy. She hasn't a clue of your involvement, has she?

FRANCOIS:

George can't disown his son like that. I'm no expert on Irish law,
but any common law jurisdiction would insist that a child is
provided for.

ELIZABETH:

Now that, I admit, is beyond my level of expertise. Tell me, does
Chrissy have any idea of what you've been up to?

FRANCOIS:

She's not the fool you seem to think she is. Christina is a very
intelligent woman. Although I daresay, the wit of our lady detective outstrips even Christina Crowley. You give the impression, I
hope you don't mind me saying, Elizabeth. But you seem like a
nosy old bag—

ELIZABETH:

Charming.

FRANCOIS:

But now that I see you in this light, I can tell you were once very
beautiful. The years have been hard for you, haven't they? If you'd
lived a life of ease . . . well, who knows what you might have
achieved.

ELIZABETH:

Ha! You can't try to make this about me, surely. Is this the official
charm that you're meant to have? Well, it's not going to work on me.

*Here we see Elizabeth's fatal flaw come back into the interview
dynamic. Disarming though it might have been, I do wonder if it*

displays a lack of finesse you'd expect from an experienced detective.

FRANCOIS:

It's rare to tango with one so adept at conversation. It is thrilling. You must have trouble with your interviewees falling under your spell.

ELIZABETH:

I wouldn't say that.

FRANCOIS:

But it's a tool that you use, isn't it? You seduce your suspects. Build an easy rapport. Let them think you are a fool, in over your head. Isn't that the case?

ELIZABETH:

You don't know a single thing about me, Francois.

FRANCOIS:

Oh, I've heard what you did with my brother-in-law back in the 1950s. He couldn't ever help himself, old Ludlow. I've struck a nerve there, haven't I! Well, if you don't use your feminine wiles on me, your only male suspect, there must be a good reason. Perhaps it didn't work out for you the last time you played that card? Because you're no fool. And age has clawed back how far flirtation carries you, hasn't it? Because who wants to flirt with a pensioner, despite how strong the stock might once have been.

ELIZABETH:

I know what you're doing. And it's not going to get to me. Let's go back to you for a moment, Francois. So, you were working on this case all week. Whereabouts were you doing that?

FRANCOIS:

In my office, of course.

ELIZABETH:

You don't bring your work home with you?

FRANCOIS:

I prefer to spend as little time as possible with my wife. I'm sure you can tell.

ELIZABETH:

You don't drink to excess. I saw how you were betting on the bridge upstairs, but you were never in the same league as Anthony. Women are your vice. And during the busiest time of your career – the week before a major murder trial – you expect me to believe that you never took an opportunity to blow off steam?

FRANCOIS:

I don't use prostitutes. If that's what you mean.

ELIZABETH:

Oh, I gather you couldn't even afford a jolly with a meagre street-walker. But you didn't have to pay Sybil, did you?

FRANCOIS:

And there you've made one miscalculation too far, Elizabeth. What's the womaniser's version of honour amongst thieves? Or shitting on one's own doorstep? She's married to my best friend. And I happen to be helping her husband to divorce her in a case that's going to be front-page news!

ELIZABETH:

It's quite understandable that you don't know what to say. You see, I'm used to seeing someone in your position. To have the intricate web of deceit and machinations that entangle your life tugged apart by a stranger such as me, well you couldn't have expected it to happen. Because I can see behind those blue eyes. Into all those little shadowy parts of your mind. I'm unearthing those bad judge-ment calls, the trick of balancing the strategic manoeuvres you've cooked up in your head, with the ache of your balls. Usually people feel relieved to be able to talk about it all with someone else. So really, you should be thanking me, for easing the burden of the past few months.

FRANCOIS:

There's a lot of things I think about you, Elizabeth. So, tell me – within this fetid little chamber of revelations, we are aside from the outside world – why do you like spending your time tugging asunder someone else's demons? Look at you there, on the edge of Sybil's bloody sofa, drinking it all in. You don't want to find any killer. You want to live in this investigation, where you are the queen and surveyor, us suspects your little ants. That's why there's such a difference between the woman who made small talk at the dinner table and this creature that you have become in front of me. Your eyes are bright and darting, the adrenaline pushing things into place. Your cheeks are flushed, you're almost breathless at the pace which we are going here. This is the moment that you live for. Everything else is just killing time. I can tell how excited you are. Aren't you? If I pushed you onto the sofa there, I don't know that you'd be able to stop yourself, would you?

ELIZABETH:

I stood up from my seat to break away from him. I touched the blade in my bag. My hand shook as I flicked my lighter. I turned my back to him so he did not see the tremor.

FRANCOIS:

Usually, they wait until afterwards to light a cigarette.

ELIZABETH:

Maybe you're right. It's been quite a while since I've investigated such an interconnected group as you. Despite what you say, it's not possible to get my knickers in a twist any more.

FRANCOIS:

How long has it been, since you've been with a man?

ELIZABETH:

Not as long as you'd think, Francois. What's with the name anyway?

FRANCOIS:

My mother was French. But she hadn't the bloody foresight to send me to Paris. I can't speak a word. Can't tell you how embarrassing it is to check into a hotel or arrive somewhere to be greeted like a Frog.

ELIZABETH:

Now, there's something to keep you occupied over the next ten years. Did Sybil tell you what she was planning here tonight?

FRANCOIS:

Sybil isn't as calculating as you or I are. If she killed Jeremy, it was a spur of the moment thing, I guarantee. Our little entanglement was just a physical manifestation of, well I don't know what. She just wanted to know if I'd heard from Anthony. I can't tell her he's planning a divorce. She's unstable, you know. Liable to do anything, as you can quite see from what's gone on here tonight. I didn't even know she was inviting us to supper.

ELIZABETH:

Why did you agree to come, if you were worried she was going to say something to Agapanthus?

FRANCOIS:

It would have looked more suspicious if I didn't come. My wife has been dying to get her bony old nose in here for years.

ELIZABETH:

He was standing right beside me, trapping me against the chimney breast with his arm over my head. His finger grazed my cheek. For a moment, time stood still as if we were in a bubble. But I would not surrender.

ELIZABETH:

I see. Well, Francois, you've been very helpful. I think we are finished. You can go back to your little love triangle now.

FRANCOIS:

That's it, is it? I was rather enjoying our little repartee.

ELIZABETH:

I can see that. Why don't you stay here and cool down?

FRANCOIS:

Oh, Elizabeth.

ELIZABETH:

He caught me by the elbow as I reached for the doorknob and pressed himself against me, kissing my neck. I pushed him, but he didn't move. I told him to stop it, but it was no use, so with as much force as I could gather, I thrust my knee to give him an almighty kick in the balls. As he roared, I got to the hallway and ran up the stairs. I needed a breath of fresh air after that heated discussion with Francois. I'd forgotten how much fun it can be to run rings around someone so much that they gave themselves up. I had almost succumbed. Francois was so busy trying to get me into bed that he managed to slip up, a few times. He thought he had outsmarted me, but he divulged far more than I expected him to. I didn't realise he'd had a fling with Sybil until I was midway through that question. If it wasn't so late, I would have made some more calls to enquire about his involvement in this murder case. I'm not a legal mind, but it struck me as odd that he would be involved in defending the man who killed his client. I stood on the landing to take a breath and consider what he'd told me in the interview.

FELIX:

What did you make of this information?

ELIZABETH:

If the victim and his client were related through marriage, perhaps they were both *ultimately* his clients? Given he had admitted to concocting this scheme with Jeremy's inheritance, I wondered was it possible he could have been involved in that murder too. My gut told me he wasn't the killer. The only thing that didn't quite sit right with me was his reluctance to accept that Jeremy was actually murdered. The evidence was indisputable. But his vehemence told me that he could be covering for someone. But who? He has admitted to having romantic connections to all three of our female suspects.

FELIX:

Did he offer up Sybil's name rather too quickly?

ELIZABETH:

That told me either he was trying to double-bluff me, or he was covering for the other two. But if he didn't love his wife any more, wouldn't sending her to prison make things easier? Unless his concern about sullying his name by being linked to this case would also extend to his wife's reputation.

More likely, I thought, is that he would be assuaging the guilt of the woman who's pregnant with his child. Although, now that I think about it, perhaps that's not the only fruit of his loin. Still, he wouldn't want her to be sentenced for any crime. And really, she had the most to gain from her husband's death.

And there, dear listener, we must end this episode of Supper for Six, *after the heated interview between Elizabeth Chalice and lawyer, Francois Langford. The newspaper clipping asserts once more the Irish ties of the group. Agapanthus was born there, as was Sybil, and indeed Jeremy was adopted to there as an infant. Only Sybil possess a muted Irish accent, having adapted once she married Anthony Anderson. The others were educated to speak with a British accent, as was commonplace with those of their position in Anglo-Irish society. This was not just a tale of Mayfair, but a story that began in County Mayo. In the next episode, Elizabeth learns that everything she believed to have happened was really just an elaborate stage set by her hostess, Lady Anderson. The pretence is about to fall apart, to deadly consequences Ms Chalice could not have foreseen. You've been listening to* Supper for Six, *with Felix Caerphilly.*

EPISODE EIGHT:

Empty Crystalware

It's the evening of 7th April, and private investigator, Elizabeth Chalice, is making her way through the suspects in the death of Lord Anthony Anderson, who died whilst disguised as punk rocker and painter Jeremy Crowley. The body is only two hours cold, the fifty-nine-year-old detective has just kicked lawyer and friend of the deceased in the balls. For despite the grand surroundings of the Mayfair mansion, with its twenty-foot ceilings and marble fireplaces, the rawness of emotions are evident. For there is still a killer on the loose. This is Supper for Six, *and I'm your host Felix Caerphilly. In this episode, Chalice interviews Jeremy's wife, Christina Crowley, a West-End make-up artist, who has been having an affair with fellow dinner guest Francois Langford. Despite how Elizabeth tugs at the threads that tie the six diners, the connections become knotted into an impenetrable mass.*

FELIX:

When did you realise that the fire was Sybil's invention?

ELIZABETH:

The radio broadcast after the card game was exactly the same as the one we had heard earlier. And the newsreader said it was the nine o'clock news, although it was well after 10 p.m. I'd seen the mother and her baby out walking on Bruton Square at the same time as two young men in flares, apparently unharmed. Then I remembered that Agapathanthus had mentioned the Balcombe Street siege, when two IRA members took a couple hostage – I was in Italy at the time, of course – and I thought it was terribly interesting that the negotiators had a false message broadcast to intimidate the IRA members into surrendering.

I mean it's so obvious now, because Sybil had staged an elaborate dinner party. But it wasn't at the time. I started to work out how she could have set up recordings to convince us there was a fire when in fact there was no such thing.

FELIX:

Did you check the radio?

ELIZABETH:

I knew I would need to closely inspect the radio for a sign that something was pre-recorded. Then there was the business of the locked doors. The electrical outages. And Anthony's disguise as Jeremy. But why would Sybil go to such lengths?

Weighing up the probability, I reckoned she had to have had help in staging this performance. And who else was involved in the theatre? Could Chrissy and Sybil, both unhappily married women, have been working together in a scheme to swap husbands? Most of all, where was the real Jeremy Crowley?

Navigating immediate danger to oneself and others can narrow the mind. Perhaps Elizabeth's concern about the immediate physical safety of herself and the other guests had clouded her judgement and ability to appreciate the larger plans that Sybil had put in place that evening.

FELIX:

How were you feeling about interviewing Chrissy?

ELIZABETH:

I remember that the air held a hint of indecency, as if my interview with Francois had left an animalistic scent. Chrissy looked a little bit better than she had done earlier, but the exhaustion was still evident in her swollen eyelids. The nurse in me just wanted to put her back to bed with a hot-water bottle until morning, but I needed to interview her about the death of the man who had arrived as her husband.

In this next clip recorded by Elizabeth, she probes Chrissy Crowley for more detail on Sybil's relationship with the murder victim. Elizabeth's nursing background is evident in her approach to the pregnant woman – but listen how she still manages to extract some important information about Sybil's potential reasons for hosting the dinner party.

ELIZABETH:

There we are. Privacy. Now. How are you feeling, Chrissy?

CHRISSY:

Jeremy's been murdered and I'm locked in with his killer – how do you bloody think I am?

ELIZABETH:

I'm afraid I may need to ask some difficult questions. I know it will be hard but you understand I must get the full picture. Who do you think killed him?

CHRISSY:

Oh, isn't it obvious who I think did it? Sybil, of course.

ELIZABETH:

But why?

CHRISSY:

Something about back when they knew each other first. The way Jeremy tells it, Sybil really let him and the lads down when the record label wanted to meet them. They were in a band for, gosh, three years? They told me that nothing ever happened between them . . . but I just don't believe that. Knowing Sybil's need for reassurance now, well, she must have been ten times worse when she was in her early twenties. So, why wouldn't she have had a fling with the guitarist? Plus, she's never had the slightest interest in Jeremy since we became friends but she insisted that he come here tonight?

ELIZABETH:

So, you think they had a relationship, what, fifteen years ago? That something happened and she's been biding her time to murder him ever since. Is that what you're telling me?

CHRISSY:

More or less. You're the investigator. Can't you investigate?

Elizabeth doesn't always get straight to the point when interviewing suspects. She leads them in a circle, from topic to topic, closing in on her prey. Listen how she moves from Chrissy's pregnancy, to Sybil, before cornering Chrissy into revealing that she hasn't seen much of her husband. But was that because he wasn't there, or because her vision was impaired?

ELIZABETH:

But Sybil is the one who asked me to investigate.

CHRISSY:

That doesn't mean anything. Of course, she would ask you to investigate if she was the killer, to deflect attention from herself and to look innocent!

ELIZABETH:

I'll bear that in mind. Now. Tell me, what's your due date?

CHRISSY:

Eh, well. I'm sorry what does that have to do with anything?

ELIZABETH:

I remember when I was pregnant, everyone would ask me all the time. From old signoras in the butcher's to girls in shops.

CHRISSY:

I suppose. Um, I believe it is August 10th.

ELIZABETH:

Now, I know it's not a precise science, from my rudimentary midwifery experience . . . that means the baby was conceived at the start of November? Francois is the child's father; he's already admitted it.

CHRISSY:

That's more than he's said to me. Do you blame me? You've seen him. How he snares you in. I . . . I have always wanted a child.

ELIZABETH:

So you weren't sleeping with Jeremy at that time?

CHRISSY:

In all the time we were married, even at the start when we were going at it hammer and tongs, I never fell pregnant. And anyway, Jeremy and I hadn't been intimate for many months. So I'm certain who this child's father is, before you look at me with that beady eye.

ELIZABETH:

I'm no one to judge. When you get to my age, you learn that life is rarely as simple as one expects. It is messy around the edges. But I don't mean to press you on this private issue; let's move on.

CHRISSY:

Thankfully.

ELIZABETH:

How do you know Sybil?

CHRISSY:

From the Lankier Theatre. She was the lead in a terrible musical; we had a lot of fun though. That's why we stayed in touch. How do you know Sybil again?

ELIZABETH:

We met in Paris, but we write to one another.

CHRISSY:

Oh, you're the pen pal.

ELIZABETH:

She's told you about me?

CHRISSY:

Sybil isn't who she pretends to be, you know. I read one of the letters she was writing to you. It must have been towards the end of last year. We were out for a coffee, and it was hanging out of her bag. She'd gone to the loo and . . . well, I didn't mean to pry. It did just fall out. She was telling you to have a good honeymoon. What was that about?

ELIZABETH:

That's personal, Chrissy. Yes, she was writing about redecorating the house. Looking for young artists. Like your husband.

CHRISSY:

Yes. I was saying, I read her letter to you. How she wanted to support local artists. And all the time she knew my Jeremy was trying to build a name for himself in the art world. His agent Bartholomew had agreed to represent him. But she never offered to buy a thing. And then I arrive here and find that up on the wall. Look at it. It's a portrait of Sybil! It's from when they were on tour together, it looks like.

ELIZABETH:

So, you think they had secretly kept in touch?

CHRISSY:

I don't trust a word out of her mouth. This entire evening has been such a Sybil show, that I don't want to give her the satisfaction. (*in mock accent*) Oh, please, Sybil, tell us all about your secret painting my husband did of you. (*in her own voice*) No. I won't play into her hands.

ELIZABETH:

But he didn't tell you he was doing the painting, did he?

CHRISSY:

No. He didn't.

ELIZABETH:

And she would have paid a lot for it, yes?

CHRISSY:

An oil like that, of course she would have. But that dealer can be rather slow in paying out to Jeremy.

ELIZABETH:

It would have taken him a great deal of time to do, no?

CHRISSY:

Jeremy worked long hours. The builder he does decorating work for pays by the job, so he works, I mean he worked, long hours to get as much work as he could. He often would be home late and out early. We could go for days without really seeing much of each other.

ELIZABETH:

Did you ever suspect him of having an affair?

CHRISSY:

Not Jeremy. He always said there was only ever one woman that he truly loved.

ELIZABETH:

You?

CHRISSY:

He was *infatuated* with Sybil, that's all. I was his only love.

ELIZABETH:

Tell me, has he been much of a help to you in these last few days?

CHRISSY:

Him? He's quite useless. Haven't seen him since the weekend.

ELIZABETH:

How long after you met were you married?

CHRISSY:

Oh, it was a brief but intense few weeks. He proposed after a month. I had wondered . . . you know, why he moved so quickly, but I was young, it was romantic!

ELIZABETH:

I remember the same feelings myself.

ELIZABETH:

Was Jeremy happy about the baby?

CHRISSY:

Thrilled, he was. But same as myself, he was rather surprised. But God works in mysterious ways, as they say.

ELIZABETH:

Let's not be coy, Chrissy, if Francois is the baby's father. Did Jeremy suspect you of having an affair?

CHRISSY:

No. He didn't. I always told him I was coming to visit Sybil.

ELIZABETH:

And did Jeremy approve of your friendship with Sybil?

CHRISSY:

He liked to pretend that he didn't want me hanging out with a lady . . . but he never stopped me from meeting Sybil. He despised the upper classes, even though he was born into them. Maybe it's because Sybil had been born ordinary enough that he didn't mind. He always wanted to know what we had been up to.

ELIZABETH:

But he stayed in touch with the other members of their band?

CHRISSY:

He's been gigging with them for years. They never asked me about Sybil. Maybe they'd sneer about the Anderson Ant, or something like that. Mikey hated her. He blamed her for ruining their shot with that record deal. He hated that she ended up smelling of roses here in Mayfair when they were slumming it. But that made them hypocrites. You know they wanted to reject the Establishment, capitalism. Spouting on about how money is the root of all evil yet furious that they hadn't got rich; it didn't make any sense. Jeremy, like the rest of them, talked the talk, but in the heel of the hunt, he still liked to see the Queen's face on those pound notes at the end of the week.

ELIZABETH:

Would you consider yourself a punk, Chrissy?

CHRISSY:

I like the drama of it all, the hair, the clothes. But I don't think it's beautiful. That look, they are like sewer rats dried up and turned inside out or something. Now I'm expecting, well, I don't want to live in a dump with junkies any more. I don't want to reject society; I just want a safe home for me and the little one.

ELIZABETH:

So, in some ways, you're glad that Jeremy's dead?

CHRISSY:

Glad? I suppose I am. Things weren't always the best between us. But that doesn't mean I killed him. I assume you're trying to rile me up to get a reaction.

ELIZABETH:

Do you think Francois could have murdered Jeremy? Apparently, he's quite the ladies' man, but could he have it in him?

CHRISSY:

He couldn't kill a mouse. Ladies' man, what do you mean?

ELIZABETH:

Sybil is a beautiful woman. She must get a lot of male attention.

ELIZABETH:

A veneer of composure has returned to our new widow as we continue our conversation. She's fiddling with her fingernails as we resume. I sense that her distress is genuine, but still, I ought to prod a little further, no matter how indelicate it may seem. But instead of pushing that point, I must capitalise on this break she is experiencing. If she believes I have let her off the hook on that front, she may reveal more.

CHRISSY:

Oh God. I mean, maybe it is Sybil. She killed Jeremy.

ELIZABETH:

Are you OK, Chrissy? Shall I get you a glass of water?

ELIZABETH:

The coal bucket was too heavy. I just about caught her vomit in an A4 envelope. Spots of watery green bile. She retched, her eyes watered and her face turned red as nothing more came up. Her frame squeezed itself as I rubbed her back. I wondered what I was doing, grilling someone who was clearly unwell. Was it possible that her illness had distracted her and she really hadn't noticed Anthony was pretending to be her husband? I stroked her hair, wiping it from the sweat of her hairline as the retching subsided, and I asked her if it had been like this through her entire pregnancy.

FELIX:

This detail was particularly relevant.

ELIZABETH:

She nodded and wiped the tears from her eyes as she leaned back into the armchair and stared up at the plasterwork ceiling where two cherubs chased one another amidst strands of ivy. Hyperemesis gravidarum. An awful affliction for an expectant mother. And she was diabetic too. I asked to see into her eye, as the doctor seemed to think she had a vitreous haemorrhage. I imagine her vision had been off for days.

When I said this to her, I was met with just more nodding. The quiet of the moment was punctuated by the sounds of a car pulling up outside. Inaudible conversation. But there were people out there. I peeked through the curtains to see the rear lights of a taxi, and a pair of elderly women bumble down the street. Chrissy could hear the same thing and our eyes met. Her eyes were dry and hard, despite the swelling on the left eye.

CHRISSY:

Have you decided who the killer is yet?

ELIZABETH:

Oh, why don't we take a break for a while. You need rest, and some fluids.

FELIX:

How did she seem?

Here Elizabeth turns the tape to the other side, she was running out of space to record that night's proceedings.

ELIZABETH:

There was a sternness and intensity to her gaze that belied the woman who had crumpled into herself a few moments before. The noise on the street did not seem to concern her. Gone was the Cockney. Instead, she clipped her vowels and drew her lips together in an accent that was standard to this part of Mayfair.

CHRISSY:

Us women are stronger than anyone else. You know, I've done things. Been places. Been other people, in fact. I was born into another lifetime. Into a childhood spent under the frolicking of Raphael and Azrael.

ELIZABETH:

Holding onto the arm of the chair, she stood. She was speaking of angels; it took me a moment to realise she meant the cherubs in the ceiling. First the left foot gained traction on the shaggy rug. Then the right. This energy, it seemed to come from nowhere. It was the adrenaline. And I knew she would be weaker than ever in a few moments when it wore off.

CHRISSY:

I've done the hardest things a woman could do. Yes, this sickness is inconvenient. But it's our penance, isn't it? Eve's curse. The rigmarole of childbed.

ELIZABETH:

What is your real name?

CHRISSY:

Oh, it is Christina all right. But we haven't time for you to consult *Burke's* or *Debrett's* for my family of origin. Sybil said you were away with the fairies. An old spinster. Well, I must say you are doing an admirable job, under the circumstances.

ELIZABETH:

You knew it was Anthony upstairs, when you saw him, didn't you?

CHRISSY:

Anthony? He's . . .

ELIZABETH:

She stumbled, taking a step back as the faintness caught up with her. The room smelled like mothballs and the envelope of vomit I'd thrown into the fire. I started to feel a wave of nausea rise in myself. Here was another assumed identity that I had failed to spot earlier that evening. Was Sybil right? Had I lost my touch?

ELIZABETH:

When you saw the body, you said it wasn't Jeremy. Multiple times. That we ought to call the police as it couldn't have been an accident.

ELIZABETH:

I knelt beside her and held her clammy hand. A hand that was soft, with manicured nails, unlike the rough skin on my palms. Her pain had a presence in the room, despite her momentary looks of strength.

CHRISSY:

Yes. Yes, I did think that. I mean, I don't know what I was thinking. So, Jeremy is not dead? It's Anthony? But how—

ELIZABETH:

Tell me the truth, Chrissy. What was Sybil planning to do tonight? I really think you are very poorly and it's no time to play around. I've walked away from lifetimes too. From people and places that damaged me. If that's what you have done, I understand. But your body cannot sustain this level of stress without collapsing. Think of your child.

CHRISSY:

The fire. It's not real. It's a set-up. We recorded tapes of the news and the air-raid siren. It . . . it was Sybil's idea. You won't tell anyone, will you? I mean I can't go to jail. I can't have this child in prison.

ELIZABETH:

I have no plan to do that. But a man died here tonight. A man dressed as your husband. Did you kill him, Chrissy?

CHRISSY:

No. No, I didn't. We never meant to be murderers, Sybil and I. We just meant to . . . let Jeremy make a mistake. You see, he was a recovering addict. Really a terribly mean and spiteful fellow. When he found out I was expecting he flung me down the stairs. I nearly lost the child. Sybil suggested we bring him over here. Put him in harm's way and let him help himself to the morphine. Hope that he would overdose and that would be the end of him. When she found you were back in England, she reckoned you could give the thing a stamp of approval. As an officer of the court, Francois would agree with the overdose. Sybil knew Francois was the father of my child and if nothing else, I felt he could do this for us. Agapanthus has been struck off for drinking on the job, so no one was going to rate her opinion. But we were never going to KILL him. I mean he was six foot four.

FELIX:

How did her demeanour change?

ELIZABETH:

She was speaking quickly. Rattling off one admission after another like a school girl recalling an argument with her sister under the eaves at a friend's sleepover. Each thing she revealed fell into place like lumber into the joists of a floor. I had felt some of these mistruths, but of course it made sense.

CHRISSY:

But now you're telling me it wasn't Jeremy at all? But Anthony? How on earth did I not see . . .

ELIZABETH:

We don't see what we don't want to see. But tell me, why did you want to have him overdose in the middle of a dinner party? Why didn't you leave the morphine somewhere else for him to find? I understand Jeremy came from a wealthy family. Just like you. Isn't that right?

ELIZABETH:

The grey pallor returned, and I knew Chrissy had no longer a single ounce of energy to speak to me. She must have been in shock, even if what she had been saying were true. I helped her to the couch where I lay her down. Her eyes were dry, not because of her resolve, but because her body could not spare the fluid.

ELIZABETH:

How long have you been seeing Francois? Agapanthus knows too, doesn't she? The two of you are worried about the other woman! She was paying a lot of attention to her make-up, and then you tidied yourself up. You're worried he won't leave her, aren't you?

CHRISSY:

How did you know?

ELIZABETH:

It was a gut thing to begin with. I've lived in Italy for almost thirty years. They live passionately, even for a Catholic country.

Extra-marital affairs are not unusual, even where the wife knows. But that balance shifts if the mistress finds herself in, well, the same position as you. But Jeremy wasn't in London when that child was conceived, was he?

CHRISSY:

Elizabeth . . . I can't go on record about this. There's too much at stake.

ELIZABETH:

Like what, exactly?

CHRISSY:

Francois seems to think that the baby could be in line for some inheritance; as Jeremy is his father's only son, this baby would be the last in that line of Crowleys. But he only said that he thought that, not that his father had asked him for help.

ELIZABETH:

So, he's a liar. And he's not going to leave Aggie for you then. At least not straight away. Because then everyone would know the child is his.

CHRISSY:

I suppose, but please don't judge—

ELIZABETH:

I'm no one to judge anyone else, Chrissy. And I know Francois hasn't a penny either.

CHRISSY:

Come to think of it . . . he started to ask me about it. It's as if he already knew . . . Well, he did know Jeremy's father. From hunting, that's it. Agapanthus still hunts when she's in Castlebar. She's in the same outfit at Jeremy's father.

ELIZABETH:

So, they do know one another. The Langfords have known the Crowley family for years, yes? Chrissy, do you think it's possible that Francois could have killed Anthony, thinking he was Jeremy?

CHRISSY:

Francois wouldn't have it in him to do something like that to Anthony or Jeremy. He's not the violent type.

ELIZABETH:

Well, someone killed Anthony.

CHRISSY:

It must have been Sybil. Must have been. But where is the *real* Jeremy?

ELIZABETH:

If the fire is a hoax, and Agapanthus is struck off, I really think we'd better take you to a hospital. You are dehydrated, Chrissy, there's a real risk to you and the baby. Come now, my car is outside and we'll get straight to the local maternity unit.

ELIZABETH:

On my tiptoes, so as not to make a sound someone else might hear, I went to the hallway. With one hand against the doorframe to shield the noise of the latch, I turned the knob, but it would not move. The door was locked! Of course it was, Francois had mentioned it. An ambulance siren wailed by outside, as I felt a sharp crack on my head, and after that, my world went dark.

FELIX:

Elizabeth? Elizabeth? Are you OK?

She snapped from her reverie to push apart two chunks of hair from the crown of her head. Just behind the parting, was a zig-zag line the length of my finger. The blood-red on her nails highlighted the size of the injury, and I thought how shocked she must have been after it happened.

ELIZABETH:

Where did you get the money to pay me, Felix? How does a teenager have a thousand pounds to spend? If someone gave you the cash, you'd really better look for their motivation.

She fixed her hair, wrapping the curly black strands into a French roll, to hide the scar that the gash had left on her head, then reapplied her lipstick. I did not want to break our conversation here.

FELIX:

I won it in a card game.

ELIZABETH:

You must be very good at cards. Poker, was it?

FELIX:

Well, my name is Felix, after all.

ELIZABETH:

This card game. It didn't happen in the company of anyone connected to the case, did it? Where was this game?

FELIX:

It doesn't matter. Why do you care?

ELIZABETH:

I need some more money.

She snapped shut her powder compact and glared at me. As she popped her raincoat closed and clacked across my bedsit floor, I could barely believe what I was hearing.

ELIZABETH:

I'm sorry, Felix, but I have to go away for a few days. You don't seem to realise that these memories are not easy for me to recall. Any good interviewer needs to be empathetic. I was in fear of my life! So were the other guests. It's all jolly well and good to posture and muse over that night as if it were a bloody crossword. But we were all victims. Even the killer. I am not a character in a comic strip, Felix.

This is not a detective story. There are two graves. Two coffins. Two sets of grieving relations. Never mind the impact such prolonged stress has on a body. When I was nursing, we'd see soldiers come home in a state of psychiatric collapse . . . Anyone who was in the Andersons' house that night is shell shocked. Traumatised!

FELIX:

What does money have to do with that?

ELIZABETH:

I need to talk to a psychiatrist. Going through all this again is bringing up painful memories. I can't speak to you again for at least a week. What's your rush, anyway? You still don't have the killer. Why don't you try and do some investigations yourself?

FELIX:

I don't have any way of getting my hands on that—

ELIZABETH:

Well, you'd better find a way, Felix.

She stood halfway out of my front door. I couldn't convince her to stay. So, I let her go. And that was the second to last time I ever saw Elizabeth Chalice. At the time, I thought Elizabeth was too self conscious about her investigating style. She was worried I would think her weak or foolish for taking care of a sick patient. I included her comments from our interview, because sometimes I feel podcasts like this commodify the murder of innocent people. And as much as I hope you're enjoying listening, perhaps let's take a moment to muse on the impact murder has on those close to the real-life victims. The great house of an aristocrat in Mayfair. Ancestral and political links to Mayo. A famous detective. Six people with secrets to hide and a dead body. Well, we have only just begun to untangle the threads from that evening. You have been listening to Supper for Six, *I'm your host Felix Caerphilly. Join me for episode nine, where my investigation leads me back to the events of that night in 26 Bruton Square and we learn how events escalated after Elizabeth's brush with disaster.*

EPISODE NINE:

MOTHER GOOSE

7th April 1977, the night of the murder. On the cold marble steps of Lord and Lady Anderson's Mayfair mansion, private investigator Elizabeth Chalice lies unconscious shortly after 11 p.m. The three-tiered Italian glass chandelier reflects speckles of light across her placid face. A pool of crimson is already growing behind her left ear, almost the same colour as her wide-skirted dress. Shards of glass from the Waterford Crystal vase that she was hit with, glisten amongst her thick, black hair. But who hit her? Welcome back to Supper for Six. I'm your host, Felix Caerphilly. This is episode nine, where we seek to peel back the layers of secrecy to tell the true tale of how Anthony Anderson met a grizzly end.

On the far side of the fanlight above the front door, sleet begins to fall as a northerly airstream makes its way across London shortly before 11 p.m. Most of the residents of Bruton Square are quietly reading in bed, or watching the end of the late news on BBC2. The nanny at number 47 is having a cup of Ovaltine, her charge finally succumbing to sleep, after a late-evening walk has placated the fussy infant. It's the third instalment in that week's book at bedtime, The Wedding Group, and the nanny stretches her stiff shoulder hoping the baby remains asleep. Three miles away in Fleet Street, newspaper editors are setting the story about a deal to settle the strike action at Heathrow Airport on the front page of tomorrow's newspaper. It's just another evening in London, and nobody knows that Lord Anthony Anderson has been murdered in his own home. That won't become public knowledge until the sun rises over the Thames in the morning. But notably absent from these headlines is any reference to a fire. Or a stay-at-home order.

Now don't be cross with me, listeners. Yes, earlier episodes of this podcast did feature snippets of the news from the evening of Lady Anderson's dinner party. I did not record these false reports. It was Lady Anderson herself; she recorded them while constructing her elaborate scheme to fool each of her guests.

Within the four walls of 26 Bruton Square there is a killer, as yet unknown, two schemers, a dead body and an incapacitated detective. To understand the next portion of the events at 26 Bruton Square, I would need to piece together the testimony of the other guests that

*night. Elizabeth's interviews survived the evening, and we will hear
from our detective in the final episode. Let's hear from the last guest I
got to interview, Christina Crowley. I must admit, this was a particularly challenging episode of the podcast for me to work on – perhaps
that's why I left it 'til now. To see Christina as such a caring, respon-
sive mother, well it was a challenge for teenage Felix. I had been abandoned as a baby, and found myself jealous of the infant and desperate
to impress his mother. Was it Chrissy's role in the events that has kept
me so interested in this story for forty-five years? Could this picture of
motherhood really have murdered someone? Here are my first impres-
sions of Christina Crowley.*

*It was a rather frosty day in January 1978, just nine months after the
dinner party, when I found a window in my reporting schedule to make
the journey to Bruton Square. I lifted my hand to knock at the door of
number 20 when it swung open in front of me. I'd decided to focus my
investigation on the Langfords. The large white wheels of a pram shuffled
out of the door with a bump, nudged by a pair of brown, platformed
boots. Chrissy Crowley blinked in the bright morning sun, encased in a
fox-fur coat. I hit the record button.*

CHRISSY:

Oh, hello. I was just, eurgh . . . Do you mind helping me down
the steps?

*She spoke with the clipped vowels of an aristocrat, quite unlike the voice
I had understood to be hers on earlier tapes. A bump in the left finger of
her gloved hand suggested a large engagement ring.*

CHRISSY:

Who are you?

FELIX:

Felix Caerphilly. I'm a reporter with the—

CHRISSY:

Oh, I know who you are. Francois told me not to say anything to you. Come on, give it a bit of welly there!

Backwards down the six steps I went, bearing the weight of the enormous pram and the small baby inside. Brown curls peeped from under his snow-white bonnet, his fingers waving into the air. Finally, his mother and I carried him down to the street.

FELIX:

There we go, on solid ground. He's a beautiful child.

CHRISSY:

He won't be so beautiful if he doesn't get to sleep very shortly.

FELIX:

Can I walk with you? Where are you going?

CHRISSY:

Oh, I suppose so. But I'm not speaking to you about the Andersons. I wanted to purchase a few picture books from Curzon Street. It's not far.

FELIX:

How old is the little gent now?

CHRISSY:

Five months. It's nanny's day off. So, I rather hope he behaves for me. Isn't that right, my little fellow?

I do wish you would leave Francois alone. We're trying to find some happiness, at long last. Don't you realise poking around in the Andersons' old pants drawer won't help anyone?

As we walked through the barren and bare branches of Berkeley Square, I remember she had these enormous square sunglasses that were popular in the late seventies. She slid back the sunglasses to reveal a sparkling pair of brown eyes and a complexion unmarred by the fatigue of early motherhood. So, she's swapped a violent man for a womaniser, albeit in more affluent surroundings. In the years that have passed, I've realised that we aren't always aware of our flaws and poor decisions at the time. On that cold and sunny winter's day, Chrissy was a mother who had at last found some security for herself and her child.

CHRISSY:

Say, don't you look familiar? Where have we met before?

But as I was about to answer, I lost my footing on a patch of black ice on the pavement. Before I could shout out a warning, her foot went from under her. She spun directly into the black railing; her gloved hands could not hold onto the handle of the pram as it flew in the opposite direction, straight through the open gateway into the path of an oncoming silver jubilee bus. The brakes screeched as I scrambled to my knees. Unable to stand, all I could do was fling myself across the gutter and grab the wheels. The baby now wailing, the Ferrari behind the bus honking its horn. I pulled the pram back onto the street where his mother stood, damp and shrieking for him to be returned to her. Safely inside the gate of the park, she tore the little infant from the pram and into the warmth of her coat. Clutching him to her chest, she thanked me, with tears rolling down her face. She agreed to the interview. The microphone was destroyed in the fall, but the recorder remained intact.

We settled down for a pot of Assam in a poky Curzon tea shop. Excellent acoustics, with net-curtained windows and pastel, velvet cushions on the upholstered chairs. With the baby dozing peacefully, the composed demeanour of Chrissy Crowley returned. The hysteria of her brush with disaster left no mark, no stained mascara. But then, she was a skilled make-up artist. Her hands then bare, I was surprised she could hold the little tea cup with the weight of the large diamond-bordered emerald that weighed down her left hand.

So now, let us return to the illusion. To the stage that was set by Sybil. The panic and fear that you heard about the fire from each of Sybil's guests was genuine. As we step back through the door of number 26 Bruton Square, taking care not to step on Elizabeth's prone form, we remember there is a killer in the house. On the right, in Sybil's formal

drawing room, Chrissy Crowley reclines for a moment to regain her
strength. Her revelation that the fire was a hoax, and that she was not
only a make-up artist, but a rich girl in hiding, well, it had taken it out
of her. For she had conspired with the hostess to cause the death of her
husband. But the wrong fellow had died. Why had Anthony imperson-
ated her husband and how had she not noticed? Where was the real
Jeremy Crowley? She had questions for Sybil. The lady of the house was
upstairs playing an uneven hand of bridge with the Langfords. The
small pool of blood from the back of Elizabeth's head had not grown any
more. The injury was not a fatal one, but just enough to slow her down.
Apologies for the sound quality of the next interview, but I was lucky to
have a back-up microphone at the bottom of my bag.

FELIX:

Who hit Elizabeth with the vase?

CHRISSY:

Agapanthus came tearing down the stairs a few seconds later. It
was an accident, she cried. She hoped no one was hurt! But how
could she have dropped a twelve-inch vase over the railings by
accident? I was feeling very poorly myself, you see. So, it is a bit
broken in my memory. I had severe morning sickness. Hadn't
managed to keep anything down in days. I should never have gone
there in the first place. Elizabeth had gone to get us a taxi from the
square, but she hadn't been able to open the door. Then I'd heard
the crash, seen Elizabeth there, and tried to help. There was a lot of
glass on the floor, so I could tell how large the object must have
been.

Agapanthus was slurring her words and said, 'Stand clear, let me
have a look at her.' I was certain that she had flung the vase at
Elizabeth, so I tried to push her away. But I was so unwell with the
pregnancy, I'd lost my strength.

'She's bleeding,' said Agapanthus. 'It was an accident. But that
vase was heavy enough to cause significant brain damage, even a
skull fracture.' She continued to insist that it had slipped through

her fingers. What could I do? She was a doctor, after all, and who was I? Elizabeth came to a few moments later. The vase had smashed on the way down, meaning only a fragment had actually hit Elizabeth's head. But the crystal was so dense, it was enough to knock her out, according to Agapanthus. The shards had lacerated the top of her head, causing all the blood. Elizabeth and I looked at each other, as much to say, we need to get out of here as soon as we can. But I was on the cusp of fainting myself. So, Agapanthus laid the two of us out in the drawing room. Found some Lucozade in Sybil's kitchen—

Chrissy's baby son disturbed his mother's story as he woke red-faced with a piercing cry that seemed to make the teaspoons on our saucers rattle. As she sat him up and rubbed his back, I thought over what she was telling me. I needed to question her a little forcefully, and the child's fussiness could have spelled the end of the interview. I'd have to move quickly. Thankfully we were alone in the tea room, even the assistant had taken a cigarette break. With a loud belch, the child released his gas, stretched, took a brief look at me, and then returned to slumber.

FELIX:

Poor fellow. Quite the release.

CHRISSY:

Now, where was I? Yes, Agapanthus had us on the couches, to the left of the armchairs—

FELIX:

Er, if you don't mind, I'd rather ask a few specific questions. I know we don't have much time, so I'd like to get right to it. Just before the vase fell on Elizabeth, you told her that you and Sybil planned the dinner party to murder Jeremy—

She sat upright in the chair. The smile of a doting mother was replaced by an entitled impatience that reminded me Chrissy, for many years, lived as someone else. At the time of Sybil's dinner party, she was penniless and living in a squat. Here she was in fox fur and diamonds.

She leaned forward with such force that the small vase holding a red rose tipped over, spilling its water onto the white linen tablecloth. Patting dry the spill, her brow knitted as she shushed me like a child.

CHRISSY:

(*whispering*) Will you please be quiet? What would a child like you know about the world? Or what happens between man and wife?

FELIX:

My uncle was rough with my aunt. Believe me, I had often wanted to push him in the slurry tank or lace his cider with strychnine. I understand why you'd want to get rid of him. But I just want to know how the plan came about?

CHRISSY:

When I told Sybil what had happened, that I'd almost lost the baby after he pushed me down the stairs. Well, she suggested it. She knew he had used dope when they were musicians, and well, she could get her hands on a large supply. He had been using again more recently, I'm sure of it. He was making fifty pounds a week painting houses and another pound or two with the gigs, it just wasn't possible he was spending it all. But he was clever, or at least he thought he was. Any time I raised my suspicions, he'd be up, fresh as ever for work the next morning.

FELIX:

When did you and Sybil make this plan?

CHRISSY:

It was the start of March. Anthony had wanted her to invite the Langfords for a dinner party anyway. Something about getting out into the world. Sybil had become terribly isolated.

FELIX:

But then Anthony went missing after the Grand National. Why did Sybil wait almost a week to ask for help finding her husband?

CHRISSY:

I think she wanted our plan to happen because it was so theatrical. She'd been a performer. She'd lived for the stage. And Anthony took it all away when they married and he insisted she stop. So, her voice got a little less sweet over the years. She'd become obsessed with recording things. Songs she would make up. Recordings of her and Anthony fighting. That dinner party was not just about helping me, it was something she wanted to do. Even Anthony's disappearance didn't stop that. You see, I spoke to her on the Tuesday . . .

The next recording comes from a fragment of tape recovered from the basement of Bruton Square and has been remastered for this podcast. At this time, Chrissy was still playing the role of Eastender, listen to the difference in her dialect. This tells us that even though Chrissy asks Sybil to take a great risk, she is still hiding her true identity from the woman she calls her best friend.

MARJORIE:

Hullo, Anderson residence?

Buzzing on the line.

MARJORIE:

Hello? Are you calling from a payphone?

Sounds of clicking as line connects.

CHRISSY:

Hello, Marjorie? Is Sybil there?

MARJORIE:

Yes, she's here reading her detective stories. Is that Chrissy Crowley?

CHRISSY:

Yes, how did you—

MARJORIE:

You're the only one who ever calls her. (*calls out*) Sybil. Phone for you.

SYBIL:

Chrissy? I'm so glad you called. Do hang up, Marjorie.

Line clicks off as Marjorie hangs up.

CHRISSY:

Is she definitely gone?

SYBIL:

Yes, she's gone off upstairs with her duster. I tried ringing you . . . last night. They told me you were in bed?

CHRISSY:

I've been off these past few days. Ain't sure what it is.

SYBIL:

Anthony's gone.

CHRISSY:

Lucky you.

SYBIL:

Well, it's not like that—

CHRISSY:

I'm sorry. Where's he gone off to this time?

SYBIL:

It's not like those other benders. There's no sign of him at any of the clubs. He lost a lot of money at the races. I'm worried he might be, well that he might have done some harm to himself.

CHRISSY:

I'm sure he'll turn up, Sybil. Try not to worry. Have you told the police? What have they said?

SYBIL:

Well, I'm trying to keep it quiet. You know. The papers would be all over it. Another missing aristocratic playboy like Lord Lucan. I do think that he'll turn up . . . But I hope before Thursday.

CHRISSY:

I'm sure he's nearby drowning his sorrows. So, we're still on then? Thank you so much for this – I just can't imagine another day walking on eggshells. He was quiet the past few days. Ain't seen much of him. But there's an explosion on the way. I can't take a chance any more.

SYBIL:

Fine. We'll do it. I've started the preparations. Got a recording of an air-raid siren. And made a few news announcements saying there's a fire and no one can leave—

CHRISSY:

Cor, you're so clever, Sybil.

SYBIL:

I don't know about that. I'll lock the doors, turn off the electricity. Jeremy will have plenty of chance to find what he really wants. And don't forget to tell him about the new diamond earrings I bought myself. That will lead him upstairs. Better go, here comes Marjorie!

A plan to end the life of an abusive husband, cooked up by his pregnant wife and her best friend. Could Lady Anderson have read too many mystery novels and thought she'd come up with the perfect crime? Wasn't she too distracted by her own missing husband? How could Sybil not have recognised Anthony dressed as Jeremy? The more secrets I uncovered, the more mired in contradictions I became. Speaking to Chrissy in that chintzy little tea shop in January 1978, I wanted to know why she had taken on a false identity.

FELIX:

Why did you pretend to be poor, Chrissy?

She looked at me blankly as if preparing to deny it. She poured the dark tea into our cups. And then added milk, whilst smacking her lips. Her right hand rested on the blue knitted socks of her baby son.

FELIX:

I've heard Elizabeth's interview tapes. The change of accent and demeanour. But why did you turn your back on a life of privilege in the first place? What was so wrong with that?

CHRISSY:

If you had a family like mine, you'd want to run away from them too. Jeremy knew how imprisoned one could be in a circle of socialites. Where nannies raised children and parents abandoned them for jaunts about the country and bloody hunt balls. As a child, I barely saw Mama and Papa, but for an hour before dinner. Our nanny was the nastiest piece . . .

Chrissy's shoulders were hunched tightly as she stared to the right. Her eyes were rimmed with tears, the pain looking for a way to release.

CHRISSY:

But then they took something from me that was not theirs to take. When I was sixteen, I went to stay with our cousins in Ireland. There was a midsummer's ball, the moon hung low over Lough Corrib, and I was bewitched. A young girl charmed into an entanglement: that was not what I wanted. A pregnancy resulted. You know, when Elizabeth quizzed me on who this baby's father was, I almost told her about my first son. It was a consequence my parents could not accept. But they pretended like I could keep the baby, right until he arrived. Then, when he was less than a day old, old nanny was back. She bundled the child away and then he was gone.

My heart was thumping in my chest. How could she not know me, her own child?

FELIX:

Did you not try to find the infant?

CHRISSY:

Oh, I did. I told them if I they didn't tell me where he was, that I would never speak to them again. And not one member of staff, not one neighbour would tell me anything. I contacted the adoption agencies, but they were no strangers to calls from desperate girls like me.

She paused for a moment as she looked off into space, returning to that time in the depths of her imagination. Her eyes returned to meet mine, and for a moment I wondered if there was some shade of recognition there, of the invisible, permanent link between mother and child. But then the the baby cooed, and she looked down to him. I inhaled sharply as I swallowed the lump in my throat, refusing to give any signal of the sadness I felt that she'd not tried harder to find me. My tiny half brother was wanted, I could see. Chrissy stroked his cheek with her finger and his slow breathing returned. I had not wanted to disturb her telling the story, but the red light on the tape was flashing. It needed to be changed or I'd lose the interview. My cheeks burned with embarrassment. I was not used to talking to grown women about such things. And yet she was trusting me with her story.

CHRISSY:

I could not stay with those people a minute longer. So, I forged a cheque from my father for two thousand pounds and disappeared, into the West End. I paid for a make-up course and met Jeremy. It's not easy, you know, to walk away from the freedom that money brings. But we left no love after us. Jeremy's parents were just as cold.

FELIX:

I'm sorry your child was taken away.

CHRISSY:

I look for him everywhere. On the Tube. In the audience of the theatre. You know even something about Jeremy reminded me of . . . him.

FELIX:

The baby?

CHRISSY:

The baby's father. I wondered if that was the reason why I fell for Jeremy, his resemblance. That I thought if we were to have a child, that infant would surely resemble the one I had lost.

FELIX:

You've seen him since the night the child was conceived?

CHRISSY:

Oh yes. But he never recognised me. Even though I've seen him a number of times. He was married to Sybil Anderson, after all.

At that moment the quaint little bell over the door tinkled with the arrival of two pristine old ladies in furs and brooches. But that little disturbance was all it took for Chrissy's baby to open his eyes with a start. A loud noise emanated from the tiny thing. The two old ladies apologised as Chrissy bundled the infant up. Did I hear it right? Anthony had got Chrissy pregnant? That also meant that Anthony Anderson was my father. That I was conceived on the shores of Lough Corrib, where other than in County Mayo. Agapanthus and Jeremy were grand families of the area, and Sybil from Ballyglass, a small village nearby. Chrissy and Anthony visited a friend's ball, hosted by none other than George and Florence Crowley, Jeremy's parents. This pocket of Ireland's west was now once again around the same table in London.

CHRISSY:

He needs a feed. I have to go.

FELIX:

Wait, please let me follow you.

I threw some coins on the table and chased after her. The sun had melted the ice on the pavement and the soles of her boots clipped along as I tried to keep up. If Anthony had fathered her first child, then she did know him – could that have been motive enough to kill him? Her revelation turned my understanding of the night in question on its head.

CHRISSY:

I have to go home now. Can't you hear he needs me?

FELIX:

Please, just a few questions.

CHRISSY:

Just leave me alone!

The traffic picked up and we were standing exactly where we'd been when the buggy had wheeled into the street earlier. Waiting for a moment to cross, she looked at me. She said, tapping her forehead with impatience, 'Oh fine then. Come back tomorrow. 9 a.m'. Something that was apparent to me, back in January of 1978, was the inability of these people to take any responsibility for their actions. Even my mother Chrissy and Jeremy, who had distanced themselves from their privileged Anglo-Irish upbringings, retained a sense of entitlement that the world owed them something. And here was Chrissy, who had returned to the world of fur coats, diamonds and nannies, despite running from them in her youth. Even in the 1970s, an era of wife-swapping and extra-marital affairs, it seemed that people could just forget about the results of those unions. Chrissy was angry with her parents for taking her child, but even at sixteen she was old enough to know where babies come from. Did she really look hard enough for me? I thought the fact that she was my mother wouldn't matter for the investigation, but that day I interviewed her, it all changed for me.

I left Chrissy's doorstep, forcing myself to shut down the hurt little boy and renew a sense of detachment about the investigation. Here was a

*woman with a clear motive to kill the victim, whether she thought him
to be Anthony or Jeremy. I returned to the* British Herald *offices lest I be
sacked from the only source of income I had. There'd been a suicide in a
school in Westminster. After the steely principal refused to give me a
comment for the paper, I slipped off to my apartment to review the batch
of recordings I had procured from Elizabeth. I had not heard from her in
days by that point.*

*Inside my dark bedsit, I sat with my coat and fingerless gloves on as
the tapes clattered against the side of the Fortnum's biscuit tin. Embossed
with winterberries, it was a new tin. Elizabeth hadn't seemed like the
type of woman who would indulge in expensive biscuits, so where had she
got it? I was stuck in my investigation. As soon as I seemed to be making
progress, it was halted by a bloody overnight train or a crying baby . . .
But perhaps there was something in this tin I had missed earlier.*

*And there was. A Philips mini casette, from a handheld dictation
device Anthony Anderson had used to entrap his wife. As luck would
have it, I had one in my coat. I inserted the tape and hit play. There's a
muffled crackle that sounds as if the machine might have been in someone's pocket. Inaudible voices. Then the sound of Sybil Anderson's voice
becomes clear. Listeners may find this next recording disturbing.*

SYBIL:

No. I told you I'm tired—

ANTHONY:

You're always bloody tired. I don't know what you have to be tired
about. You can't even keep the house clean, you had to drag my
mother in like a skivvy. It's not normal Sybil. The way you are
cooped up—

*There's more buzzing on the tape with the sound of high heels clacking
on a marble floor. Anthony sounds incensed. His voice is clearer, he must
be the one recording the conversation.*

ANTHONY:

Wait, come back here!

SYBIL:

Can't you leave me alone! I don't want to go to the bloody races to watch you squander the last of our money just to be seen to gamble with the rest of the big boys.

ANTHONY:

What sort of a wife are you anyway? I should have known better than to marry someone from the back fields of Ballyglass.

SYBIL:

If it wasn't for you, I would have signed that record deal. I had a talent, you know. You stole that from me—

ANTHONY:

You haven't even given me a son. You just live here in your own little world. There's a whole life out there. If you'd look.

Sybil can be heard protesting, she squeals in objection. It sounds like Anthony is pulling her somewhere.

I've heard this over and over again. Wondered if it was even fair to include it. Victims of domestic violence or coercive control might find this next part difficult to listen to.

ANTHONY:

Look out of the bloody window, Sybil. Life goes on out there.

SYBIL:

(*crying*) Get off me!

ANTHONY:

(*angrily*) Look, you see. People getting into cars and going to lunch at Sheekey's or to work in an office.

SYBIL:

(*shouting*) You get your hands off me. You did this to me. I was made to be on the stage. But you stuck me here. Why don't you look at yourself—

A sharp smack cuts through the muffled noises. Someone has been struck.

ANTHONY:

You bitch.

SYBIL:

(*upset but firmly*) You lay a hand on me again. And I will kill you. Do you understand? I will kill you in your bloody sleep.

ANTHONY:

My wife, ladies and gentlemen. Sybil Anderson. Now you see the sort of recluse I'm living with? All I asked was for some company at the races. Just as a wife ought to do.

The tape clicks off.

Anthony Anderson was not the first aristocrat to record his wife. The way he finished the tape – who was he speaking to? Had he intended to share the tape with someone, a court perhaps? Listening back over these tapes as a grown man, I see that the marriage was volatile, toxic. The pair re-cover the same well-worn tracks. The insults, the name-calling, the belittling. I am taken back to a dusty corner of my aunt's kitchen as I hid from a rowing couple. My small child's body tight with the stress. Thank God the Andersons had no children, is all I say. Although we now know that is not strictly true. Anthony fathered Chrissy Crowley's first child. A boy who was forcibly adopted against her will. That boy who grew up so possessed by this case that he is now recording a podcast.

But one thing we cannot ignore is Sybil's threat. That she would murder him, in his sleep. It's an ominous statement sprung from the lips of a downtrodden wife. But it is a death threat to a man who died not long after the tape was recorded. From the person most likely to have killed him. When did Elizabeth get this tape? Where did it come from? Surely Elizabeth couldn't have had access to this tape on the night of the fire. And what about Chrissy's admission that Anthony was the father of her first child? There's something about these pieces of information that confuses me even more. I need to reorient myself to the night in question and rifle through the tin of tapes again.

When I returned to Chrissy's house the next day, there was no answer. I stood by the door for ten minutes, before a wizened old lady in a neat little purple suit and smelling of powdered lilies appeared. She smiled, revealing a smidge of pink lipstick on her dentures.

'Oh, you've missed them,' the old lady said. 'They left for St Moritz this morning. And poor Agapanthus has been turfed out of her own house. I had to take her in, you know, after it all happened. She's heart-broken, was so attached to the fellow. It's wrong what that girl did. You can't go about taking other people's husbands.'

I thanked the old woman and stood in the street for a moment, unsure of where to go next. I checked my watch; it was after 11am. My absence from the office would have been noted. My editor would be looking for copy. As I walked towards Fleet Street, I wondered what possible reason the pair would have had for absconding suddenly other than guilt. In my confusion, I had walked in the wrong direction across Bruton Square. I stood outside the door of number 26. I decided to ring the bell, and Lady Anderson opened the door. Lady Marjorie Anderson. You have been listening to Supper for Six, join me for the next episode where we will uncover another deadly secret hidden upstairs in 26 Bruton Square. A second dead body.

EPISODE TEN:

FROZEN GOODS

Lord Anthony Anderson left behind two women when he was brutally murdered in April 1977. His wife, Lady Sybil Anderson, who we know was planning to kill Jeremy Crowley with the assistance of his beleaguered wife Christina, whom we will examine in more detail in episode eleven. But there was another woman who had to watch his oak-and-brass coffin being lowered into the grave in Brompton Cemetery: his mother, Lady Marjorie Anderson. What did she think happened to her only son? That cold, January morning in 1978 I doorstepped her to find out. In this episode of Supper for Six, *we consider our detective, a strong Bolton lady, in the role of killer. An accusation made by none other that the victims' mother, Lady Marjorie Anderson.*

Marjorie, a redhead in her seventies, answered the door wearing a black-and-cream Chanel suit with polished mother-of-pearl buttons. There wasn't a hint of smoke damage in the home in which Marjorie lived alone. Even the thickly powdered Pan Stik could not conceal her dismay at seeing me there. Later we will return to recordings of that fateful evening, but first let's hear Marjorie explain why she was certain that Chalice killed her son.

MARJORIE:

That woman was known as a fixer. I'd crossed paths with her over the years, from Juan-les-Pins to Amalfi. Each time someone had pointed her out to me. She'd usually have been lurking in the shadows with some bloated whale of a chap, drinking wine on his tab. I don't wish to name names, but I know of two instances where a fellow was murdered by his wife. Both times the old codger deserved it. And death was preferable to a divorce. Elizabeth was sort of an angel of mercy, by all accounts. I'd known that Sybil and Anthony had had their troubles, I used to pop in. You know, she couldn't manage a home in Mayfair by herself, she hadn't the skills. It took me years to learn how to keep a townhouse. So, when I heard that Elizabeth had been at dinner that night, the night my Anthony died, I just knew she was behind it.

I didn't take the woman's claims seriously, given the lack of evidence. But Marjorie had me questioning how reliable this detective indeed was.

I could not think how I could replicate the winning streak that had left me with the thousand pounds in the first place, and I was still no closer to finding Anthony's killer than I had been at the outset of my investigation. I went back over all the tapes I had already listened to, looking for some nugget that I had failed to examine properly. There was nothing new.

And then, something curious arrived in the post, with a Swiss stamp. Remember earlier the old lady, Mrs Townsend, told us that Francois, Chrissy and Henri had travelled to St Moritz? But it was not from them. It was another tape! Enclosed was a note:

E Chalice

ELIZABETH:

Dear Felix, Elizabeth Chalice here, I do hope you'll be able to meet our little bargain. I've been further delayed in my travels, but did want to share this recording for your investigation.

Now, back to the night in question. I want to tell you about how I uncovered the second body. With a stiff brandy and a moment to collect myself after the crystal vase hit my head, I knew my time at Sybil's had almost concluded. So at this point, I just wanted to find Jeremy. Then I remembered how put out Sybil had been at the mention of the freezer. My head was thumping. I almost considered taking some of the morphine, but could not to relinquish my remaining mental capacity. As soon as I could stand, I made Sybil show me around. It wasn't the time to challenge her about Anthony or the phony recordings!

The next portion of this episode will be told by Elizabeth herself – if you can believe a word she says.

ELIZABETH:

Can we have a quick look around this floor? I know you have the Ouija board set up and the other guests are waiting in the dining room, but I'd like you to show me all the rooms in this house. As quick as you can. Are all the bedrooms upstairs?

SYBIL:

Eurgh, I don't see why. You've had a terrible blow to the head. I think you should have a lie-down.

ELIZABETH:

Sybil, this evening has been exhausting. Please just let me look around. Unless you're hiding something. There are no bedrooms on this floor. The dining room here extends the entire length of the house.

Pause.

ELIZABETH:

How many bedrooms are upstairs? Come on then, will you please hurry! Take my arm.

Pause.

ELIZABETH:

I said, how many bedrooms? There's no time for pleasantries now. The police will be here any minute.

SYBIL:

My dressing room used to be a nursery. My room, which you have already seen. There's Anthony's old bedroom and here – blue room.

I opened the door to a room the mirror of Sybil's, but in a royal blue. No one was in there. She scratched the back of her head. She seemed rather . . . peaceful. Or pensive. What was going on in her mind?

ELIZABETH:

I didn't think titled ladies changed their own sheets.

SYBIL:

Oh, of course, where are my manners? Of course, you'll all need to stay.

ELIZABETH:

That's not why I asked.

SYBIL:

I forgot to ask Marjorie to do it. She just comes in for a few hours in the mornings, she has a little flat across the square. It's too late to call for her now. And indeed our arrangement is an unusual one. I mean she is also a 'titled lady'. Of course, I wasn't expecting you to all be staying. And God knows how long they have been on the bed for. This is usually quite a noisy room, right in the corner of the house. But I daresay you won't have much disruption tonight.

ELIZABETH:

Marjorie? As in Anthony's mother?

SYBIL:

She may seem like a society doyenne, but she came from a family of washerwomen. She'd just die if anyone found out. But she liked to clean the house. Said it kept her connected to her roots. I wonder how that fire is coming along . . .

ELIZABETH:

There's no sign of any fire, Sybil.

She fiddled with her bracelets, deliberately avoiding eye contact. It was safer to let realisation dawn that I was onto her than to have a direct confrontation. After all, there was a very unwell pregnant woman, a killer and one dead body. As far as dinner parties went, it was certainly memorable, for all the wrong reasons. Something caught my eye on the bedside table. It had gold lettering.

ELIZABETH:

What's that doing up here, Sybil?

SYBIL:

Well, I haven't a clue how it got there.

ELIZABETH:

Could Anthony have put it there? Is he here, Sybil?

SYBIL:

Why do you think I would concoct a lie? I told you: I don't know where he is. Francois knew all along but won't tell me a thing. But what does it matter? If Agapanthus gets word of where you found it, well there would just be more drama that none of us need tonight.

ELIZABETH:

I already know about you and Francois, Sybil. He admitted it to me.

SYBIL:

That bloody fool. Well – he is the most awful cad. He took advantage of me, you know. I suppose with Anthony abandoning me – I'm certain he's going to divorce me – well, I just wanted to feel desirable. It shouldn't have happened.

ELIZABETH:

I'll return the address book once I've had a chance to take a look.

SYBIL:

But—

ELIZABETH:

But nothing, it's evidence in a murder investigation. Right, next room please.

The hinges on the old, heavy door squeaked open as the beige colour scheme of the landing was replaced by a bright red-and-brown-striped bedroom, complete with four-poster bed.

SYBIL:

I'll put the Langfords in here. The red room on the third floor.

ELIZABETH:

Well, I wasn't expecting this.

SYBIL:

Yes, it's very oriental, isn't it? Anthony's stepmother Idabel redecorated this as the main guest room. She redecorated the entire place when Anthony's father took her on as the new châtelaine.

ELIZABETH:

Where was it that Idabel, the stepmother, died?

SYBIL:

Francois told you that sorry story, did he? Anthony found her in here. And his father. But this isn't where I feel her. No, she's in the dining room.

ELIZABETH:

How do you mean, you feel her?

SYBIL:

It's as if she's standing over my shoulder. Once, I felt her breath on my neck. But mostly it's her perfume that I smell. A heady, oud-y sort of smell. As I said, she loved everything about the East.

ELIZABETH:

I smelled that earlier, I thought it was yours.

SYBIL:

Oh, no, I'm a floral woman. You don't believe in spirit energy?

ELIZABETH:

Having a closed mind is the worst trait in a detective. So, I would never say never. But considering the time I have spent in the vicinity of the dead, I haven't had what you could describe as a ghostly encounter. Although I very much believe in another sense . . . that may or may not be informed or influenced by something bigger than us. Intuition is important in my game.

By this stage I was digging my nails into my hand trying to hold my tongue. If I'd risked confronting her about Anthony, well not only could it have been dangerous, but she would have clammed up altogether and I would never have an opportunity to look for Jeremy. But how could I get rid of her? The ache on the crown of my head told me I would need to get the wound stitched rather soon, so I had to act quickly.

ELIZABETH:

Say, Sybil, I have an idea. I'm sure everyone is getting rather bored of bridge downstairs. Perhaps we could ask the spirits?

Her eyes flitted to the final bedroom on the fourth floor but the suggestion brightened Sybil's form. I remembered the Ouija board she had set out in the dining room, where Chrissy, Francois and Agapanthus were waiting.

SYBIL:

That's a jolly brilliant idea, Elizabeth. Will you help me?

ELIZABETH:

I will in a moment. I just want to put some towels down around Jeremy. You know, a dead body can leak all sorts of fluids.

She scrunched her nose up. Death can bring out the most squeamish reactions even in someone like Sybil who was leading us all on a merry dance throughout the evening, from our initial invitation to the contrived menu options and fiddling with the electricity, playing false news bulletins. She was starring and directing in her very own production – with deadly consequences.

SYBIL:

I guess this fire in Soho will have the undertakers very busy tonight. Well, don't take too long.

Had she started to believe her own lies about the fire? She spoke with such conviction but nonetheless tentatively handed me some towels from the airing cupboard and floated downstairs, her black dress lending her a spectral appearance. The fifth bedroom was a replica of the red four-postered room. Nothing but a bed, two lockers and a small, French wardrobe. There was no body. No freezer. I started to doubt my instincts, when something dragged me back to the airing cupboard. The door of the cupboard seemed modern, without elaborate ornamentation. I pulled it open to reveal a six-foot square space with shelves on either side and a curtain hanging on the back wall. Drawing it back, I found another door. It was just as large as the bedroom doors. The airing cupboard had been built to conceal this entrance, and the strong smell of paint and wood glue told me it had been done recently. I froze, hearing Francois on the landing calling my name. Had the fellow a sixth sense that a woman was alone near a bedroom?

FRANCOIS:

Elizabeth? It's time we got Sybil to let us go, don't you think? This has gone on long enough.

Or was he our murderer? I reached for a screwdriver from a painting bucket on the floor, lifting it over my head. I turned to Francois in the darkness.

FRANCOIS:

This is new! But they've put up this terrible flimsy little thing to hide the entrance to the attic. Let's see what they're hiding.

He squeezed past me, over a pile of dustsheets, in the tiny space before I could put him off. On the inside of the doorframe were several long, thick scratch marks. The carpet on the stairs was torn in two spots, and the scratch marks continued up the walls of the stairs. Someone had moved something very heavy and large up here. Something like a freezer. As we reached the attic, Francois flicked the light switch, but the light fitting hung empty. The only source of illumination was the glow of the moon through the small half-windows. I did not see any freezer. I began to worry that Sybil could simply shut the airing-cupboard door and we would be trapped.

FRANCOIS:

This used to be Nanny's room. I know Anthony had planned to convert it into a home office. You know, when we came through, I half expected to see him in a robe, with a glass of Scotch, laughing at us.

ELIZABETH:

Let's go. The others will be looking for us.

Francois was looking out of one of the windows, when under the eaves on the other side of the room, as my eyes adjusted to the darkness, I noticed the bright edge of the freezer. The moonlight was reflecting on its white surface. It was here after all! Francois noticed my attention had shifted.

FRANCOIS:

Strange he would have a freezer for food but no loo. Unless he was planning to use a bucket.

ELIZABETH:

I don't think it's frozen peas in there, Francois.

FRANCOIS:

No, you're right. There's nowhere to cook the bloody things.

Well, this was the moment I'd been waiting for. With the faint illumination from my lighter to see inside, I lifted the lid. I didn't feel any sense of achievement. Just intense sadness. There is something about the vulnerability of a person's body. Jeremy Crowley was in there. Folded into a ball. Ice dusted his top lip. His hair had been shorn; his clothes removed. Torn, red flesh was gnarled at the back of his head, revealing the bone of his skull. He looked so cold. Even though he could not feel anything, I had a motherly instinct to try to warm him up. Only then I remembered Francois was in the room with me. He was on his knees, retching.

FRANCOIS:

Dear God. Dear God. Anthony! She's a bloody psychopath.

He stood to glance in again, unable to bear the sight of the man he thought was his friend. My doubts about Francois knowing the victim's identity evaporated. His reaction was visceral, emotional. Unlike the cold way he had observed the discovery of the previous body.

ELIZABETH:

It's not Anthony.

FRANCOIS:

What do you mean? Who the bloody hell is it?

ELIZABETH:

It's Jeremy Crowley.

Francois tentatively approached for another look and I handed him the lighter. He managed to look a moment longer, blinking through angry tears. His slicked-back ponytail grazed the collar of his shirt as he bent to look at the frozen face of the murdered corpse. He looked at me in total bafflement, trying to process what was in front of him.

FRANCOIS:

Oh, Tony, what happened?

ELIZABETH:

I'm afraid Anthony is downstairs.

FRANCOIS:

But he looks so like him— this is Jeremy? So that was Anthony downstairs earlier and I didn't even recognise him?

ELIZABETH:

Sometimes our brain won't let us see what we believe to be impossible. And you don't have your glasses.

FRANCOIS:

But why was he dressed like Jeremy? Why was he pretending to be someone else? And how did I not see?

ELIZABETH:

It seems whatever happened to Jeremy here is the answer to those questions. From what I can gather, Jeremy must have come here and had an altercation with Anthony. There's rather a big gash on Jeremy's head, you see here under the hairline. So, Anthony was impersonating Jeremy with a view to swapping the bodies, once the witnesses could attest to his being at the dinner party. But of course, the plan went awry when Anthony was murdered.

He was holding his head in his hands. The upset changed to an angry snarl as he was beginning to unravel what happened.

FRANCOIS:

Bloody Sybil. So, she killed Anthony. The locked doors, the fire. Who else—

ELIZABETH:

I know it's a shock, but we had better get downstairs. There's no handle inside the airing cupboard. Whoever did this could simply close the door and trap us—

As if my words heralded it, the curtain rail squealed from the door between the airing cupboard and the attic stairs. Slow footsteps paced up the steps and I closed the freezer. Pushing Francois back to the wall, I held my finger to his lips as I wrapped my legs around his waist.

ELIZABETH:

(*whispering*) Don't say anything, Francois. If Sybil thinks she's getting away with it, she will reveal herself more. The police have to be here shortly. There's no fire – she recorded—

FRANCOIS:

(*whispering*) What station did you ring?

ELIZABETH:

Belgravia, why—

FRANCOIS:

Dammit, Elizabeth. That's where the chap on trial works. I told you the big murder case that I'm working on is involving a police officer who works at Belgravia station. A few of his colleagues were even at court today – giving me intimidating looks. If you called that station . . . did you say that I was here?

ELIZABETH:

Of course, they asked—

FRANCOIS:

Dear God, don't you see how dangerous that is? That they could try to pin this murder on me? They'd do anything to win and throw the case off.

The footsteps came to a stop as I pushed my lips onto Francois's. I tasted the salt of his lips momentarily before he pushed me away. There at the doorway was Sybil, with a grin on her face.

SYBIL:

Not even Ms Chalice is immune to his charms it seems. You really ought to be more discreet. Don't worry. I won't tell anyone.

FRANCOIS:

(*angrily*) It's none of your business, Sybil. Now if you don't open the bloody front door, I'm going to throw you out of the window.

ELIZABETH:

Francois—

Turning to look at me, Sybil began to laugh. Her eyes betrayed her concern about the freezer. My lighter! In the commotion I'd dropped it right beside the plug. She snatched it up, recognising it immediately.

ELIZABETH:

Oh, that's where it is. I was um, checking the windows were locked.

She glared at us both before handing the lighter back to me. Standing over us, her presence was almost eerie in the half-light of the attic.

SYBIL:

Well, your fly is still closed, Francois. Pull up your knickers, Elizabeth. It's time for the last part of this dinner party.

ELIZABETH:

I really ought to get this wound sutured, Sybil.

SYBIL:

Oh, don't you know everywhere is going to be full to the brim with this fire business? Can't Agapanthus do it?

She shot me a look of disgust. Francois could barely contain the rage he felt towards Sybil. He reached forward as if to push her down the stairs, and I only stopped him by a hair. Calm yourself, I conveyed with a stern glance. As we followed her into the false entranceway of the airing cupboard, I rested my hand on his chest, hoping he could read my mind. The paint smell was replaced by the scent of turpentine, as I noticed a bottle had spilled all over the dustsheets.

SYBIL:

Chrissy has rallied quite a bit—

ELIZABETH:

Sybil, wait. This needs to be cleaned up, it will destroy the carpet and leave an awful stench on the bedclothes.

SYBIL:

Ah, the angel of carpet protection speaks again. Leave it. You didn't put anything down around Jeremy. I suppose you were too distracted.

FRANCOIS:

Why did you put that ugly piece of construction on the landing?

I was glad to be on the landing again. Francois was agitated, biting on his flexed knuckle. It was quite a change to see in him. He seemed to live like the Italians, passionate, emotional. He was a little bit dangerous. And not in the way I usually liked to take my men. We continued down the stairs following Sybil's innocuous prattling.

SYBIL:

Oh, I thought it would be fun to have a little secret hideaway. You and Anthony had one as children, didn't you? He wouldn't tell me where it was. I just wanted my own spot. I'd quite like to start writing crime novels. It would let me look all about the square.

SYBIL:

Gosh, Francois, what's the matter with you?

FRANCOIS:

A man has died, Sybil. And you're playing stupid games. I'm going to call the police and see where they are.

He threw open the hall door and we could hear him begin to swing the mechanism furiously. Chrissy, lipstick reapplied, and Agapanthus, her blouse now neatly tied, were sitting at the drawing room table with freshly poured glasses of wine. I began to feel like an outsider. There was something about how these three women could just act so normally. A growing sense of dread in the pit of my stomach pushed me to consider that perhaps I could have been their next victim. It was only Francois's shouting down the telephone that grounded me in the reality of the moment.

SYBIL:

But Elizabeth is here to investigate it.

Francois pointed at Sybil and gestured for me to get her out of earshot. I encouraged her over to the portrait that hung over the fireplace.

ELIZABETH:

You'll have to tell us the story behind this painting Jeremy did of you, Sybil. Chrissy was rather upset to think you sat for it secretly—

CHRISSY:

Oh, I'm quite fine now, Elizabeth. But do tell me this, Sybil. Was yours the Mayfair house that Jeremy was working in this week? Oh it was, wasn't it?

Sybil ran her finger down the canvas. Chrissy and Agapanthus were swivelled in their chairs, nursing a bulb of wine like a pair of fat duchesses. Chrissy had dropped the Eastend act, and in the lamp light, I could see the haughty privilege that held them straight up in their seats. This was all a game to them! A cold chill rose in my bones as I began to think that I had been lured into a trap. For I had excused Chrissy because of her nausea, and Agapanthus's drunkenness. The line between fact and fiction was blurring. Agapanthus, the snob, who was born to a builder's daughter, just like Sybil. Chrissy born to money, like Jeremy, but refusing it. My head began to spin as I reached out for the chair. Francois surveyed me. His reaction to Anthony's death was unscripted. I listened into his conversation. His ponytail was flapping as he shook his head in annoyance.

FRANCOIS:

(*on the telephone in the background*) I'm calling to report a murder. 26 Bruton Square. No, I can't get through to Belgravia. We need an ambulance too, someone has a serious head injury, and there's a pregnant woman here in need of medical attention. I said 26 Bruton Square. Do hurry.

SYBIL:

Let's go up to the dining room, I feel we would all be more comfortable there.

Francois seemed calmer now, and I noticed his eyes were rimmed red from the earlier tears. I leaned over to whisper to him as he helped me up the stairs.

ELIZABETH:

Now, remember to just wait for them to come. Placate Sybil. Did you know much about where Christina comes from?

FRANCOIS:

No . . . I don't know what to believe any more.

His eyes moved to Chrissy, now toasting with Agapanthus. Sybil looked back at us with an unknowing smile. Does she know she's been caught? It's the grin of someone who is about to have their entire world collapse. Even if she didn't kill Anthony, she was an accessory to murder. She had lit dozens of candles, and the candelabras, each holding six candles were lined up in the middle of the long, dining room table, either side of the Ouija board, now covered with a black chiffon scarf painted with golden stars. The mantelpiece and sideboard each held two candelabra. Francois took his seat opposite Chrissy and Agapanthus. His earlier confidence was replaced by dejection. The candlelight cast tall shadows up the 20ft walls. The shapes looked nightmarish, as if a coven of witches was at work on the other side of the board. As if a spell had been cast. We watched the ominous little flickers, all over the room. Waiting to set every piece of upholstery, rug and curtain ablaze. Candle grease from one off-kilter candelabrum was dripping red splodges onto the white tablecloth. The dark crimson reminded me of the wound on Jeremy's head, and the lack of blood within Anthony's body – their faces were just as waxy as those tall candles.

AGAPANTHUS:

What is the latest with this fire business?

SYBIL:

The radio is dead.

AGAPANTHUS:

Don't you have a television anywhere?

SYBIL:

Oh, but this will be fun! It's almost twelve anyway, there won't be anything on.

FRANCOIS:

The police will be here shortly, I'm sure they can update us.

AGAPANTHUS:

Let me use the telephone myself.

SYBIL:

In a few moments. But first, please, I have one last piece of entertainment for you!

AGAPANTHUS:

Entertainment? Is that what you call what's gone on here tonight?

FRANCOIS:

Hear her out, Agapanthus.

SYBIL:

We are going to connect with the other side. I feel that there are spirits there who could shed light on the current state of the world. I've felt this draw to the other side for some time now. But I need help to get there. In fact, Jeremy's untimely death was a sign to me that now is the right time. He could in fact, help us. When spirits shed their physical selves, they often don't know it. Especially with his wife, his unborn child in this room. It's almost four hours since his death. If we reach him, he could act as an intermediary. You know, he could help put us through to the spirit world. A sort of telephone exchange of the other-worldly kind.

It may have been his wife, but it was not his child. To dull the ache on my scalp, I poured myself a large glass of wine as I reviewed the events of the evening. Could Jeremy and Anthony have fought over something as simple as some home decoration? Was that sufficient motive for Anthony to actually murder someone? Or had he become enraged in the moment? With the police about to arrive, I thought back to how I conducted my investigation. Had I missed anything? I'd managed to keep everyone else alive, which was something.

For there was a killer at the table. I looked carefully at each of the suspects. Sybil was leaning backwards with her head tilted to the ceiling as her black veil slipped off her blonde hair. Agapanthus was looking at the face of her wristwatch with great concentration. But with the other hand, she pinched her wrist. She was trying to take her own pulse! Why was she monitoring herself? A medic would understand just how a fast heart rate leads to sweating, and adrenaline flooding the system. Her chest rose and fell as she took deep breaths to slow down the nervous system. Chrissy took a small sip of her wine. Even a few mouthfuls could have made her tipsy if she hadn't been used to drinking. Especially if she had been nauseous. But how could she stomach it after vomiting earlier? Perhaps the tiny sips were enough to just relax her. Francois was fiddling with the tablecloth. He folded a triangle of the corner over and over itself until the wine glasses began to move. One of these four was a killer, possibly even two of them. Never had I dealt with such a smooth bunch. I closed my eyes and asked for my own intuition to guide me to the next clue. For despite this unravelling evening, there was still more to be uncovered.

SYBIL:

When contacting the spirit world, ensuring a high quantity of emotional energy on this side of the veil, I have been engaging with the other side, for some years now. I've had varying degrees of success. The truth is, I don't know where my husband really is. Spirits will tell me where he is.

Francois coughed his wine in outrage, the red droplets dribbled down his chin as his eyes widened. Be patient, I urged him with a look across the table. Then he said something that struck rather a bit close to home.

FRANCOIS:

I bet he's somewhere off Grosvenor Square. Brooks Mews or somewhere like that.

SYBIL:

Where his heart is. The heart he shared with me. You've all met him. You all know him. But it's not just Anthony – these other energies need you all. You all know me well, we have a mental connection, of heart and of head. As Anthony's father would say, you're juice for the tank. You are here with me now to reach through to the spirit world.

Sybil's statement did not sit well with the others. But I was perturbed at Francois's mention of my address. I had rented a small mews house around the corner from Claridge's. I always gave another address to potential clients. For I did not want anyone looming over my doorstep in the dead of night. I let it pass, as did the others. If Anthony had been staying there, wouldn't I have seen him?

Agapanthus rolled her eyes to heaven, and Chrissy just looked annoyed. Sybil was swirling her fingers around a lit, black pillar candle.

Tiny, jerky movements. The sight was entrancing. From her lips emerged a sort of humming noise. There was a feeling of, well, of something in the room. A presence. I do not believe in ghosts, but over the years I have learned to listen to the voice that seems to come from nowhere. An intuition for invisible information. Was it all an act? She did not break her trance when Agapanthus pushed her chair back from the table to stand.

AGAPANTHUS:

You're all as absurd as a company of circus performers.

FRANCOIS:

Oh, we'd best do as she says or she won't bloody shut up. Come along, Agapanthus, take your seat. Also, perhaps we might call upon Anthony senior, see if he has any tips for the Guineas. He was always more of a Newmarket fellow, you know. Or the Curragh.

CHRISSY:

Don't make fun, Francois. The other side won't want to be made fun of.

SYBIL:

Thank you, Francois. Here. You'll need another drink. Brandies for you all. Elizabeth, will you help me pass these out?

AGAPANTHUS:

Oh must I take part in this charade? This evening has dragged on rather long. I fancy a stiff brandy, and I suggest the rest of you leave our over-excited hostess be whilst we wait for the authorities to arrive.

CHRISSY:

Oh, just let her do what's she's doing. I'm curious now.

FRANCOIS:

(*imitating Chrissy*) I'm curious now. (*as himself*) Who are you, Christina?

AGAPANTHUS:

You're not the only one who has secrets, Francois.

SYBIL:

There are no secrets from the spirits.

Sybil was waving her hands methodically across her face with her eyes still closed. Francois looked like a confused child. Not surprising, considering he had just learned his best friend was dead, that the killer was amongst us, and that his mistress was not who she claimed to be.

FRANCOIS:

Maybe you do believe in this old tosh, then, Christina, if that's even your real name.

SYBIL:

Oh, Francois, but she does. Chrissy visited all manner of mediums in her quest to have a baby, didn't you? I know I'm betraying your confidence now, my friend, but it feels that we have perhaps moved past it. Come. I know the rest of you have . . . queries. That slim gold cross you're wearing, Elizabeth. And your little book of common prayer, Agapanthus. Francois aside, you all have a strong faith. Hmmm.

Felix here. One side of the tape finished just as my telephone was ringing – it was the office! The editor was looking for my copy on the tragedy I had meant to be reporting on. There, in the middle of Sybil's final grand performance, we take our break.

EPISODE ELEVEN:

Raising a Toast to the Dead

Dozens of flickering candles, four suspects and an investigator sit around the long mahogany table of Sybil Anderson's dining room. Despite a fractious evening of interviews and two dead bodies, the hostess convinces her guests to partake in a chilling after-dinner activity whilst they wait for the police to arrive. Investigator Elizabeth Chalice had rumbled Sybil's role in orchestrating a palpable sense of uneasiness through the evening. There had been no fire. There were no electricity strikes or news reports demanding Londoners remain indoors. The man who had arrived as Jeremy Crowley was in fact Lord Anderson, whose disappearance, claimed his wife, was the reason for the dinner party in the first place! As Elizabeth unravelled her hostess's large production, she allowed the next portion of the evening to proceed, in the hope that the true killer would be revealed and there would be no more victims. The Anderson residence at 26 Bruton Square was caught between life and death, as we return to Elizabeth Chalice's recording of Lady Anderson's séance. Welcome to Supper for Six *– this time our investigator asks the dead for answers. Felix Caerphilly handing over to Elizabeth Chalice to recount the night.*

Our hostess began to, well, growl, as with a dramatic flick of her wrist she lifted the scarf from the Ouija board she'd set out earlier. I didn't mean to, but I shifted in my seat. It shouldn't have bothered me, whatever Sybil was trying to channel. My ears tricked me into thinking I heard the doorbell. But no one else seemed to stir.

SYBIL:

Take a deep breath as we are all settled into our seats. Now, can't you feel . . . there's something in the air. It's not just the candlelight. It's not just the dead body in the attic.

The attic! A dead body in the attic! I opened my eyes and met Francois's. The exchange was not lost on Agapanthus who looked perplexed for a moment, but let it go. Chrissy and Sybil were lost to the moment. Our hostess's voice became lower, no great feat for a performance artist like her.

SYBIL:

The air has a richness, as if imbued with some highly combustible material. On the table I have laid out an Ouija board. Chrissy, you may have seen one before when you had your little habit of visiting mediums for answers . . .

CHRISSY:

Let me out of this, Sybil, please. Don't you think I've been through enough?

SYBIL:

Fine. Each of the twenty-six letters, the first ten numbers, and the word GOODBYE. With this small glass marker, spirits will guide our hands to communicate more than we could possibly know ourselves. There are more energies present than just ours. This house was built in 1837. Lanes of hovels. The homes of the poor. Babies were born, from labours leant against clay walls, grown up into soldiers and sent across the Irish Sea to rob the Irish of their lands and hovels. Mayo and Mayfair . . . The sick and ailing were tended to; rainy days passed inside, trying to keep dry. Life as cheap and worthless as the leavings of the rag-and-bone men. They were cleared away, of course, to make way for the perfectly appointed gardens, the elegant shapes and forms of our high ceilings. To house the *ton*, the new residents, solicitors, merchants. But the old residents come to me at night. Take the hand of your neighbour.

I signalled for Agapanthus to close her eyes and she complied with a little grunt. Our doctor was still loath to take instruction from a nurse.

FRANCOIS:

Oh, come on, everyone, might as well get into the spirit of things, ha-ha! Well done on your choice of after-dinner entertainment, Sybil.

SYBIL:

Chant!

How indeed did I find myself submitting to a séance when I should have been investigating a murder? I was used to unexpected happenings, but this was folly. Throughout the entire dinner party, we'd been led on a merry dance by Sybil. I ought to have seen what she wished to achieve with this venture. It wasn't my first experience with spiritualists – in matters of life and death, where no salient or reasonable explanation can be found, humans seek solace through any means. When the Conte child went missing, his mother used the services of an old crone, to no avail. I looked around the table from under my eyelids, opened just enough to regard the others. Dark shadows danced across their faces in the flickering candlelight. I couldn't allow my guard to drop, for who knew what she was planning. Our hostess may have been a petite woman, but we were in her lair. She'd had all the time she would need to prepare a trap, poison the drinks, set a fire, anything at all in that house of horrors. I wondered what she was distracting us from with this ludicrous performance.

Sybil's head flipped forward so that she was bowed to the table. I could see the thin line of grey breaking through her hairline. Her shoulders were rounded as she brought up a great, guttural growl. Chrissy's eyes were closed, she was a willing participant in the proceedings. Their friendship was renewed, as Chrissy clasped Sybil's hand. Across the table, Francois reached for Chrissy's fingertips with a degree of tenderness. The fondness defied her deceit. Agapanthus appeared once again to be taking her pulse. But then I realised she was, in fact, massaging her wrist. I squinted to see a raised line of white flesh with a scratch of blood at its peak. Something thin and narrow had scratched her. Like a needle. Murder is a physical business. Especially when the victim is six foot tall. If she had been trying to administer morphine, and the victim had moved, might the syringe have turned back on itself to scratch her?

For a moment, it no longer felt that we were a motley crew being led along by our hostess. No, Sybil and I were the outsiders. Either side of that duplicitous man of law, his wife and his lover. I was waiting for the right time to arrive. I had been paying close attention to all of the guests. You can't trust the words that come out of anyone's mouth. I've learned that the hard way over the years. I wouldn't be fooled again. Eventually the body gives us away. We are animals. The animal within outs us. The giving and taking of life seem to sit on the cusp of heaven, or some other sacred place. But it is firmly rooted in our basest of desires. Survival. Attraction. What I had just seen with my own eyes shifted the focus of my investigation. Francois Langford couldn't be discounted as a killer.

I glimpsed a slight shift in the far sleeve of Francois, as he squeezed Chrissy's hand. She returned the gesture, and he stroked her fingertips with his own. Oddio! There still was something genuine between them. Francois, the hapless lawyer. Could he really be our killer? His eyes flashed open to look at me. I remembered the taste of salt on his lips. I closed my eyes quickly. My heart was racing, for there was something animalistic about Francois's look. It was the gaze of a hunter. Perhaps he is not just a skirt-chaser, but an individual that feeds off others. I felt the uncomfortable itch of goosebumps against the sleeves of my dress. The room had grown cold.

SYBIL:

Keep your eyes closed. So here they come. One face after another flashes onto the screen of my mind's eye. I feel many of them just want to make themselves known to me. Here, they have arrived. The crinkled and dirty face of a woman whose kindness in life prevails despite a mouthful of rotten teeth. The saccharine smile of an innocent infant, golden curls sitting around a grey and deathly pallor of poverty. We may view death as a terrible affront to life, but our ancestors didn't. The millions of Londoners on the other side . . . centuries of mortality, pestilence, murder, starvation. Well, they must look at us, and laugh. Unholy souls. Unrested souls. Join us this evening. Come to this side of the table. It is 7th April, in the year of Our Lord 1977. We seek your counsel. We wish to find our lost friend. One of our own, who has moved from the bosom of his family.

SYBIL:

Together we ask the spirits this night, to send us only the blessed. We claim protection for everyone here, and no evil can come near. Come ye, to this table. From the other side. Join our hearts. Jeremy Crowley. If you are here. Please come. Please join your earthly friends.

CHRISSY:

Ah!

SYBIL:

Keep your eyes closed.

FRANCOIS:

Why, that's just the breeze blowing open that curtain . . . Why on earth is this window open? I didn't notice it earlier.

AGAPANTHUS:

She's on another plane, Francois. Close it and sit down.

SYBIL:

Jeremy, are you there? This is Sybil. Sybil Pritchard. Your old friend. Remember, the times we had. Making music. Creating together. Jeremy, your wife is here. Your unborn child.

ELIZABETH:

The sideboard door slams shut, and with it I jump.

CHRISSY:

What was—

ELIZABETH:

It's just the breeze—

Another slam, this time it's the door of the dumb waiter, ten feet away on the other side of the room. I'd been so occupied looking behind me . . . My hands were damp with sweat, Agapanthus gripped my knuckles, she was rattled too. But Sybil was a perfect image of stillness, the only moisture between our hands was from my nervous palm. Relax, Elizabeth. It was all part of the ruse. The chill in the air was not because of the open window, it was freezing and I could see my breath. I detected the scent of wet coal . . . or was it plasterwork? My senses had heightened. My inner animal was awoken to danger. Francois slunk back in his seat, warily. In fact, I believed he'd been snared in the illusion. His eyes opened wide, darting around the room to the banging furniture.

SYBIL:

Thank you for joining us, Jeremy. I know you are angry, Jeremy. We are separated by the thinnest of veils, but you have passed on to the afterlife. You must not linger in this world for long. You must seek the light, find the salvation, your peace. Let us all place our hand on the glass marker. Do not resist the movement but do not encourage it. The spirit requires our earthly hand to guide it to the letters. Did you die by your own hand, Jeremy? Tap once for yes. Twice for no.

RAPS TWICE.

CHRISSY:

I told you! Didn't I tell you! Ask him who did it.

SYBIL:

Thank you, Jeremy. Now, if you can, tell us, do you know who killed you?

RAPS ONCE.

SYBIL:

Are they in this room?

RAPS ONCE.

SYBIL:

Can you point out where they are?

The glass marker was sliding over to Sybil. It was impossible to tell who was pushing it. But I didn't for a minute believe that the spirit of Jeremy Crowley, or Anthony Anderson, was there to tell us his killer. What a load of old rubbish! But what was helpful was how everyone was react-ing to the spectacle. Sybil had fully submitted herself to the part of a psychic in a trance. Eyes closed; her lash line was flickering. She had her ceremonial knife at hand, along with a deck of what I could only presume to be Tarot cards. The white of her fingertips flickered with the candle wicks on the table. She was wearing her large, diamond earrings and the warm orange glow twinkled across the facets of the cut. She must have been in her dressing room to get them, when Francois and I were in the attic. What else had she been doing in there?

Each of us had a hand on the glass marker encased in a wooden triangle. I could not detect force being applied by any particular hand. I lifted my fingertips from the surface to watch who may be pushing the device, but I couldn't see anything. It continued to move. I was under the glare of Francois, who also lifted his fingers from the marker – as if to tell me it had nothing to do with him. His defiant look ebbed as the marker moved to the letters of the alphabet on the Ouija board. We simultaneously replaced our fingers. I was feeling for anything that would tell me who was leading this. Perhaps it was a magnet? There was nothing metallic in that device. With my free hand I reached into the centre of the table. I felt only the smooth material of the tablecloth, no strings or wires. Sybil retracted her hand suddenly. She swished the air before splaying her palms into the air. Still the marker moved.

SYBIL:

Jeremy . . . Oh. You're not Jeremy. Anthony? Is it you?

Francois thumped his fist on the table and leaped up, more livid than I thought the fellow had the propensity to be!

FRANCOIS:

Enough of this charade! I know you killed Anthony, Sybil. And you killed Jeremy. Both of them are in this house!

SYBIL:

Who is this? I-D-A-B-E-L. Idabel. Idabel. Is that your name? Rap once for ye—

Chrissy regarded her friend with a growing suspicion. There was another loud knock. What mechanism was she using? I remember the sound seemed to come from the top of the sideboard. The marker kept sliding across the table, like a beetle approaching a worm.

SYBIL:

Our friend Jeremy is there with you. He has just died. He was going to tell us who the killer was.

AGAPANTHUS:

It's moving again. Oh, my God. Look.

SYBIL:

F-I-N-D, find, M-Y, my. Find my . . . What is it, Idabel? You want me to find your K-I-L-L-E-R? Were you . . . murdered? Idabel?

Another rap. This time against the plasterwork beside the doorframe. It was a hollow, sickening sound.

SYBIL:

Do you know who killed you?

Yet another rap came from the ceiling. The noises were coming so quickly – I felt my body react. Fear was making my cheeks red hot. Those raps . . . I seriously wondered if they could be caused by a spirit. My rational mind still struggles to explain the locations.

SYBIL:

When did you die, Idabel? 1-9-6-5. 1965? You died in 1965, Idabel?

There was a knock on the table this time. I felt the vibration with my own hands. The Langfords and Chrissy exchanged glances with each other. Then Chrissy jumped further into her chair removing her hand from the marker. There was a movement of air and then beside me, Francois's brandy glass shattered as if squeezed by an invisible hand. I am a woman of science. Of evidence. But I could not hold in a shriek. Dr Langford ran from the table. Her chair clattered on the floor, jangling our nerves further. Throughout these events, Sybil remained entranced, unbothered by the distress this event was causing.

SYBIL:

This spirit wants you to talk, Francois. 1965. You must know who she is? We'd better answer her to get Jeremy back speaking to us.

FRANCOIS:

I don't know who she means—

CHRISSY:

Answer her, Francois!

A sliver of glass skimmed my eyebrow as my own glass shattered – this time as if squashed from the top. Ground into the table as if with a great strength. I swept the shards away, thinking of the gash on my scalp. I lightly touched the spot on my head now matted with blood. The hair knotted into a solid chunk. But I could barely feel it as the adrenaline coursed through my body. Sybil was the only one touching the marker now, as the rest of us moved away from the centre of the Ouija board.

ELIZABETH:

I think that's quite enough, now, Sybil—

CHRISSY:

That almost hit me in the face! Will you answer . . . the woman, or ghost or whatever she is.

SYBIL:

It's moving again. A-D-U-L-T-E-R-E-S-S.

CHRISSY:

For God's sake, Francois, will you just answer her!

FRANCOIS:

OK. OK. Idabel was Anthony's stepmother. She . . . she died here.

A rap from the sideboard. These were quieter now as if agreeing with her.

FRANCOIS:

But I don't know much about her.

Two knocks came from the sideboard. I wondered if Sybil could have a hammer rigged to a battery.

SYBIL:

Look, it's moving again, L-I-A-R.

FRANCOIS:

OK. OK. I thought she died from a heroin overdose?

Two angry knocks came from the window. Francois swivelled his head and addressed the ceiling, seeking the source of the conversation. Agapanthus was kneeling, her hands wrapped around her head. Chrissy sat resolute, her hand re-joining Sybil's on the marker.

FRANCOIS:

Idabel, that's what Anthony told me!

SYBIL:

Do you know who killed you, Idabel? Can you spell their name? Idabel? Do you know where my husband is? Has he . . . crossed over?

The marker moved again to spell M-A-R-J-O-R-I-E. And then the heaviness in the room evaporated. Whatever that was . . . whoever that was – Idabel – had gone. I looked to the door, to the sideboard, to the window. A stillness as disconcerting as those loud noises kept us frozen. My breathing returned to normal. How had I let myself become so rattled? Francois investigated the sideboard, as I inspected the doorframe. Agapanthus was rocking back and forth on the floor, daring to raise her eyes from behind the protection of her shielded arms. Sybil's face was calm and untroubled as she opened her eyes. She wore a serene expression, as if awaking from a night of unbroken sleep.

Then a sly smile crossed her face. She threw her head back in amusement. I wouldn't be outwitted by a spirit or Sybil or her ludicrous game.

In the distance, the noise of traffic, of movement in the square, were the only disturbance. Chrissy's eyes were rimmed with tears. The candle flame reflected in the pupils of her eyes. Next the marker slid towards Francois. A parlour game, was all it was. Victorian con artists used to run them. Looking back on that night, even at the time I could see the tricks that Sybil used. I read somewhere that those con artists only need to push a little bit at the very start, that once everyone realises the direction it's intended to go, they will subconsciously push it along. Our suspects were doing exactly what Sybil wanted without realising it. The glass marker – planchette, that's what it's called – moved over to Chrissy. Could she have been guilty? I hadn't ruled her out as a suspect, but at that point I considered her motivation for murdering Jeremy. If money was tight . . . well, sometimes a mother's instinct can take over. And she'd believed she would receive a life insurance payout, which would have given her and the baby security. She seemed genuinely perturbed. Which would be understandable if she was the killer. Taking a life is no small matter.

ELIZABETH:

It seems like whoever was here . . . has gone. What did you want to find out, Sybil?

SYBIL:

They are here somewhere. There may be some sort of confoundment on the other side. It's not unusual, you know, if there are new, angry spirits. Like Jeremy.

AGAPANTHUS:

We don't even know if that was Jeremy or not. Sybil, how do we know that was anyone at all? It's probably just another one of your party tricks. The amateur dramatics of a washed-up starlet who feels she isn't interesting enough to host a dinner party.

That movement of air came again. This time it was more forceful, as if a person had passed right by me. The candle flames were blown to one side but did not go out. The candelabra were thrown across the room. The sticks thudded along the Persian rug. There were no strings, no wires. But things don't just fall over like that? Or so I wondered. But my immediate attention was to the fire hazard. Brandy from the broken glasses had drenched the carpet.

ELIZABETH:

Oh, no, the candles! The candelabra! Quick, help me put it out before the candle grease takes the flame.

SYBIL:

It's Jeremy. He's back.

I jumped despite myself as I heard a long, slow knock against the table. Agapanthus shrieked, trying to turn the door handle but it wouldn't open for her. Sybil smiled to the air.

SYBIL:

Please don't burn down my house, Jeremy. The wax is terribly hard to get out of the carpet. Look, he's moving the marker again. T-H-I-E-F. Thief. Who's the thief, Jeremy? Who killed you?

With that, the radio kicked into life. The static cleared to the voice of the newscaster. Agapanthus was throwing her weight against the door.

BBC NEWSREADER:

Good evening, from the BBC, this is the nine o'clock news. Twenty people have died and dozens have been injured as London Fire Brigade fights a blaze that broke out in the Plortex Factory earlier this evening. Residents of Westminster and Mayfair have been warned to stay indoors with doors and windows shut. If the situation deteriorates, residents may be evacuated from their homes, and should make preparations. Radios should be left on, and residents should be prepared to shield their faces against the toxic gas. Catherine brings you this report . . .

CHRISSY:

It's a tape! It's a tape! That's not real. Sybil just invented this entire event. She meant to kill Jeremy! That was the plan.

AGAPANTHUS:

I knew something didn't make sense about the fire!

ELIZABETH:

Deep breaths, Chrissy. Calm down, now. It will be OK.

Sybil is laughing ominously.

SYBIL:

Jeremy, speak to us. Did your wife kill you?

One quiet knock came from the sideboard. Francois leaped to the door, the soles of his shoes creaking as he patted down the interior.

FRANCOIS:

Nothing! There's nothing there!

He rushed to his seat, wiping the sweat from his hands onto his trousers. In a frenzy he'd lost all reason.

FRANCOIS:

It's time to bloody go! I can't stay here another bloody minute. Come on, Christina.

The planchette began sliding again, this time towards me. Francois and Chrissy seemed transfixed. Sybil must have rigged up some sort of knocker, because I could see both of her hands. Hmm, I didn't want to attract attention by pulling up the tablecloth. Maybe she had someone else doing the knocking. I suppose now we'll never know.

FRANCOIS:

Watch out. It's coming for you, Ms Chalice!

For a minute, as they all looked at me, I felt as if I've been found out.

AGAPANTHUS:

There, we have our killer! The investigator herself. You ought to know how to get away with murder.

FRANCOIS:

I bet she wasn't expected to be outed by a ghost.

CHRISSY:

Oh, stop it, all of you.

Chrissy jumped up and her chair fell over. The exhaustion was replaced by anger – her arms raised. Shrieking, she stomped away from the table, kicking the chair from the rug to the varnished floorboards. This physical violence was a side of her I had not seen, although I did see a hint of this in the actions of Sybil and Agapanthus. Francois held Chrissy's shoulders as if restraining a wild dog. In the moment, with the rising candle flames, it passed as a neutral intervention. Something any fellow might do to stop a hysterical woman from hurting herself. Agapanthus was bemused. She stood tall, laughing as she slowly turned the handle of the door. It opened wide.

CHRISSY:

Stop it now. You're there making jokes. Don't you realise my husband has died? Jeremy is dead! Whatever you're up to, Sybil, it's not funny or amusing. I know you're desperate for attention now that you can't get on the stage any more, but this is not the right time. Don't you get that? I want to know which one of you really did hurt my Jeremy. I'm not taking part in this ridiculous venture for another minute. What do you even want to know, from the spirit world?

Chrissy's outburst summoned Sybil from her trance back into the room rather promptly as her eyes flashed open. The vein under Sybil's left eye was spasming. The mask had fallen; our killer revealed her true plan.

SYBIL:

(imitating Chrissy) My Jeremy! Whatever you're up to, Sybil. (*as herself*) Good God you're ungrateful, Chrissy. After everything I've done for you—

Agapanthus turned on Chrissy then too.

AGAPANTHUS:

You're missing a husband? Well, by the looks of things so am I, my dear! You've made it further than most. You're a better actress than Sybil will ever be. But spare me the heartbroken widow routine—

Francois sidled up to Sybil, and with two fingers he jabbed her bare collarbone. His red face contorted with anger, the loose strands of hair against his sweaty forehead. He pushed her again, this time to the floor.

ELIZABETH:

Stop it! Leave her alone.

I tried to pull him off her, but he was gripped with outrage as he screamed into her face. The fire had broken into flames along the edge of the rug, and as I had been so distracted by the slap I failed to see the smoke grow.

There were two dead bodies in the house by now, Anthony and Jeremy. Two widows. Did that mean two killers? This I leave my investigation in your hands, Felix. If you can't pay me any more, I wish you the best to solve it.

The occult, spirits, Ouija boards. As I've tried to understand Sybil over the past few decades, it is this particular episode that jars with me the most. Was Sybil a master manipulator, or a misguided dreamer with a preoccupation with the occult? It could be argued that the entire performance was a distraction from the murder of Jeremy Crowley that she and his wife had planned. But, if Sybil knew that the man who had died was, in fact, her husband, why would she have gone ahead with these events?

The further I delved into the supernatural aspect of the evening, the more questions it raised. In preparing this podcast episode, I shared the recording with a paranormal investigator, Manley Addams. Here's his opinion:

MANLEY ADDAMS:

Séances have been used as a form of after-dinner entertainment for the best part of the past 150 years, so there are a number of tricks that people use to arrange such an experience for their guests. The first thing I look at in a case like this is the tape itself. These days anyone can add in bangs, knocks and noises easily through an online audio editing app. In 1977 this would have been far more difficult. The first thing to consider is the location of the raps that respond to Sybil's questions. These noises come from the sideboard, the doorframe, the ceiling, and the table they were sitting at. This points away from the use of mechanisms, but does not rule them out. Elizabeth, a confessed cynic, reported the movement of air and a cold feeling in the room. The events of the evening before this, the phony blackout, radio broadcasts and air-raid siren, along with the discovery of not only one but two bodies – Elizabeth had found Jeremy in the freezer by this stage – would have been deeply unsettling and could have created the conditions in the minds of Sybil's guests that something was really happening. Suggestion is a powerful thing. Then there is more . . . kinetic activity. Both Francois's and Elizabeth's brandy glasses are shattered, and the door handle is stuck. Opera singers can shatter glass with very high notes, which can be recreated by high frequency recordings and tuning devices, but it can be rather unpredictable as to which glass would actually smash. If each guest had a red, white and water glass, that's eighteen glasses, more if there were also liqueur glasses. So it's possible this noise was activated in the next room by an unseen accomplice? Sybil would have been able to achieve these effects with planning. In my experience, with true spiritual energies, they don't always act as you would expect. Sybil's 'spirits' were extremely well behaved, giving an answer just at the right time. Ultimately, that leads me to conclude that the séance was not a genuine one, but a collection of tricks masterminded by the hostess. However, I am less certain about there being a rational explanation for what happened immediately after the séance.

I have long suspected that Sybil orchestrated the events; she was an avid reader of crime fiction with ample time on her hands and a propensity for performance. Once lockdown had ended after the pandemic, I went back to Mayfair. Hoping to find something in the square, in the park, in the streets that could unlock the Anderson puzzle. I did not find the smoking gun, but I did find something rather fortuitious. Remember when I met Chrissy Crowley she mentioned she was going to a book shop to buy her son some picture books? Well, I revisited that second-hand bookstore. Perusing the shelves, I came across the spiritual section, and what title did I find? A navy hardback book with the title in gold lettering: Phenomena of Materialisation *by German physician and psychic researcher Baron von Schrenck-Notzing. When I opened the cover, I felt the colour drain from my face. Inside was stamped 'Ex Libris Sybil Anderson'. From the library of Sybil Anderson. It details séances with Frenchwoman Eva Carrière the author witnessed between 1909 and 1913. This phony medium caught the attention of Sir Arthur Conan Doyle and Harry Houdini, before the ectoplasm she had produced during the sessions was found to consist of chewed-up paper and faces cut out from the French magazine* Le Miroir. *Carrière would ask her audience members to put their fingers inside her vagina to check for 'ectoplasm' both before and after a session, which could explain why her performances were tolerated for a number of years.*

Just like the sexual aspect of Carrière's mediumship distracted from the facts of reality, so too had Sybil's preoccupation with the occult acted as a distraction from the real killer. For Sybil did not kill her husband or Jeremy Crowley. Join me in the next episode as we learn exactly when and where the fire took hold of 26 Bruton Square and who the real killer of Lord Anthony Anderson was. Come back peckish for the last episode of Supper for Six, *won't you?*

EPISODE TWELVE:

A Bitter Aftertaste

Thick black smoke now obscured the disco ball that hung in the dining room
of Lord and Lady Anderson's Mayfair residence. Just six hours after five
guests arrived for a highly unexpected dinner of avocado salad, country
chicken and Black Forest gateau, a series of stomach-churning events had
led to terror and panic throughout the five storeys of the Mayfair mansion,
with the discovery of two dead bodies. Trying her best to identify the killer
and keep the innocent guests safe was private investigator Elizabeth
Chalice. For nothing at all was how it seemed. The first murder victim was
not Jeremy Crowley, but Anthony Anderson in disguise. And where was the
real Jeremy Crowley? Under the attic eaves on ice, having been murdered
by Anthony five days earlier. The posh doctor was really a builder's daugh-
ter. And the Eastend make-up artist an aristocrat in hiding. Even Francois
Langford, the womanising lawyer, had a motive for killing Jeremy. The
enchanting, mysterious and reclusive hostess, Lady Anderson, had cooked up
more than the meal, with a scheme to murder her friend Chrissy's abusive
husband; at the same time, her own marriage was in tatters.

Throughout this series, you've heard the threads that I have pulled in
an attempt to unravel the case to its finale, from Sybil's occult leanings
to potential terrorist links to the IRA – an unfortunate suspicion many
Irish Londoners fell under in the 1970s. Given the strong links to the
West Coast of Ireland, the potential of political motivation I have
explored without recovering any evidence of espionage. The motives for
the murders of Anthony Anderson and Jeremy Crowely were deeply
personal. These might make for a good story, but they only serve as
distractions, dead ends. In the forty-five years I've studied this case,
there's always been a piece of the puzzle missing. The smoking gun that
would confirm beyond all doubt who the killer really was. But we are
almost at the end. A night that began in perfect order, with a beautifully
set table and pleasant conversation has devolved into the scene that now
lies in front of us. The following recordings are the last Elizabeth made
of that evening, interspersed with her recollections of events.

FRANCOIS:

Oh, shut up, Sybil, your husband is in your dressing room dressed
as her husband. But her husband is really in the bloody freezer in

the attic. No one is missing a husband. Someone has murdered your husbands. And I don't plan to be next.

ELIZABETH:

He stood up and dusted himself, leaving Sybil in the foetal position on the floor, paying heed only to the palms of her hands. Shock and surprise sent Chrissy's hands to her mouth, but no tears came. She knew much of what Sybil had been planning, but did she know that Jeremy was in the freezer? As she'd been planning to let him overdose, she clearly wanted him dead. Agapanthus was at work trying to escape the flames, but it was not a battle she could easily win. She arched her eyebrow at Francois and smiled, as if she were considering pushing him into the flames.

AGAPANTHUS:

Oh, I don't know about that.

ELIZABETH:

Quick – go and get the towels. Agapanthus, we need water to quench the flames. We haven't long or the house may be lost.

AGAPANTHUS:

There's smoke coming in through the door – I thought it was just the candelabra.

CHRISSY:

Shouldn't we get out? Before we burn to death?

AGAPANTHUS:

You heard it on the radio. It's a chemical fire from that bloody factory. It will be worse outside.

Everyone turned to the doctor – and I remembered then that she didn't know that the Soho fire was Sybil's hoax! Francois and Chrissy had begun coughing, so I stayed close to the floor.

CHRISSY:

It's not real! Sybil made it up—

SYBIL:

To save you from that monster, Chrissy!

AGAPANTHUS:

Well, what on earth are we still doing here? Sybil, you must open the front door. Stand back, Francois.

Flames climbed the lamp beside the door as Francois, Agapanthus and Chrissy ran from the room. Black smoke poured from the landing – as if there was another source of fire. At that point I realised we were trapped between two walls of flame. I couldn't stay there, but I couldn't leave Sybil either. She watched the others leave with resignation. The danger of our situation was not apparent to her. In fact, she was smiling. Split from the reality of the flames, she lifted her hand to her ear.

SYBIL:

I suppose I'll ring the fire brigade. Hello, my house is burning down. Can you send an engine? There's five of us here, and I've lost the key.

I had a daughter to see. I had to go but if Sybil were to survive, I'd have to stir her from the delirium. I dragged her onto the landing, and she was blathering into her hand. We met a wall of angry flames so loud I could barely hear Sybil. Breathing was difficult by this stage, so I forced her to the floor. We made it down to the ground floor, but the drawing room was ablaze. Was there another source of fire down here?
   Sybil and Elizabeth are coughing heavily.

SYBIL:

There's a pregnant woman here. Can you send help. Yes, it's 26 Bruton Square. It's terribly smoky. Yes, I realise there's a . . . just do what you can.

ELIZABETH:

Will you help me to smash a window? Sybil, you don't want to die here. You don't want to have another death on your hands.

I found a path to the kitchen window, still no sign of the others.

SYBIL:

Don't throw those cushions out there. Don't you realise they're antique?

ELIZABETH:

It's kindling for firewood, is what it is. Now, stand up here, good girl. You need to jump past the balcony, see? It's a good six feet – the garden is lower. Sybil, I am getting out. I need to get help. I can't wait for the brigade. Stay if you want, if that's how you want to die.

SYBIL:

A good captain goes down with his ship. Isn't that what they say?

The sirens – I heard them over the beastly roar of the flames. If I didn't find my way out now . . . I'd never get Sybil out either. Our hostess may have invited us here, but I couldn't just leave her behind. How could I get her out?

FELIX:

Dear listeners, we are reaching the end of our journey into the murky Anderson family. To lose one Lord Anderson may be regarded as a misfortune. To lost both looks like carelessness. The first of these twelve episodes began with our logline, of course based on Lady Bracknell's line from Oscar Wilde's The Importance of Being Earnest. *That, dear listener, was your first clue that appearances can be most deceptive. The Anderson Affair echoes the play, where the protagonists maintain fictitious personae to escape social obligations. But at Lady Anderson's dinner party, appearances were not sometimes deceptive, but always deceptive. Each one of Sybil's guests was the opposite of who they claimed to be. Jeremy and Chrissy Crowley maintained the appearance of impecunious anti-establishment rebels. Jeremy no longer spoke to his wealthy father George, and Chrissy Crowley was not an impoverished make-up artist, but a bohemian aristocrat. Both sported a decent Eastend accent.*

The Andersons similarly wore a disguise. Lady Anderson was not the titled society maîtresse her bi-annual appearance in the Tatler *would portray, but an insular individual who could only engage with people through elaborate schemes and performances. Lord Anthony Anderson was not missing at the time of the dinner party, but in attendance. Assuming the identity of Jeremy Crowley, he had pierced his nipple and dyed his hair to take the role of a punk. When he was murdered, Elizabeth had to decide if the killer had been taken in by the disguise and meant to kill Jeremy. Or if the perpetrator, who had injected their victim with morphine, had planned to murder Anthony all along.*

When it came to the Langfords, lawyer Francois and doctor Agapanthus hid an unhappy marriage and a lack of finances. Striving to keep up appearances, Agapanthus forewent her medical oath to supply drugs to addicts. Francois schemed to put Jeremy back in touch with his estranged father. But their secret links to the Crowleys further tangled the web of motives that investigator Elizabeth Chalice attempted to unravel.

And in reviewing her recordings of that evening, I too found damning evidence that the sage sleuth carried her own secrets. With Elizabeth uncontactable in Switzerland, I discovered Francois Langford – returned from his ski trip – lurking outside the court café. We will hear from Elizabeth at the end of the episode. But first, to Francois.

FELIX:

Tell me about what happened when the fire took hold.

FRANCOIS:

Good God, it was an inferno. I might be a weak man. A man who hasn't done much to be proud of, but that was my moment. I was lit up like Superman, the strength I felt as I lifted Christina's limp body from the landing. It was as if I could just fly out of there. I managed to yank the downstairs curtains off their pole. I covered her face and the exposed skin on her legs. Her belly was firmer than I could have imagined, as if she had a watermelon under the dress. My child. My love and my child. The smoke was choking. But I got her downstairs, one slow step at a time. I wondered if somehow I was detached from was happening. It was as if I was observing myself from above. Even at the time when it was happening. All I knew was that the front door was open.

FELIX:

But Sybil had locked you in. The doorhandle had been too hot for Elizabeth to open it. How could it be wide open?

FRANCOIS:

Well, someone must have opened it from the outside. Marjorie arrived shortly afterwards and would have had a key. It was only a few steps away, the burnt carpet singeing as I made my way down. But in the moment I was distracted because I saw her. Not Sybil but Agapanthus, still on the landing. I decided that once I got Christina to safety, I'd go back for Agapanthus. As soon as we were outside, the cold burned my throat, my nose, my eyes. It was worse than the smoke. But I could breathe. A woman was standing there. It was Anthony's mother, Marjorie, asking who else was left inside. She wanted to know where Anthony was. I could have told her more kindly, but I just blurted out that he was dead. She sort of crumpled for a moment. But something in her stopped her going into despair. She was ready for action.

'Yes, I know. I found him in the freezer,' she said, waving the smoke from her face, but without a shred of emotion. 'That's why I set this fire. A mother knows her own son.' And just like that, she walked back towards the front door, despite the blaze.

'It's Jeremy. Jeremy Crowley, in the freezer. Not Anthony,' I shouted as best I could. She swivelled around, her face falling into her hands before getting another wave of resolve to step into the flames. And she was gone. Before I could dwell on what Marjorie had told me, I had to help Christina. She was shaking and coughing uncontrollably. It took all that happened to make me appreciate her. I remember watching the police car pull up, the ambulance behind, and thinking that if anything happened to her, I would never forgive myself. I called out to God to let her live. That's the

day I put my womanising behind me. And then another object of
my desire, Elizabeth Chalice, appeared around the corner of the
street, soot black, telling me to sit Christina up. She'd escaped from
the back.

FELIX:

And what happened next?

FRANCOIS:

That is the point where things get blurry. The lights of the
ambulance, the neighbours spilling out into the street. I swear I saw
Mrs Townsend with a grin on her face. Sybil and Agapanthus were
still inside . . . but then the fire brigade arrived. I went into the
ambulance with Chrissy soon after. And that was how it ended!
Agapanthus made it out of the fire . . . Mrs Townsend took her in
when she left our house. A week later Christina moved in. Poor
Sybil, well you know what became of her. But I can't be too sympathetic. If you ask me, I think Sybil did both chaps in. You know
where she ended up, she was wild. Now, I've told you everything.
Kindly leave me and Christina alone!

*His eyes were following a smartly dressed young barrister crossing the
cobblestones to head back to court. Francois seemed trustworthy, but I
could not accept his account without question. Francois no longer
wanted to discuss the matter. He refused to be drawn further on how he
felt about the loss of his best friend, or the trauma of dragging the mother
of his child from a fire. Alone in a multi-centre blaze without any help,
once Elizabeth ran for her life, it seemed that Sybil's demise was inevit-
able. From the earlier tapes we heard the difficulty she had in breathing
with all the smoke, but in fact, Sybil did not die that night. In fact, she
survived the fire. But if her reclusiveness up to that point had forced her
to live in her own world, the events of that night led to a complete breakdown. Was she really the killer? I knew Elizabeth was certain of the
murderer's identity.*

*After my interview with Francois back in dejected. I took myself to a
little cards club off Curzon Street and bought into a hand of poker. This*

investigation was eating me alive. I could not return to the newsroom to cover funerals, and fishwives who resembled movie stars. A Tuesday afternoon was a good time for a game, the professionals never came in to play in the daytime. The chaps gathered there had already lost their money. It was only a matter of the right cards coming to me. And they did. I commanded court of aces, diamonds, clubs and spades, as Royal Flushes and Two Pairs passed through my hand. By teatime, I had the five hundred pounds Elizabeth wanted, and more. I knew that she didn't rate me as having any investigative abilities. So, I listened back over her last tape. Was she testing me? Of course, she had mentioned her address. Brooks Mews, behind Claridge's. Not the lodgings of a woman unable to buy cigarettes, but an esteemed investigator of means. She had been conveying a particular image to me, one that I had bought. From the half dark of an April evening, I peered in through the windows of the mews houses until I spotted her. Thrusting back and forth on a rowing machine, illuminated by Tiffany corner lamps, was Elizabeth Chalice. She opened the door with her hair tied back in a loose ponytail, fully expecting my arrival.

ELIZABETH:

When did you realise where I lived?

FELIX:

It took me about twenty-four hours.

ELIZABETH:

You'll improve. Don't worry.

She poured me a highball of gin. I was glad of something to disguise the Scotch of the club on my breath. The small mews house was crammed with Persian rugs, the walls covered in Italian movie posters. A baby grand piano took almost the entire dining area of the two-roomed house. Black-and-white pictures of a couple, a baby at the beach, and a young girl in a cap and gown took pride of place. This was not any old digs. This was a home someone had lived in for many decades. This was Elizabeth's London home, for everywhere were

touches of Elizabeth. She had misled me to believe her financial situa-
tion was more precarious than this. A large, crystal ashtray beside her
gold lighter. A shelf with three tape recorders of varying size, and three
large chests of what I could only presume to be tapes. There was so
much to take in, but there was only one thing I really wanted to know.
I stepped over the rowing machine and allowed her worn green
armchair to take my weight as I threw a handful of crumpled bank
notes on her crammed occasional table. This conversation was the last
one I ever had with the enchanting sleuth, for it was the very last time
I would ever see her.

FELIX:

Five hundred pounds. Now will you please tell me who the killer is?

She sat astride the rowing machine, nursing a glass of water, as she
stared into the Tiffany lamp, and mentally returned to 7th April 1977.

ELIZABETH:

The first thing to consider is why would Anthony want to
impersonate Jeremy in the first place. A few days before the dinner
party, Jeremy had been in the house to install the airing cupboard.
But given their resemblance was so striking, Jeremy must have realised who his biological parents were.

FELIX:

But how did that lead to Anthony murdering Jeremy?

ELIZABETH:

Let's imagine things got heated. Accusations and confusion.
That Anthony lost his temper. He cracked Jeremy over the head
with a Waterford Crystal vase. The matching one of which
Agapanthus threw over the balcony at me a week later, but Jeremy
ended up dead.

This was not the first time Anthony had helped to cover up a death. Ten
years earlier he had ensured the circumstances of his father's death, also
an overdose of heroin, were not made public. Newspaper coverage

*printed that Anthony senior and his wife Idabel died in a car crash.
Anthony managed the cover-up. This shows Anthony's ability to react
quickly.*

FELIX:

So what happens after Jeremy is dead?

ELIZABETH:

Anthony remembers the freezer that Sybil has ordered. I can only
imagine that they moved it to the attic to avoid the dinner party
guests making the discovery. Moving such a large appliance up
several flights of stairs would have been a great challenge, and the
scuff marks around the door point to the difficulty Anthony must
have had in doing that. A final attempt to protect his mother from
uncovering the body of her first-born son. So he deposits Jeremy
there to give himself time to think. He hatches the plan. Sybil will
host a dinner party. Witnesses, including a doctor, a lawyer and a
private investigator, would give statements that Jeremy was there and
alive and kicking. Then on the night of the dinner party, Anthony
would pretend to be dead, keeping Agapanthus at arm's length, until
Sybil could get the guests out of the house, where he would deposit
Jeremy's body in his place, albeit with a rather significant head
wound. Yes it would mean that her plan with Chrissy could not come
off – but perhaps Sybil thought that she and Anthony could then sail
off into the sunset for a new start, evading the authorities, disappear-
ing just like Lord Lucan did a few years ago.

FELIX:

And Chrissy never noticed Jeremy was actually Anthony?

ELIZABETH:

A stroke of good luck for the pair came in the form of Chrissy's
illness. She was so unwell in the days after Jeremy's death, that
Anthony was able to visit Chrissy's home, dressed in her late
husband's leather jacket and torn T-shirt. With the vitreous haemorrhage and terrible morning sickness, her vision was blurred. All she

could see was a tall fellow with a green mohawk dropping in and out whilst she rode the waves of nausea.

It was never going to be a straightforward meal with pleasant conversation. Sybil and Anthony needed to distract their guests, especially his oldest friend Francois, in case they recognised him despite the disguise.

FELIX:

But, who killed your fellow diner? Had they meant to murder Jeremy or Anthony? Had they recognised Anthony under his disguise?

ELIZABETH:

My deductions centred around this question. I also became suspicious of Sybil's behaviour after the body was discovered. According to their plan, one would presume, Anthony was going to lie upstairs and pretend to be dead until the guests had gone home, until they could deposit Jeremy's body in its place. She did not seem concerned when two medics, Dr Agapanthus and myself announced that he had no pulse. We confirmed he was dead. Sybil's behaviour began to look erratic. During our interview, she did seem greatly perturbed, and she still had all of her guests locked in.

Agapanthus's temper was evident throughout the evening. From the stinging remarks she made on her first meeting with Elizabeth, to the comments to Francois, and ultimately throwing the vase on top of Elizabeth's head from the landing. Did such a hot temper fit with a quick and organised kill?

ELIZABETH:

Then there was the matter of Francois. How could he not recognise his oldest childhood friend, whom he'd known for most of his life? He did not seem too perceptive. He was short-sighted, without his glasses, but also just a bit stupid. But say he had recognised Anthony. What would his motivation to murder him be? He was a lawyer in need of money, and the legal fees he could earn from

Anthony's will would be considerable – enough to keep him going for years.

FELIX:

Was money alone sufficient motive for him to commit such an opportunistic murder?

ELIZABETH:

Francois also possessed a callous motivation for murdering Jeremy Crowley, as he had been having an affair with Chrissy Crowley. Chrissy had told him about the vast fortune Crowley had walked away from. Francois realised the infant Chrissy was carrying could be entitled to a share of Jeremy's will, in turn making Chrissy a very wealthy woman, and a single mother. He would propose and they would live together in abundance with the child. That much has transpired as the skiers of St Moritz witnessed last week.

FELIX:

Could Chrissy have been involved in the murder with the father of her child?

ELIZABETH:

No. Given how unwell she had been, and the fainting and weak spells throughout the evening, I don't believe she would have been physically strong enough to carry out a murder.

Then I considered Dr Agapanthus Langford and her question-able behaviour throughout the evening. How could she fail to recognise Anthony when she was examining him so closely? First of all, she was already drunk when I arrived. I'd say she'd had another two bottles of wine and a few brandies to drink in the very short time we were at the table. That would be enough to floor most people, so her vision would have been blurred and her judge-ment impaired. Sometimes people believe what they want to see, so perhaps she had fallen for the ploy and thought that it was really Jeremy Crowley lying in Sybil's dressing room? The initial tension that I witnessed between Anthony-as-Jeremy and the doctor convinced me that they knew each other, but did she recognise Anthony or believe that it was Jeremy?

For she had a secret connection with Jeremy. Remember, Agapanthus knew her husband was unfaithful. But the single most important thing to her – something she would kill for – was her reputation as a doctor. And Jeremy had threatened to take that from her. She had been involved in a scheme to sell prescription drugs through Jeremy, for well-connected society members, and even rock stars who did not wish to dally in street drugs. Had she believed the fellow to be Jeremy, she would have been terrified he would reveal her secret to her husband and the others at the table, which could have led to her being struck off from the medical register. But if Chrissy was correct, she'd already got in trouble for drinking on the job. Was she a woman with nothing, or everything to lose?

ELIZABETH:

Something about the way Anthony was murdered bothered me. And remember, Agapanthus had scratches on her wrist, when none of the other guests had any injuries at all. If you prick someone with a needle, they jump. They don't just stay still until you've managed to drain the syringe. Morphine, when injected subcutaneously, behaves differently in the body than if plunged directly into a vein. The opioid takes longer to reach the blood stream, to reach the heart and cause the cardiac arrest I initially believed to be the cause of death.

Given there was only a very short window, I'd say about nine minutes, between the time he left the room and Agapanthus discovering the body, it seems a stretch to think that the morphine could have acted so quickly, so Elizabeth ruled that out.

ELIZABETH:

That left two other options. Either Anthony injected himself, but he was known to be vehemently anti-drugs. Especially as the first Earl of Edale, his father, and his stepmother met their end so tragically. Even ten years ago he understood the reputational damage if such a story got out, and managed to have their true cause of death to be disguised in a car crash. The second option is more likely – and I'm ashamed that it's taken me until now to pick it out. Anthony wasn't injected with morphine, like the empty vials suggested, but with a fast-acting poison.

Substituting the morphine for another poison would require an element of premeditation. We already know that Sybil and Chrissy had planned the evening in the hopes that Jeremy would voluntarily inject the high-strength drug. That means Sybil was simultaneously planning two separate murders with two separate co-conspirators. Rather a lot to keep in mind, with the other aspects of the evening. I can barely cook a dinner without getting into a tizzy.

FELIX:

What drove them to plan the murder?

ELIZABETH:

Two best friends, both unhappily married and engaged in extra-marital affairs with the same man, their plan hinged on the fact that Jeremy was hopelessly addicted and would not pass up the opportunity to indulge when he discovered the drug freely available in Sybil's bathroom. They encouraged him to go to Sybil's dressing room with talk of her new diamond earrings. Chrissy says that they did not plan to actually kill him, but it's impossible to assess the truth of such an admission. Perhaps Chrissy did not want to risk the failure of their endeavour by leaving it up to Jeremy.

FELIX:

But it wasn't Jeremy. Why why would Anthony have injected himself? The simple answer is, he didn't. Can you explain the motives of the two wives, Sybil and Chrissy. Did you think they both planned to kill their husbands, Anthony and Jeremy?

ELIZABETH:

The two friends had certainly planned to kill one husband, so why not the other one? Is it possible Chrissy didn't notice that Anthony wasn't her husband? Given the disturbances in her vision and generally being unwell that night, this is possible. But the other half of this plotting pair knew all along that it was not Jeremy, but her own husband. Chrissy claims Sybil never told her this, which would indicate that Sybil wanted to murder her own husband. Throughout the evening, Sybil fooled guests into thinking that Anthony was missing and she was terribly concerned about him.

But of course, the truth is, the reason Sybil and Anthony hosted the event in the first place was to cover up the first murder. I knew the freezer was somehow important from the start of the night. She almost jumped out of her skin when Chrissy mentioned it. Initially I pegged the reaction to worry that such cost-efficient food preservation might be perceived as common. With Sybil's preoccupations about class apparent all evening, it was a reasonable assumption to make. But it held the corpse of Jeremy Crowley, who was placed there five days earlier, after a row with Anthony resulted in his murder. Had Anthony meant to kill him? Why would he want to murder someone he barely knew?

Here is situated a mystery within a mystery. Like Russian dolls, the more I picked away at the events, the more complex they became. You see all of us are layered. We wear our experiences, our life histories, our jobs, our relationships slathered all over our very essence, our very core. For Sybil was masquerading as an aristocrat, Chrissy and Jeremy were hiding their own privileged backgrounds. They had abandoned country estates and controlling families for the freedom that came with the disguise of shedding their accents.

FELIX:

How had you been fooled by Anthony's charade as Jeremy all night?

ELIZABETH:

At first, I dismissed it because I had never met Jeremy and hadn't seen Anthony in ten years. But when I discovered Jeremy's body in the freezer, I could not ignore the striking resemblance. Both looked almost identical. Just like their father, Anthony senior. For Anthony and Jeremy were not strangers, but brothers. Jeremy was born as Jeremy Benton, to Marjorie Benton before she married Anthony Anderson senior. Jeremy was later adopted by George and Florence Crowley when they returned from London to County Mayo after the war.

This point was later confirmed to me, when Francois refused to speak to me any more, and sent me the copy of Marjorie Anderson's will that he drew up after her divorce, before her boys were murdered.

ELIZABETH:

George accepted him as a son, continued to make financial provisions for him, even when he refused to see him. Jeremy hated George for his poor treatment of Florence. A situation which is sadly ironic, given he repeated many of his adoptive father's behaviours on his own wife, Chrissy.

FELIX:

Why had Anthony senior and Marjorie had their first child adopted?

ELIZABETH:

They were not married until a year later. Unwed and not yet achieving the success that warranted a peerage, Anthony and Marjorie gave their first-born son up for adoption.

This much was true. It wasn't until Anthony Anderson, a private in the 168th (2nd London) Brigade was sent home injured from the Allied invasion of Sicily in 1943, that he started his business.

ELIZABETH:

So, for each suspect we have two things to consider. Who did they believe the man in the punk's outfit was? We now know that Sybil knew it was Anthony. But how could Francois not recognise his best friend? It's one thing to pass a chap in Hyde Park and not see them, but Francois was in Anthony's house with his wife telling us her husband was missing. Yes, he had forgotten his glasses and was potentially distracted by the presence of his mistress and wife in the same room. A few weeks before the dinner party, he'd also bedded Sybil, and perhaps had his sights set on me. Francois Langford is a man gripped by an addiction to carnal pleasure. With the burden of a big day of court, it is plausible that he was so self-consumed he believed it was Jeremy.

But if he believed it was Jeremy, and he knew of the inheritance that awaited Chrissy when her baby was born, could he have opportunistically sought out the poison and followed the chap upstairs? I do think this is a stretch too far for Francois.

FELIX:

How did you rule Sybil out as the killer?

ELIZABETH:

Let's go back to a week earlier. On one hand, if Sybil is to be believed, she had an expectant friend desperate to escape a brutal husband; she'd agreed to arrange circumstances so as to allow Jeremy to kill himself, thereby ridding her friend Chrissy of the ball and chain. But since then, Jeremy had been killed by Anthony, and Sybil had gone along with Anthony's new plan. Everything was on track for the dinner party, where Anthony, as Jeremy, would pretend to overdose. The witnesses would be there to confirm what had happened and Anthony would be free to return to his aristocratic life free from murder charges, although perhaps in need of a hat to disguise the buzz cut he'd have to have to get rid of the mohawk.

FELIX:

But Sybil masterminded the entire evening?

ELIZABETH:

If Sybil's goal had been simply to free Chrissy from her abusive husband, the job was done. Jeremy was dead. But she never told Chrissy her husband was dead. She proceeded with the other plan to get her husband off the hook. But something shifted in Sybil. Now she had the chance to kill Anthony too. A crime fiction addict, Sybil had read every Christie book multiple times. She had read about poisons that included belladonna, arsenic, strychnine. Despite having no medical skills or experience with syringes, Sybil had ample time to put this together. She set the stage with the recordings of the air raid and the news bulletins, locked the doors and turned off the lights. A repressed stage creature finally had her chance to play with a captive audience, and she would be rid of the husband who was about to divorce her. She would inherit the Anderson fortune and be free to sing again.

None of Sybil's guests was innocent. Agapanthus had been selling prescriptions to the black market. Anthony, a spendthrift and gambler, murdered his own brother. Jeremy had been abusing his wife. Chrissy was about to have Francois's baby.

The marriages of everyone at that dinner table were tumultuous However, the 1970s was a different age to the one we live in today. Rape was not a crime if it occurred within a marriage, and although there's no evidence of rape in any of these marriages, there is clearly evidence of psychological and verbal abuse. Even physical violence was commonplace – Francois audibly slaps his wife in front of a party of people. The story of the Anderson family is a lesson in the damage that parents can inflict on children.

In every story like this, coincidence and circumstance have a hand to play. In this case, that no officers responded to Elizabeth's report of murder to Belgravia police station. This could not have been predicted by the killer, or indeed those who were plotting to murder that evening. The woman at the centre of the very evening in question. Sybil Anderson.

FELIX:

How did Sybil survive the fire?

ELIZABETH:

She refused to leave with me, so I left her. The fire had over-taken the stairs and landing, so I was very worried that she wouldn't make it out. But Sybil must have been concerned with fire safety. Remember her mother had started a fire in their home, and that's why she was committed to an asylum? The Andersons had also renovated the house in the sixties. Like many of those tall Georgian houses in Mayfair, there was a rope ladder in the dining room. She fought as far as the window and threw it out. By this stage, the fire brigade were almost in control of the fire in that room and quite a little crowd had gathered in Bruton Square.

FELIX:

What did it look like?

ELIZABETH:

She emerged blackened and singed at the very front of the house. All you could see were the whites of her eyes. What had been immaculate white stucco when I first arrived that evening was a wash of thick grey plumes of smoke. Sybil jumped from the ladder into the arms of a waiting fireman, but miraculously wasn't too badly injuried. Francois went with Chrissy in the first ambulance. Paramedics gave myself, Marjorie and Sybil oxygen, but I could not talk to Sybil. I was so disgusted by her actions. While my empathy for our deranged hostess has returned, but that night, well I was so furious with her. How could someone who had so much make life so difficult for her guests? Why did she have to go so far?

Sybil received no criminal charges. Once her physical symptoms from the fire, a few burns and scratches, had been treated, medics realised that Sybil had suffered a mental breakdown, and she was retained in a psychiatric unit. Marjorie, her mother-in-law and only relation, ensured that she paid for her role in that evening's events by moving her to a secure facility. Despite Felix's claim that Marjorie admitted setting the house alight, the first was declared as accidental. Sadly, Sybil remained in residential care until she died in 1995, aged fifty-two. Did you consider her to be the killer? This may be a podcast, but I had to spin a yarn out of things, didn't I? But if Sybil was not the killer, who is? I put this question to Elizabeth as we spoke in her little house, that rainy evening in 1978.

ELIZABETH:

Let us consider Agapanthus. Heavily drinking from the outset of the evening, her ability to think clearly was hindered by the sheer quantity of alcohol she consumed. You would imagine a woman would recognise her husband's best friend. But given the similarities between the two brothers, Anthony's disguise as Jeremy was a very good one. And Jeremy was certainly someone that Agapanthus would not want to see. She could not conceal her unease when Jeremy walked into Sybil's dining room. I could feel the hatred immediately. When I put it to her that she'd been selling prescriptions to Jeremy to distribute illegally, she was incensed. But considering how Anthony actually died, injected with poison, it is obvious she is the most skilled of all the guests. But given the volume of Kangarouge she'd consumed, how could she have committed such an opportunistic crime? Is it possible she could have brought poison to a dinner party?

Then I thought back to my walk over to Bruton Square. I'd seen a punk outside the famous Clermont Club. At the pace the disguised Anthony was walking he most certainly would have arrived at his own home before us. But he was the second last to arrive. Surely Agapanthus had been at home right before she came here, a mere hundred yards up the square at number 20. Anthony, dressed as Jeremy, would have walked right by her window. Perhaps their eyes met through the window pane, as Anthony couldn't help but look at his old pal's drawing room window. For Agapanthus, who wanted to clear her name and get back to practising at the hospital, the presence of the man in her neighbourhood, who by all appearances threatened to put a stop to her career forever? Well, it was simply unacceptable. But then he continued to number 26, where she was heading for a dinner party!

So, Agapanthus went to her medical cupboard, put her hand on the syringe and prepared it. With the needle primed and ready to go, she was just waiting for the right moment to pounce, and kill the man who was the absolute pebble in her shoe.

She could not have known about Sybil and Chrissy's plan to kill Jeremy, as it began to unfold. The taped air raid and news report began to play. Although Agapanthus was on edge that it might mean a nuclear strike, she could not bear to let the pre-loaded syringe go to waste. The perfect moment arrived when Anthony, still dressed as Jeremy, went upstairs to Sybil's dressing room. Without realising, her crime was aided by Sybil, who turned off the lights by removing the fuse.

FELIX:

And with Agapanthus finding the body . . .

ELIZABETH:

She announced that he had no pulse. Given the very short window the killer had, the doctor's presence as first on the scene was very relevant. Agapanthus then realised that Sybil had been plotting someone's death, so she did her best to place as much suspicion at Sybil's door as possible. For clearly Sybil and Anthony's plan wouldn't have worked if Agapanthus hadn't decided to murder who she thought to be Jeremy, but in the end, Anthony paid the ultimate price.

Perhaps it was her Dutch courage that meant she was not concerned about the police detecting any wrongdoing. But she was unnerved by my interview. The smashing of her glass, her physical animosity was more than just the demeanour of a rowdy drunk. I could see her body was in a sustained state of stress so that she could no longer think clearly or properly control her emotional thermostat. She couldn't sit and play bridge with her husband, so she watched my interview with Chrissy. When she saw me approach the front door, she saw her moment and threw the vase down the stairs. Thankfully, her aim was off. It hit the handrail at the turn in the stairs, breaking the lead crystal.

FELIX:

How did you know that Anthony Anderson did not die by accidental overdose, perhaps by accident after a moment of desperation?

ELIZABETH:

Punk guitarists these days don't always use plecs and often have butty, broken and callused fingernails. Jeremy Crowley did not, because he was, of course, Anthony Anderson. Then when it came to the crime scene itself, the tourniquet was put there to make it look like an overdose. When I looked closely at the arm, there was no puncture mark. Instead, there was a line of bruising perpendicular to his chin. I realised someone had jabbed him with a syringe face on.

The upper floors of 26 Bruton Square were saved from the worst of the fire damage by the timely arrival of the London Fire Brigade. The body of Anthony Anderson was recovered from Sybil's dressing room, and the body of Jeremy Crowley, intact in the chest freezer in the attic, both underwent autopsies. Elizabeth's observation was corroborated by the coroner's court, who confirmed the direction that the needle entered Anthony's neck would have been impossible to perform on himself. And indeed the real Jeremy Crowley had broken and callused fingernails on his left hand.

FELIX:

How could you have been so certain of Anthony's murderer?

ELIZABETH:

There were six of us there in total, including the victim. Everyone could have gone to the room he was in during those ten minutes – that's what made this mystery such a difficult one to solve. I took very careful notes of exactly who was where in the house. Can I read from my notebook?

She produced a crocodile-skin notebook, flipped it open, revealing curled pages covered in her precise script.

ELIZABETH:

Our hostess had told us that her husband was missing, so, they wanted to go and look for him. Anthony, identified as Jeremy at the time, announced that he was going to the toilet. Agapanthus decided to follow who she believed to be Jeremy, and managed to make it to the second floor without anyone downstairs noticing, stopping on the way to collect a syringe of morphine from the medicine cabinet on the first floor. The carpet was so thick, it muffled her footsteps. He had no idea she was following him. But he turned around when she opened the door. He knocked the lamp in shock. Agapanthus then came down a flight of stairs after killing him, where she met Sybil and the pair returned to the dressing room, where they found the body.

FELIX:

What other evidence did you notice?

ELIZABETH:

Dr Langford's thumb was swollen, probably from the force it took to ram the syringe into a man both taller and broader than her. Over the last few months, new memories from that evening came back to me. Like when I handed Agapanthus the dessert. She almost dropped the plate, which was unusual, because the couple had argued about who was clumsy earlier in the evening. She was using her left hand. She is left-handed, I notice. She had wrapped some ice in a muslin on her own thumb. Then when I took her hand . . . later in the evening, well, she flinched but tried to pretend she didn't. Which no innocent person would ever do. In my entire career as an investigator, I've never been wrong. She had a very strong motive to murder Jeremy, who she believed him to be. To think Anthony might have survived had Agapanthus realised Jeremy was already dead. For Agapanthus, who adopted a fancy Greek name over her birth name of Agatha to distance herself from her humble roots, was deeply concerned about what other people thought of her. But she wasn't a well-respected doctor. I learned the morning after the fire that she hadn't worked in the hospital for a year. Had Chrissy been lying when she said Agapanthus had been suspended for drinking on the job? Perhaps that was a line Francois told her?

In the four decades before this podcast launched, I've come to the conclusion that Chalice was perhaps the best investigator of her generation. Elizabeth Chalice did very well in uncovering the truths that she could find that night. She was an unquantified element to Sybil's dinner party. If they hadn't bumped into each other in Hyde Park for Sybil to invite her along, well, things would have gone a whole lot more smoothly. But the testimony of Elizabeth Chalice only takes us so far.

No formal complaints were ever brought against Agapanthus Langford by the medical council, although she never worked as a hospital doctor again. Elizabeth was certain that the disgraced doctor was Anthony's killer, but how could I be certain? That is the question I've tried to answer. Throughout the eighties and nineties, I listened to the tapes over and over again . . . But in many respects I moved on with my life. Then, in the long and slow days of the pandemic, I began work on this podcast. I became obsessed with getting justice, finding the evidence to convict Agapanthus.

The key to this mystery was particularly personal for me, as it came in the form of a deathbed confession from my birth mother Chrissy Langford. Our relationship had never been a close one, despite how being forced to give me up had made her turn her back on her own family. Several times a year we would meet for tea, but I did not have the same relationship with her as my younger brother, Henri, her child with Francois. Even that first day I met her, in that Mayfair teashop when the buggy almost ran into the road, I fell in love with her – my mother. Had she really done all that she could to find me once I'd been adopted? Along with my obsession with unfolding the Anderson mystery and my

drive to make it as an investigative reporter, what I really wanted was
her love. How could I be impartial when assessing her role in the deaths
of Anthony and Jeremy Anderson? Plainly put, I couldn't be. But
Elizabeth could, and she called me out on it that miserable rainy day
sitting astride her rowing machine. I removed and reinserted this
particular clip from this final episode many times. But as a show of
transparency, I've decided to include it. Remember I was just a teenager,
no match for an experienced investigator like Elizabeth.

ELIZABETH:

Now, Felix, there's something else we ought to address here.
There's the small matter of your mother. Your birth mother.
Christina Crowley—

FELIX:

What about her?

ELIZABETH:

Oh, please, Felix. I realised almost as soon as I met you. First of all
there is the dates. You're about seventeen, and Chrissy's baby was
born about seventeen years ago. Then there is the matter of your
resemblance to both Christina, and of course your father, Anthony.
I wondered why such a young person was investigating this story,
but you are really investigating the circumstances of your birth,
aren't you?

FELIX:

Perhaps on some level I am . . . but I do think that I've done a
good job in this investigation—

ELIZABETH:

Which would be one thing. But your relationship with the
victims: Jeremy was your uncle, and, of course, Anthony was your
father. If your adoption was a fully legal one, then you would have
no automatic right to the Anderson fortune. But if it is as Chrissy
described, an illegal arrangement, then there could be a chance that
a claim on the estate would stand—

FELIX:

That's not what this is about, Elizabeth.

As I listen back to that tape now, as an old man, I'm struck by the naivety of my youth. In one way, I was glad that Elizabeth had seen through my bravado to the hurting child that lay beneath. But handle me with kid gloves she did not.

ELIZABETH:

Perhaps it's not the only reason for your obsession with the Andersons. But we ought to call a spade a spade, Felix. You are a person of interest in this case. Marjorie, your grandmother, who had herself let Jeremy be adopted, could perhaps be persuaded to allocate some funds to you. I'm no expert in British probate, and the whole thing could take years to bring to a resolution in the courts. But there is a chance that you could be the next Earl of Edale, isn't there? And people have killed for far less. So, Felix, I'd like you to tell me, where were you on 7th April 1977?

FELIX:

Why do you always ask questions that you already know the answer to?

ELIZABETH:

You're bright, I'll give you that. That day you interviewed me in your apartment, I found a letter from your adoptive mother sending you some money. The Caerphilly family is one of the wealthiest in Cumbria. A fortune amassed from, ironically, a dairy-processing plant. That day I also found a copy of your A-Level results. A's across the board. So, I phoned the local library and they confirmed you were studying late there on 7th April. You're a boy who has everything, a loving family with plenty of money. You've the refined but mischievous grin of your father, and the abundant brown hair of your mother. So you came to this investigation to solve the mystery of Felix Caerphilly, not that of Sybil and Anthony Anderson. As long as we're clear about that.

She was right, of course. In time, Elizabeth helped Christina and me to meet again, as mother and son. But it was not easy. It was as if I represented a great wound to her that it pained her to look at. At first we met every few months, for boring conversations in Bruton Square. As Henri got older, and more jealous of me, Christina met me perhaps once a year, not in her home though. In the seven years before she died, I had only met with her twice. But in the strange cyclical, echoic nature of life, it was this woman – who had delivered me into this world – who delivered the final piece of damning proof to confirm the Anderson killer.

From an isolation room in the corner of Chelsea and Westminster Hospital, she had a care assistant record the following message, shortly before she was ventilated for Covid. At her age, and given the severity of her underlying conditions, she knew that the chance of waking up was slim. Ten days later, she died.

CHRISSY LANGFORD :

(slow and pained with wheezing) My boy. Felix, the irony of the name your adoptive parents chose for you has not been lost on me. If I never told you, I loved you the moment I set eyes on you. Your obsession with that night in Sybil's house . . . I could not tell Elizabeth, I could not tell either of you the truth. With Henri on the way . . . there was too much at stake. I could not risk being arrested. But the truth is, I watched Anthony die that night. I was looking for the toilet. But I saw Agapanthus go into Sybil's dressing room, the syringe in her hand. Oh, she knew what she was— *(coughing fit)*

CARE ASSISTANT:

That's enough, Mrs Langford, put the mask—

CHRISSY:

No! I cannot take this to the grave. She snuck through the door; as Anthony turned around she went for him. Shoved the needle right into his neck . . . Then when he started to slump on the floor, she grabbed a towel and held it over his face . . . I ran back downstairs— *(coughing fit)* But it was her. She is your killer. I loved you, son. And I wish . . . I wish . . . things could have been different.

It's not an easy thing to listen back to, even now, when I've heard it dozens of times. Agapanthus Langford may well have disappeared to the British overseas territory of St Helena, five thousand miles from London, in the winter of 1979. I had paid a visit to Mrs Townsend, where she had been staying. The old lady insisted that Agapanthus had just gone back to County Mayo. But there on the telephone table, in full view, was a postcard sent from a remote tropical island, signed simply with the letter 'A'. We can't be certain if that was Agapanthus Langford, but as she hasn't been seen since 1979, it is a possibility that she would send that postcard to the woman who took her in when she was at her lowest ebb.

Now, I hope you've enjoyed Supper for Six. *May dining on the misery of others not leave you with indigestion.*

This has been Supper for Six, *and I've been your host, Felix Caerphilly. Thank you to our production manager, Sarah Chalice-Piper, and to Henri Langford.*

AFTER-SUPPER DIGESTIF

A podcast by Elizabeth Chalice

Well here we are, dear listeners. Like you, I've followed each episode of Felix's podcast closely. Who would have thought a woman aged over 100 could keep up with podcasts? With some help from my technologically-minded daughter, I have produced my own episode in order to add a few final details. The paltry fee Felix paid for my tapes in the 1970s pales in comparison to the large revenue he's earning from a podcast at the top of the charts. So I'm releasing this to clarify a few things. From time to time, I've sat and mused on it; these are the tapes you will now hear.

You see, Felix, was obviously motivated by more than just fame and fortune to publish his investigation into the Anderson Affair. Despite an early knack of winning at the Texas Hold 'Em table, Felix never again succeeded at cards, despite many, many attempts. This podcast was his last bid to squeeze some money from events which happened decades ago. Really, something like this should be conducted by actually independent journalists, not the children of those involved. His grandmother Marjorie refused to acknowledge him, despite Chrissy's eventual admittance some time in the late eighties. She and Francois were divorced within five years, and neither went on to have more children. Agapanthus moved to St Helena in December 1979.

I suppose you're all wondering what became of me? I have lived a long and contented life in the sun, under false names, avoiding the enemies I have accrued across a career peppered with murderers, adulterers and thieves with an axe to grind. You'll have to bear with me, if I'm a little slow. But I still walk three miles a day along the beach. This tape, I'm told, is from 2015 in an interview my daughter Sarah recorded.

ELIZABETH:

Of course, with all the melted Gruyère and kirsch wine, I'd forgotten about Felix and his investigation that January, 1978, just after the inquest. I was in St Moritz, you see. I hadn't wanted to stay in London, musing over the same old story from months earlier. When an old client invited me to Switzerland, I was glad to accept. She'd paid an exorbitant price for a false painting, and had instructed me to track down the snake-oil salesman who'd taken advantage of her. After a snowy morning ballet on the ice rink, I didn't ski. My days were spent leafing through art history books and making telephone calls to galleries where the fellow had been in operation. I couldn't quite believe it when about ten days into my stay, I heard a little infant crying outside the hotel. You see, it wasn't really the done thing in those days to bring children to places like the Badrutt. I peered into the pram and lo and behold, it was Chrissy and Francois's baby, who closely resembled his parents. Nanny told me the pair had just gone for a skijouring. She was Norwegian and began to explain this unusual sport and the ins and outs of how a skier is pulled by a horse. This struck me as odd because Francois was a city boy. I waited for twenty minutes to speak to them.

The waiter came to signal my usual table was ready; given the heat of the sun I did not think it advisable to stay out for much longer.

But it all began to get a little close to home. Why had they left the country if they weren't involved in the murder? In any case, after Sybil's dinner party, I realised that I'd been very lucky to escape with my life. It's a cliché, really, but after a close shave with the grim reaper, it changed what I thought was important. I was deliberately evasive with Felix. He was a tabloid journalist, and an inexperienced one at that. I had to keep you safe, Sarah, and out of his sordid sights. For in Felix, I saw something untamed. Yes, he was motivated to make a name for himself by solving the Anderson mystery. And he was bright enough to turn a large profit at poker. Perhaps it was beginner's luck. But I knew he saw me as nothing more than a commodity. It was a hopeless scenario, to be pinned as a devious detective or totally incapable. I should never have accepted his money. I did not even need it!

But there's something about spending so much time on managing on a budge: it had left me with an unrelenting urge to take cash when it was on offer. The further we went into the events of 7th April 1977, the less human I became to him. My return to England had not gone as planned. Charlie was out here, in this anonymous island that I will not name. Every London street just reminded me of the war. And my clients were international, so as long as I had a forwarding address, they could reach me anywhere. So, I disappeared. I'd watched people do it before. I'd seen them slip up. But Sarah is every bit as clever as her father. She knew I'd find her when it was safe, didn't you, dear?

Then there was the time I went to see poor Sybil. It was in September 1994, I believe. John Major was the PM. Anyway. The place she was in, a sort of long-term facility, was nice enough, I suppose. Well, the part where they allowed visitors was. We had some lemonade by the lake. Only the healthiest of residents went down there. They even had a radio-controlled boat chugging along. It was Charlton House, in Kent.

SARAH:

She stopped for a moment, smacking her lips and looking for a glass of water. She held my hand with her soft and feathery fingertips. Her skin was as thin as paper. She pulled down the sunglasses to give me one of those meaningful stares she did when she really wanted to hammer something home.

ELIZABETH:

Oh, it's times like this I wish you hadn't made me give up smoking. Anyway. I am glad you made me give up. There are no smokers here. They are all long dead.

Right. Sybil. The expensive mental health facility was Marjorie's attempt to buy herself out of guilt. I should have gone earlier and was quite prepared for the worst type of situation. But there Sybil was, nicely dressed in slacks and a cardigan. An orderly had helped her with a French roll. It was her youth that disturbed me the most. She looked so well and healthy, and I couldn't fathom why they were keeping her there. But Marjorie was gone, and she had no relations. So, where else could she go?

SARAH:

An ancient gentleman with a boater and a gold tie pin that shone in the midday sun stopped to tip his hat in her direction. He tilted his head back to signal a drink.

ELIZABETH:

Oh, don't mind old Bazalgette. He's a pervert, by all accounts. Anyway, I hadn't wanted to upset Sybil by going over the events of the night of fire, but she was so lucid, even making jokes about my disappearance! I eased my way into it. She told me that at first, she really did feel unwell and could not properly distinguish what was real, and what she might have imagined. If the case had ended up in court, she could have been prosecuted for a number of things, so her lawyer told her behind the safety of the padded cell. In reality, she was in very comfortable surroundings, but used her mental illness as a shield. But she wasn't a social creature. She enjoyed the large library at Charlton House. Anyone who wanted to could visit her. It was no different from the self-imposed isolation in which she had lived in Mayfair, with the exception of the excursions with Anthony that tortured her. But yes, we got to talking about that night. She swore that she didn't murder Anthony. That earlier that day she'd tried to cancel the dinner party, but he had insisted.

SARAH:

Oh no, Mum, my phone doesn't have much battery left. We only have another minute before it dies.

ELIZABETH:

(*speeding up*) But even though Felix wasn't declared publicly as Anthony's heir and the title had gone by the time he sought it, Anthony had set aside some money for him. Francois Langford had told me that it would be a long and complicated probate as Marjorie had survived her son, and with the circumstances of Anthony's death. But he was Chrissy's son too.

SARAH:

Who was Chrissy, really?

ELIZABETH:

Christina Smythson! The first cousin of Peter Smythson, whom I had been previously acquainted with in Lake Como for the Caswell-Jones case in, oh, it must have been '53 or was it '56. A very nice boy, if not a bit foolhardy in love, but who isn't when they're young. You see, Peter's mother was Black and American. The marriage had pushed some family members, including Peregrine Smythson, Christina's father and Peter's uncle, into being ultra conservative. For them it was unacceptable for their daughter to have a child out of wedlock. She made the right decision in dumping them, I do think. Perhaps things would have turned out differently for Felix had he remained with his mother and been acknowledged by his father. We're all victims of our parents, aren't we?

SARAH:

Not me. I'm down to 5% now, tell me the answer to two questions. When did you have time to get the recordings from the basement?

ELIZABETH:

I went back in the morning and sweet-talked my way past the police. It wasn't all sealed off and official like it would be now. The fire hadn't touched the basement, so it was quite safe. Recording things was very important to me. You see, the word of a woman didn't carry as much weight. Even then. Even in the 1970s. I had to have the proof.

SARAH:

And then why didn't anything happen to Marjorie? If she had set the fire?

ELIZABETH:

Proof, my dear! Where was the proof? The people who assess fires are particularly skilled at identifying how they start. And it was the spilled turpentine in the airing cupboard. It had been built over a vent, so the air had become very hot. And it ignited. Now, I think we'd better make our way in for lunch, dear. That's quite enough murder for now.

Author's Note

When I was fifteen years old, I watched my father, stepmother and best friends stumble in terror, drenched in the blood of the victims of the IRA bombing of Omagh. The attack killed 29 people and injured about 220 others, making it the deadliest single incident of the Troubles in Northern Ireland.

The blood and terror I was watching was not real, they were extras in the 2004 film about the bombing, which was filmed on Watergate Street in my hometown of Navan, due to its similarity to Omagh's Market Street. As a child growing up in the Republic of Ireland, the atrocities committed by both sides during the Troubles were relegated to news packages, something far removed from me. But that day on the movie set has forever brought home the reality of the blood that has been shed between Ireland and Britain, and nothing will excuse the actions of the Real IRA and Provisional IRA in murdering innocent people.

In writing crime fiction, there are tropes of the genre that must be subscribed to. But from Agatha Christie to Dorothy L. Sayers, the issues of a shifting society are omnipresent. In the fourth draft of *Supper for Six*, as I sought to distil some truth of my own creative soul into the text, I begged of myself to find another way into the story that felt authentically connected to me.

For in the 1970s, my grand-aunt, Auntie London, dampened down her Meath accent, as she aspired to climb the social ladder in London. My own aunt, uncle and father have recalled to me the discrimination they received in Britain throughout the 1970s and 1980s. When I walk out on the driveway of my house in Bective, on the River Boyne, I see the wheel at the local mill, where a century ago

British soldiers tortured and drowned an innocent man accused of treason. A mile ahead, as I drop my children to school, I pass through the village of Robinstown, the site of a vicious attack that took place a century ago. At lunchtime on Ash Wednesday, 9th February 1921, eleven lorries arrived. They contained a mixed force of Auxiliaries, regular RIC and soldiers. They terrorised the occupants, damaged buildings, destroyed belongings and stole a large amount of food, drink and other articles.

Human memory may no longer record the atrocities the Irish experienced at the hand of their colonisers over centuries of British rule, and the history books never capture the extent of violence experienced by the ordinary person. These are the wounds that my fellow countrymen and women carry, an intergenerational trauma.

It is my job to write a murder mystery, but it is also my job as an Irish writer to avoid moral injury and tell *Supper for Six* within this context. For crime fiction is a reflection of our society at a particular point in time.

Acknowledgements

To the oldest and youngest people in my life, who feed my creative soul, thank you. My children, Sephie and Archie, are my constant motivation and inspiration. My grandmother, the subject of my dedication, Monica Sherlock, encouraged me to write from an early age. Her belief in my storytelling abilities set me on this path, and I will forever be grateful for her influence.

The creative process would not have been possible without the generous funding and support of The Arts Council, Meath County Council Arts Office, Creative Ireland, and Meath County Library. The Hinterland festival organisers, Heather and Les Hanlon, deserve a heartfelt thank you for showcasing my work and providing a platform for local authors. Their dedication to promoting literature has been invaluable to me and many others. Thank you to Midge Gillies and the Institute of Continuing Education at Cambridge University.

To my local bookshop, Antonia's Bookshop in Trim, Co Meath, Antonia, Helen, and Barbara, your support in championing my work is deeply appreciated. Your belief in my novel has meant the world to me (and they also ship worldwide). Thank you to Jody Corcoran and Alan English in the Sunday Independent, and those at Screen Ireland for supporting my work.

I am also immensely grateful to my incredible agent, Lina Langlee, whose guidance, expertise, and unwavering belief in my work have been instrumental in bringing this novel to fruition. Your dedication to championing my writing and negotiating on my behalf has been a true blessing.

A heartfelt thank you goes out to my editors, Sorcha Rose and Sara Nisha Adams, for their keen eyes, insightful feedback, and dedication to shaping this novel into its best possible form. For their proofreading, editing and illustration skills, and production skills, Helen Parham, Swati Gamble, Mike Parsons, Lewis Csizmazia and Claudette Morris, your expertise and encouragement have been invaluable. To all the talented individuals on the editorial, audio, and marketing teams at Hodder, I extend my gratitude for their hard work and dedication. Your collective efforts have brought this novel to the attention of readers far and wide.

I am also grateful to the group of individuals who contributed to the development of "Supper for Six" and helped envision London life in the 1970s: William Sherlock, Ita Sherlock, Megan McNicholas, Fiona McNicholas, Margaret O'Brien Lynch, Helen Crafter, Faith Wilson, George Bridges, Karen McCourt, and Andrea Ryder. Your insights and assistance have enriched the story beyond measure.

My parents Deirdre White and John Sherlock have been my pillars of support, stepping in with childcare and offering a helping hand whenever I needed it. Their understanding and belief in my passion for writing have allowed me to pursue this creative endeavor wholeheartedly.

Last but not least, a warm thank you to Helen Tuffy, Emma Gill, and Barry O'Brien Lynch, who plied me with tea and pints during moments of procrastination. Your companionship and care have been a soothing balm on this creative journey.

About the Author

Fiona Sherlock is an Irish author, entrepreneur and newspaper columnist from who lives in Bective Co Meath. Her mystery games are played all over the world. She is completing a MSt in Creative Writing at Cambridge University.

www.fionasherlock.com

TikTok - @fionasherlockauthor Twitter/Instagram: @FionaSherlock

Want to discover another thrilling mystery? Read on for an extract . . .

EPISODE 1

Catherine Caswell-Jones

ELIZABETH:

Now, interviews. Suspects. Let's get going. There will be twelve interviews in total, for we must interview Argento once he arrives. Please do take note of each one in turn, if you can. Where shall we start? Naturally, I should begin with Catherine herself. After all, she is the person who called me here, the one who found Jonty's body, and, helpfully, she is the person here I know the best – she even lets me call her Kate. Once upon a time, we were friends. But I am not here for friendship, not today. I need to know one thing: what would motivate a wife to kill her husband?

Here we go. She sees me beckoning her into the elaborately corniced drawing room to begin. She is as perfectly put together as ever, not a hair out of place. There isn't a sweat patch or mark on her immaculate wool pencil dress. It's a wonderful claret, as red as the bow on the front door wreath.

CATHERINE CASWELL-JONES:

Elizabeth, I'm so pleased to be able to talk with you. Frankly and openly. I know on the phone you wanted to know his movements before I found him. I've been thinking long and hard about it, trying to get every detail right. After dinner, he just stormed off. I must say, it wasn't like Jonty, really, to go off in a sulk like that. I had noticed at dinner there was some tension between him and Ludlow. I had been too distracted orchestrating the various courses. It wasn't until halfway through the soup that I noticed Ludlow had completely turned his back on Jonty's end of the table. It was very rude. Jonty, I'm sure, would have hated it.

(Pause as tears catch her)

I'm sorry, Elizabeth, it's just, I used to love spying down towards the end of the dinner table to see what was going on. I would save it up as ammunition to tease Jonty with at night. To think I will never— (Her voice breaks up)

ELIZABETH:

Take your time, Kate, you've had quite the shock. I'm very grateful to you for thinking of all this detail. Can you remember who was sitting beside Jonty at the table?

CATHERINE:

(*Composing herself*) Matilda on his right; Sally – Ludlow's wife – was on his left. Ludlow is a man who *cares* about etiquette. It shocked me to see that he had turned his back on Jonty – they're so close, you know? – but I was perhaps even more surprised to see his back turned against his best friend's mother, Matilda. Ludlow would never normally be so impolite. This behaviour continued throughout the main course and into the *secondi* – we tend to do a mixture of British and Italian courses for Christmas, you may remember; this time it was roast turkey followed by a wild boar ragù.

ELIZABETH:

Yes, yes, that sounds delicious. Can you take me back to Jonty? So, he was sitting between his mother and Sally. Presumably Ludlow's rudeness was clear to all the guests. Did your husband seem put out by Ludlow's behaviour?

CATHERINE:

You know how much Jonty hated any conflict. All these years he's spent mediating between his mother and me because of that very fact. He just hated Ludlow's disruption, I could tell. The way he was smiling, but with dead eyes – like he was putting it on. There was something bothering him, clearly. But then again there seemed to have been something bothering him all week. Before we arrived on the twenty-third, the children and I hadn't seen him since September, when he left for the South American tour. I was shocked when he opened the door to me and the girls, he looked so wan. Unhealthy. I wondered if he was ill. But today Jonty seemed . . . I don't know . . . they have been friends since Stowe . . . Jonty always looked up to him and Ludlow didn't appreciate his friendship . . . it always seemed so one-sided. It has always upset me. Maybe today was the day Jonty realised it for himself . . . Oh, Elizabeth – how rude of me. Would you like a light for your cigarette?

ELIZABETH:

My cigarette is clutched between my teeth. My not-so-subtle hint . . . I'm sorry, I should have told you, my investigative brain doesn't quite work without some nicotine. But it has proved a good distraction technique, too . . . While Kate rustles around the marble-topped sideboard for matches, I must tell you what I know of Ludlow. He proved himself quite the cad to me in those first Christmases I spent at Villa Janus. I must file away my prejudice against him for the purpose of this situation.

A broad man, over six feet three, Ludlow's sheer physicality could have divided the dinner guests, causing a rift among the table perhaps. Kate has never worked very hard to disguise her dislike of Ludlow, that much was obvious even when I first met her during the war. I have always wondered whether her haughtiness towards Ludlow was out of concern for her husband.

CATHERINE:

Here you go. Well, where was I? Yes, it was always Ludlow this and Ludlow that, Ludlow hosts the grand garden party, is next in line for a peerage, Ludlow gets Thomas, our eldest, the job at Banc Le Bennet . . . Jonty followed him around like a lapdog. It was disgusting to see. *(Suddenly distracted)* Oh, look. Someone's out on the lake. It does look so beautiful at this time. So peaceful. It almost makes me forget . . .

ELIZABETH:

What? *(Slight pause)* Why is the skier chap – Peter Smythson, is it? – why is he taking a speedboat out in the middle of the night?

CATHERINE:

Thinking, I expect. Apparently his father was the same. Terrific fishermen, the two of them. Peter has been out there the past three nights. He just drives out so far, and comes back in.

ELIZABETH:

Ah ... I see. Smythson ... Smythson ... Is his mother American?

CATHERINE:

Yes! How did you know that? He's an *Olympic* skier, you know? We've known him since he was a child. He's from three villages over in England.

ELIZABETH:

I can tell because of the little stars and stripes on his lapel. But Smythson is a British name. So that leaves an American parent to meet the citizenship requirement.

CATHERINE:

How in God's name can you see, let alone deduce all of that?

ELIZABETH:

That's why I'm here, isn't it? I noticed his lapel earlier when we met in the hallway. But sailing out on the lake in the middle of the night? It really is most peculiar behaviour, *especially* after a murder. But in my experience the strangest of actions are often the most readily explained. Nonetheless, it will need to be investigated, I'd better take note. *(Slight pause)* Now. Sorry, we got distracted. This view you have here ... it's a wonder anyone gets anything done, isn't it?

What did I mean to ask you? Ah, yes. Today I saw the six hefty trunks and an array of suitcases at the bottom of your sweeping staircase with Ludlow's and Sally's initials. Were they arriving or preparing to leave, Kate? Is there anything you need to tell me about your Jonty and Sally?

CATHERINE:

(Laughing) Ha-ha. Ah, yes. The star-crossed lovers.

ELIZABETH:

I have always been amazed, during my stays here, that it never seemed to bother you. Jonty and Sally having once been engaged. And she was *always* around.

CATHERINE:

Elizabeth . . . there has never been anything to worry about. He married *me* in the end, didn't he? Sally is *completely* self-absorbed, of course, but it makes her easier to deal with. She's a very clever businesswoman and makes a good role model for Flora and Polly. I don't mind having her here. It's Matilda who can't stand it these days. Of course, she blames Jonty for not managing to sustain the interests of highly marriageable Sally. Such a slight would *never* have happened to William, Jonty's golden-boy brother. You know how Matilda is forever comparing the two? And who can compete with a dead man forever placed on a pedestal? I can't imagine how difficult it has been for Jonty to always feel like his mother would have happily traded which son died in the war . . . *(Gasping)* Elizabeth! Now that I mention it, one thing really did strike me as strange this year. Matilda took a decidedly back seat on this year's guest selection for Christmas. The inevitables aside, it's not like her to leave it to me. It really is very odd.

ELIZABETH:

Old age has begun to take its toll, perhaps? Maybe she felt she needed a rest.

CATHERINE:

Oh no, I don't think we are that lucky. I heard them arguing last night, on Christmas Eve – Matilda and Jonty, that is. She always insists someone walks her to her room at night, and of course Jonty is so *desperate* for her approval, the inheritance, everything, he just obliges . . . Well anyway, here's what happened: she's upstairs, directly over this room but at the back, overlooking the Orangery, and we hear a terrific banging, and the two of them just *shouting* at each other. In all the years I've known Jonty, I have never heard him raise his voice to that woman. Matilda used to tear shreds off him – but not so much in recent years. The argument, and Jonty's response . . . it was unusual.

ELIZABETH:

That must have been shocking for you all. Does Matilda speak about William often? And in front of Jonty?

CATHERINE:

I think her singular joy in life is recounting the life and times of William Henry Caswell-Jones. The right and true heir of Avonlea Hall. And yes, always in front of Jonty. That's part of her pleasure.

ELIZABETH:

So with William gone, and now Jonty, who is the heir now?

CATHERINE:

Well, it should be my eldest, Thomas . . . *(Growing angry)* Besides, why do you even need to know that? Jonty's not even cold out there . . . I haven't had time to think about—

ELIZABETH:

Oh dear, Kate, I'm sorry. I didn't mean anything by it. It's only . . . it's just for my investigation. Do you want to take a break? You must be heartbroken.

CATHERINE:

I'm sorry, I didn't mean to . . . Yes, I am heartbroken, but I am also still in shock, so I've been trying to capitalise on that. I want to lay things out for you before I really fall apart. Elizabeth, I know someone in this house killed Jonty. There is a murderer here, right now. I need you to find them.

ELIZABETH:

Here . . . someone is coming. A pair of hard-soled shoes heralds another Caswell-Jones into the room.

CATHERINE:

Polly, whatever is the matter—

POLLY:

Mother, there's been a theft . . . someone has stolen my notebook, you know, the one with the drawings?

ELIZABETH:

I would expect Kate to laugh at the absurdity of a missing notebook at a time like this when her husband, Polly's father, has just been murdered. Instead, a shadow of panic crosses her brow. Yes, she composes herself quickly, but not quickly enough. Clearly, this trivial news seriously disturbs her. There's something in the notebook she doesn't want anyone else to see, or notice. Polly, of course, is simply ignoring my presence, wholly consumed by her own distress.

CATHERINE:

Sorry, Elizabeth, that break might be a good idea after all. I need some coffee. Would you like some?

ELIZABETH:

I agree and watch mother and daughter leave in a forced show of calm. The room still smells of lily of the valley perfume, Matilda's signature scent, and cigarettes. Although I am sure I detected a hint of guilty sweat from the earlier congregation, too. Kate originally wanted me to contain them all here, in one room, but I prefer to let them roam. What they do with their freedom will be far more telling than keeping them cooped up. Kate is my chief suspect, despite her protestations and tears. It has not gone unnoticed, Kate's tiptoeing around my questions. Have you noticed it, too? She hasn't responded about the suitcases . . . skilfully sidelined . . . but I will give her time. I have nursed men back from the brink of death with Kate, through those wartime experiences . . . well, she was once a good friend to me – I know her well. But I need to be firm, direct, for we all know it is usually the person closest to the victim who has the most to gain from their murder. And Kate was jolly quick to change the subject from Sally and Jonty's engagement, despite the fact that she said herself it hardly bothers her now, almost thirty years later. Plus, while Matilda is the grand dame of the Caswell-Jones family, I suspect that Kate has since secretly superseded her dreadful mother-in-law as the true matriarch. Matilda isn't so happy to see me here . . . have you noticed? In the past, Matilda has always found my presence acceptable, so long as I offered the dual benefits of socialite gossip and medical knowledge. Now I'm here for a very different reason, to investigate her son's murder, I can sense I am not so welcome.

I settle back into the armchair. The golden-panelled drawing-room is illuminated by the dark waters of the lake. I have the peculiar sensation of being in the centre of a raindrop about to break the water's meniscus. My thighs are sticky from the travel, and the lining of my dress is stuck to my nylons as I peer into the winter dark. The distant lights of Bellagio are twinkling, tapering to tiny communes across the lake edge. The console behind the sofa looks rather empty; I remember years ago Catherine had travelled with framed photographs to put around the villa. Not now, it seems. But there is a bunch of little dolls. Four of them in rag dresses with bright red lips. They are from South America, I'm not certain if they are Peruvian, or perhaps made by the Tarahumara tribe in Mexico. They do look out of place.

Kate and Polly are gone quite a while, but now Kate returns alone with a rattling tray. She pours coffee into squat espresso cups, the crema dribbling down the porcelain edge. Her hand shakes. I wonder what they spoke about. I wish you could be a fly on the wall for me. The whole situation smells off to me. A notebook. Why on earth is it so important? When I arrived, Polly had not been uncontrollably upset. She'd seemed tired, certainly, a little snarky and rude, too – but not upset. But then, ever since I've known that child, she's always been good at hiding her feelings. However, it seems to me she is considerably more distressed by this, her missing notebook, than she is by her father's murder.

CATHERINE:

Sorry that took so long, I had to make the coffee myself.

ELIZABETH:

Polly seemed quite upset. Is she okay?

CATHERINE:

She's always been rather disorganised. She's managed to misplace her art portfolio.

ELIZABETH:

It must be terribly important to her.

CATHERINE:

It's everything to her, the poor child. I'm sure it will turn up. Polly will be fine, you remember how wretched it is to be that age.

ELIZABETH:

All too well. Tell me, are those little dolls Flora's?

CATHERINE:

(Confused) What? Oh, these dolls, from the Andes, I believe. Can you imagine a girl of seventeen *still* collecting them? Jonty used to always bring home bits and bobs for the children, arrow heads, baskets, all sorts. There are shelves and shelves of curios at home in England. I insisted he stop.

ELIZABETH:

So, where did they come from?

CATHERINE:

Peter, our neighbour must have brought them for Flora. They are spooky little things, aren't they? Oh dear, you don't seem to be enjoying the coffee, Elizabeth.

ELIZABETH:

It's quite lovely.

CATHERINE:

It's far too strong. I'm sorry. Argento hasn't arrived yet.

ELIZABETH:

Please don't worry. Remind me, who is Argento again?

CATHERINE:

Argento di Silva. He called earlier. Poor chap. Used to be our Italian lawyer but got himself into a bit of a scandal . . . We have him here to help out – he looks after the house, helps us with various other things, and he's terribly passionate about cooking, so he usually caters for us, too. It means he can make a little money. He has joined us for dinner the past few years. We're all awfully fond of him. His mother lives in Milan and hasn't been well – that's where he is at the moment – but he should be here shortly. He actually has some important papers for us all . . . it might be useful for you to see, too. Speaking of important papers . . .

ELIZABETH:

I spot Kate's eyes fly to the chequebook sitting on her desk. I prepare myself for the awkward conversation that may follow – it is hard to get paid in my line of work, so the cultivation and maintenance of friendships with those much wealthier than me takes up much of my time. It makes me feel cheap, but alas, it is essential.

CATHERINE:

Before we get back to it, I wanted to raise the matter of your fee.

ELIZABETH:

I have known you for years, Kate, I don't expect payment.

CATHERINE:

Please, I insist. I'd rather we settle the matter now. Sterling or lira?

(Scratching of a pen on paper – sound of Elizabeth writing down a figure)

ELIZABETH:

Here you go.

CATHERINE:

Very well.

(Scratching of a pen on paper – sound of Catherine writing the cheque)

CATHERINE:

The reason we are hiring *you*, of course, is that we want to keep this private, a family matter. For now, anyway. Until we know where we are with things. Are you sure you understand?

ELIZABETH:

Of course. I understand. Remind me again, how and when did you find Jonty's body?

CATHERINE:

It was just after four o'clock. I knew the time because I was waiting for the limoncello cake to cook in the oven . . . It had been in there for almost half an hour and was still cold; I was worried it would be dried out. Jonty came to tell me he had something urgent to do and to call him when the next course was served. I asked what could possibly be urgent on Christmas Day. But he just walked off in a huff. I stoked up the coals a bit and put the cake back in. I'll admit the lunch was poorly organised without Argento; they were all getting restless. I went in to top up the glasses and saw three more empty chairs. Polly, Ludlow and the writer chap had disappeared. Matilda was bent over the table completely incapacitated by alcohol. It was very unlike her to be that rude . . . she must have had quite a bit to drink. In all the years I've known her she has never been prone to drinking like that, especially in front of so many guests. I spotted Polly out on the patio and signalled for her to come back. Instead, she turned around to light a cigarette. When I went out to drag the child back in, I saw there were tears in her eyes. She wouldn't admit it, but that young chap, the writer . . . I think something is going on between them . . .

ELIZABETH:

I'm sorry to push, I know this is hard, but can you tell me about . . . about the body, Kate?

CATHERINE:

Yes, well, when I got to Jonty's study to call him for food . . . the door was shut firm, which was the first sign that something was not right. Jonty didn't like to close his office door. When I opened it, well, there he was. Lying flat across the desk – almost exactly like Matilda had been at the lunch table. You know, I thought at first that's what he was doing, making a joke because she had been so drunk – but I realised he hadn't seen her like that, and the way his eyes just focused into the corner . . . He was still warm. *(Pause for a gutturalsob)*Ididtrytoresuscitatehim. . .butIknew,therewasnopulse—

ELIZABETH:

Oh, Kate. I'm so sorry. Can you tell me what you did next?

CATHERINE:

I must have let out a wail. The children came running. I know they're grown, but, well, I didn't want them to see . . . But it was too late. Thomas came in first – his face was red, like he had been shouting. Tears still rimmed Polly's eyes – she looked forlorn. I tried to get them out. Flora appeared quite a while later, thank God – I wouldn't want her scarred, she's still so young, only seventeen – not quite a young woman yet. Thomas called the doctor, he came quickly. Hmm. I hadn't thought about who called the undertaker, but it is important. Now I think about it, Thomas must have called the undertaker, too, as they arrived together from Bellagio. Within thirty minutes. Anyway, the undertaker was a small man with a thin moustache. I remember he said to me in slightly broken English: 'The dead do not know it is Christmas.' It was like a dream . . . but at some point, when they were wrapping him up to take him off, I realised I should have called the police. Thomas objected, accused me of dramatics . . . but I went ahead. I know they would need to preserve the evidence . . . and moving the body had already disrupted things. The officers looked around – two local chaps – they sighed and commiserated but shrugged it off as one of those things . . . Thomas, I'm sure, encouraged them to think I was mad.

His Italian is quite good. Better than mine. Margaret had to translate for me.

ELIZABETH:

(Sternly) So why am I here, Kate? If the local police said there is no crime?

CATHERINE:

Elizabeth, they weren't going to get a detective involved. They just wanted to get back to their Christmas lunch. They certainly didn't look likely to disturb a superior officer for some mad woman claiming her husband was murdered. After all, there wasn't a mark on the body . . . But I just know. I *know* Jonty was murdered. You're a detective, Elizabeth, I'm sure you know the importance of following your intuition.

ELIZABETH:

Of course, but he *did* have a heart condition, didn't he?

CATHERINE:

Yes, that's true. But, well, there's something else. I didn't even try to explain it to the investigator, but a few months ago, when Jonty was at home in Berkshire, he was very on edge. Screaming at me and the children . . . refusing to answer the telephone. One night I overheard him crying in the study. Not that I'm one to pry . . . but I needed to find out what was the matter with him. I went into the study and found a letter in the wastebasket.

ELIZABETH:

What did it say?

(Catherine shuffles around)

CATHERINE:

Here, read it for yourself. I brought it here with me as I wanted to ask Jonty about it. I thought he might be more relaxed here.

ELIZABETH:

Very well. Thank you. *(Reads aloud) Jonathan, watch where you are stepping, there are loose rocks and steep cliffs. You don't want to lose your footing, or worse, get pushed. (To Catherine)* It's typed – not signed, there's a brown mark here, it looks like—

CATHERINE:

It's tea, it had been spilt all over the bin.

ELIZABETH:

Who do you think sent it?

CATHERINE:

Heaven knows! Jonty is a coffee trader, after all – with all that travel, he meets hundreds of people a year. The reference to the cliffs, I wondered if it was a metaphor or if it was referring to something directly. For ages, I could not narrow it down to any situation . . . but then I remembered Villa Janus, this villa. All along the eastern edge is a loose cliff. Do you remember it?

ELIZABETH:

I remember we used to jump off it in the middle of the summer. But falling from it wouldn't cause death, would it?

CATHERINE:

Perhaps not in the summer, but that water is freezing right now. A few seconds would shock the system, for someone like Jonty.

ELIZABETH:

A shock big enough to cause a heart attack . . .

CATHERINE:

Exactly.

ELIZABETH:

So he had an enemy, who perhaps knew of his heart disease. But that isn't how he died – and the fact is, he did have a weak heart. I need to ask you again, Kate, *why* are you so certain that he was murdered, and didn't just die of natural causes, a very likely heart attack in a man with chronic and ongoing heart issues? You must have a suspect in mind. Who do you think killed your husband, Kate?

CATHERINE:

If you want my honest opinion, Elizabeth, I wouldn't put it past any of them.

ELIZABETH:

That is a chilling thing to say, Kate. But you need to be honest with me. You are so certain he was murdered. Do you have one single suspect in mind?

CATHERINE:

This is difficult for a mother to say. I *never* want it to get back to him, and it's one of the reasons I knew I could only trust you with this – for you know this family better than most. But, Elizabeth, I believe Thomas killed my husband.

(Pause)

He is capable of anything. He was so keen for the police not to get involved, and he has never got along with his father. It was the main reason I tried so hard to get him out of the country as soon as he finished university. They fought all the time. Thomas wanted to become more involved in the estate, the company, but Jonty would *not* let him. Thomas has been *so* different lately. He has always been difficult – I'm sure you remember from your stays here, years ago – but recently it's as if he has been possessed by . . . some sort of evil. Ludlow thinks I'm crazy, too, of course; he does not believe it's murder, and he'd *never* suspect Thomas, but . . . out of everyone here, Thomas posed the biggest threat to Jonty.

ELIZABETH:

How old is Thomas now?

CATHERINE:

Twenty-one. But don't let his youth fool you. There was an incident . . . in school. He must have been about twelve. Thomas claimed it was a horse-riding accident. They were going for a morning out on the gallops, him and this other chap. They get split from the rest of the group on the way back, then Thomas arrives back at school with this chap's body across his lap on the horse, with the other horse following behind. Says the horse reared on the friend and crushed his skull. It was *Ludlow* who convinced the headmaster to let it all go. I've never trusted either of them since that day. We all knew there was something not quite right about it.

ELIZABETH:

So Ludlow and Thomas are close?

CATHERINE:

Very. Ludlow and Sally have no children, so Ludlow takes his role as godfather very seriously. I had been glad of their relationship, if I'm honest. Jonty came back from the war a totally different person. He had no real interest in Thomas. Or the rest of us. Jonty just never seemed to get over William's death, or the shadow William left behind.

ELIZABETH:

His brother, William, what happened to him? I heard once that he was in a prisoner-of-war camp.

CATHERINE:

That's right. Vincigliata Castle. Near Florence. Lots of high-ranking officers. William died in the camp. Dysentery, I think, not that Jonty ever wanted to speak about it. They were unspeakably lucky, to find each other in there, to have that time together. Matilda always said the wrong son came home, you know, when they were arguing.

ELIZABETH:

I can only imagine that made for a difficult relationship.

CATHERINE:

To say the least.

ELIZABETH:

And how did you and Jonty cope during the war?

CATHERINE:

It was hard. We saw each other four times in six years. Not that that was unusual, even for officers, but each meeting just became more awkward. I'm sure you know much of this, but he was stationed at Aldershot initially, then went to France, then was captured in 1943 and taken off to the camp. The children were lucky – they stayed in Berkshire with Matilda, though they won't remember much. Flora was only a toddler when it started. But the war – it changed us all, didn't it? Tell me, do you ever think about that night?

ELIZABETH:

What . . . You don't mean . . . ?

CATHERINE:

Yes, you know.

ELIZABETH:

All the time, Kate. But you and I both know that fellow deserved it.

CATHERINE:

It's taken me a long time to shed the fear, Elizabeth. You know, anytime some official sort turns up at the door, people recording statistics or that sort of thing. I worry it will come back to me.

ELIZABETH:

What he did to that girl, it ruined her life.

CATHERINE:

But it's not for us to decide, is it? Judge, jury and executioner.

ELIZABETH:

I doubt anything would have happened to him otherwise. He was a Captain or some other high rank.

CATHERINE:

We got a good dark night, I suppose . . . *(Snide laugh!)* You know, Elizabeth, I am sorry that we stopped, you know, having you here. I noticed after you came the first time – I realised how much your presence brought back to me the shame. Seeing your face just reminded me of that night.

ELIZABETH:

I know I am not here to discuss what happened all those years ago, but do you think – and I'm not going to leave until I've got to the bottom of this – do you think you could be reliving what happened to that chap now, and that's why you're so jolly certain Jonty was killed?

CATHERINE:

(Sharply) I want an investigator, Elizabeth, not a psychiatrist.

ELIZABETH:

Look, Kate. It is coming up to ten, I am an *investigator* and I really want to interview as many people as possible before bed tonight, so I will want to revisit some things with you. A few last things and then I'll wrap it up. I need you to be honest with me. Any affairs? You or Jonty.

CATHERINE:

Me, no, haven't the time or the inclination. Jonty, probably. His great tours take him away for a while, to all sorts of interesting places. I'm no fool. I know how the world works.

ELIZABETH:

What sort of travel is it that he does?

CATHERINE:

The winter tour, which he's just come back from. It's a public relations exercise mostly. He visits the brokers who haven't ordered enough coffee this year. Tells them what innovations and improvements to the coffee planting and harvesting and processing have taken place. Presents expensive cigars and Scotches, generally wines and dines them.

ELIZABETH:

Where did he go?

CATHERINE:

Buenos Aires, New York, Montreal, sometimes to the plantations themselves – the largest is in Guatemala.

ELIZABETH:

I would like full details of his trip. Can you ask his secretary or assistant to send it to me?

CATHERINE:

I may be able to convince her to go into the office, but it is Christmas Day, Elizabeth. I'm not even sure she's at home or near a telephone. There are some notes in his study – you might be best placed to look in there.

ELIZABETH:

Fine. One last thing. And please don't take offence.

CATHERINE:

I can't promise that.

ELIZABETH:

I know this chap Argento was meant to be here, but you have no other help for this trip, no one to clean?

CATHERINE:

My family have spent their whole lives being pampered with staff. I wanted them to realise, you know, how important the cooks, the cleaners all are. I wanted them to see that they can't always expect to be waited on hand and foot. They take things for granted, but times have changed. They needed to realise that. Jonty is – was – the worst of them all. He was slovenly, and I wanted more than anything to teach him a lesson. Of course, you're right, even with

Argento here there wouldn't be a full dinner service, no housekeeping. But they need to learn, Elizabeth. It's about time they realised the world does not revolve around them . . .

ELIZABETH:

Without waiting for further interrogation, Catherine Caswell-Jones leaves me alone in this room. So, what do you think? Do you believe her? Kate is certain her husband has been murdered by one of their guests, and, in her view, his own son, but that does not discount her as a suspect in my mind. Wives have been known to kill their husbands for the most trifling of reasons. And no staff, what could that possibly be about? Surely the family could spare a few lira for some help. Now, throughout my interview with his widow, a woman I nursed with during the war, a woman who invited me into her home as a friend – I watched for signs of guilt. I am very aware that she avoided some of my questions. She was leading me to certain areas of inquiry, wasn't she? But for what purpose? While there is something bothering her that I can't quite identify, in the end, what can we note down as her only clear motive for murdering Jonty? The fact that she hated how slovenly he was? How very . . . unconvincing. Not quite what I've been looking for . . .